THE FOREVER MOUNTAIN

A LONE MCGANTRY WESTERN

WAYNE D. DUNDEE

WOLFPACK
PUBLISHING
— EST 2013 —

WOLFPACK PUBLISHING
— EST 2013 —

Paperback Edition
Text Copyright © 2021 Wayne D. Dundee

Wolfpack Publishing
5130 S. Fort Apache Road, 215-380
Las Vegas, NV 89148

wolfpackpublishing.com

Paperback ISBN 978-1-64734-260-9
eBook ISBN 978-1-64734-259-3

THE FOREVER MOUNTAIN

CHAPTER 1

"Based on all my medical training and subsequent years of practice, I would not expect anyone in his condition to be alive. The fact that he still is, in my opinion, can only be explained by his sheer iron will to keep hanging on until he was able to have this chance to talk with you."

The assessment was grim, as was the expression on the face of the middle-aged doctor presenting it. As he listened, Lone McGantry's own countenance was somber, concerned. He was a big man, crowding forty, tall and solidly built with thick brown hair overdue for a trim spilling around his ears and down the back of his neck from under a battered Stetson. He had a square, weathered face, prominent nose, and dark blue eyes that were normally restless and alert. At the moment they were somewhat subdued, conveying an anticipatory sadness that recognized what was left unspoken in the doctor's words. After the patient *did* have his talk with Lone, what then of his will to continue hanging on?

The two men, along with a stout, elderly woman, were standing in a narrow, colorfully wallpapered hallway outside the closed door to the room in which the man under discussion awaited. The latter was known as Peg O'Malley, a former mountain man who had years prior lost his right leg to a grizzly bear hence the moniker "Peg" for the wooden prosthetic he wore from the knee down. The doctor was named Hurlbert and the elderly lady was known to one and all as "Ma" Sharples. The room containing O'Malley was one of several in the boarding house Ma had operated in North Platte, Nebraska, for years.

"Iron will, you call it," said Ma now, echoing the doctor. "All the time I've known that old rascal, I thought he was nothing but plain stubborn."

Dr. Hurlbert smiled wistfully. "Apply whatever term you wish. In any event, it has sustained him far beyond ordinary expectations. That's all I know. I find it remarkable and rather admirable."

"He could be that," Lone allowed.

Ma frowned. "Along with cantankerous and loud and uncouth and… But never mind that now. I didn't mean to speak ill of the…"

She stopped short of saying "dead" but may as well have finished it. The doctor, in slightly fancier terms, had already set the tone for that inevitability, even stressing how it was overdue.

Lone took a deep breath, expelled it slowly. Squaring his shoulders, he said, "I sure ain't lookin' forward to goin' through that door. And I don't mean for my sake. Might sound crazy but, based on what you're tellin' me, I can't help feelin' that if I stay on this side he'll somehow keep hangin' on."

Ma put a hand on his shoulder. "He's *been* hangin' on, son. For weeks now. Hurt and sore and in a mighty bad way. It's time for you to help him out of his misery."

******

He sat with O'Malley for the better part of an hour. He listened to the main message the old man had stayed alive to give him. Then he listened to some disconnected ramblings beyond that. And then he listened to the final raspy breath sigh out and it was over.

When he emerged from the room, the doctor and Ma were there waiting. "It's done. He's past his hurtin' now," Lone told them.

Without saying anything more, he stepped past them and went outside to start making arrangements for what he needed to do.

CHAPTER 2

"Me and my deputy, Keith Overstreet, we rode on out there first chance we got," Elmer Dalrymple, the town marshal of North Platte, was saying. "It's out of our jurisdiction and all, but seeing as how it was Peg and we knew you'd be gone a spell longer—well, we thought maybe there was a chance we could spot something worthwhile, something that might give some idea who was behind that nasty damned piece of business.

"Unfortunately, too much time had passed. Six or seven days. The ground all in close around the cabin was chewed up too bad by horse tracks to make much sense—first by the owlhoots who stove in Peg to begin with, then even more by the Circle L wranglers who happened along and found him. Plus, by the time me and Keith went out, there'd been some rain and even a light dusting of snow." The marshal wagged his head. "Neither one of us are any great shakes as trackers, I'm afraid—nothing like you or Peg—even on dry ground. So there was nothing we could make heads or tails of. Same for the half-burnt cabin—just the wreckage they left after rummaging through and taking what they wanted before setting a torch to it. Damned sorry I can't be any more help, Lone."

Seated in a straight-backed wooden chair hitched up in front of the marshal's desk in the front office area of the jail building, Lone gave a dismissive shake of his head. "You did what you could, Elmer. I appreciate it."

Dalrymple leaned forward where he sat behind the desk and rested his palms flat on the desktop before him. He was a smallish man just past the forty mark, lean and spare almost to the point of appearing frail. As a lawman, he was popular, effective, soft-spoken and mild-mannered in his day to day dealings with the general public. But for those who knew what to look for, there was evidence of a muted flintiness in his pale gray eyes that warned he was quite capable of turning hard and no-nonsense should the need arise.

Continuing to display his milder side now, Dalrymple said, "It goes without saying, I trust, that my deepest sympathy goes out for the passing of Peg. I won't pretend he wasn't a rascal sometimes when he came to town, but I never found the ruckuses he got into ever stemmed from mean-spiritedness or nastiness, not on his part. At any rate, I'm gonna miss seeing him come around from time to time."

"Yeah, I hear that," allowed McGantry. "He was one of a kind."

Dalrymple eyed him a little closer. "Talk around town is that you had Cobb, the undertaker, pick him up from Ma Sharples' place and proceed with preparing him for a proper funeral and all but that you intend to haul him off to the mountains somewhere for his actual burying. That right?"

"Uh-huh." McGantry met the marshal's gaze levelly. "Ain't nothing illegal about that, is there, Elmer?"

"Not illegal, no. Leastways not no law against it I know of. But it's a mite peculiar, you got to admit that."

Lone sighed. "Yeah, I reckon it is. But it's what Peg asked of me. Had some particular notions on where and how he wanted to be laid to rest and put it to me to see it done."

Dalrymple's eyebrows lifted. "You mean that's what kept him hanging on for so long when it didn't hardly seem possible, hanging on just to give you those particulars on how he wanted to be planted for eternity?"

"How a body dies and how they meet eternity is mighty important to some folks, Elmer," Lone said solemnly. "All the travelin' we done together, I gotta admit, I never knew such about Peg. But seems they was there all along, those particular notions, like I said, on how he wants to go over. So now that he's laid it in my hands, I aim to do my darnedest to see they get met."

The marshal regarded him some more, this time a little less mildly. "That all he had to say, Lone? He didn't say nothing about the ones who left him for dead and stole the horses?"

"He put his hardest focus on the burial details. That was the main thing he wanted me to know," Lone answered. "He rambled some other stuff, all foggy-headed from medicine and pain. Didn't make any sense."

"And you're willing to settle for that?"

Lone cocked an eyebrow. "What's that supposed to mean?"

"It means I know you pretty well. Hard to buy that you'd accept so easy not having any kind of clue who did your best friend that way."

A spark flared in eyes that had previously been mostly dulled by sadness. "If, by 'accept', you mean do I *like* it?

Hell no, I don't! But with nothing to go on—no idea who or how many they were, no indication which way they went—what am I supposed to do? Peg lay in that bed at Ma's place for weeks," Lone pointed out, "did you get any details out of him, Elmer, as far as who attacked him?"

"You know doggone well I didn't. I tried questioning him a half dozen different times, but either he was too out of it to respond at all or he just kept mumbling about finding you, wanting to talk to you. That's why I thought maybe he was holding out to tell you something. something more than his burial wishes, I mean."

"No such luck," Lone said bitterly. "But you're right about one thing. I haven't *accepted* this. Not yet, not by a bucketful. First, I have to honor Peg's burial wishes. Once I've done that, though, I'll be back. I don't know how, exactly, but some way or other I'll scrounge up a whisker of a lead and then I'll start to follow it until, whisker by longer whisker, vague sighting by clearer sightings, stench by increasing stench. I mean to track down the rotten bastards responsible for what was done to Peg. Only then will I consider it settled."

"There's more like what I'd expect to hear from you," Dalrymple replied. "But, as a fella who wears a badge, I guess this is where I should also remind you to give proper law and order a chance if and when you catch up with those varmints."

"It's already a cold trail. Be even colder if I have any luck with my catching up," said Lone. "In other words, after so much time it might be hard to convince a representative of proper law and order the right of things. Don't mean I won't try, though, Elmer. But, in the end, I'll have to do what *I* see as right."

Dalrymple grinned wryly. "Wouldn't count on anything different. I said my piece, can't say I didn't try. Now, sort of off the record, here's something more: Comes time when you *do* get any kind of lead, let me know and I'll help any way I can."

"Obliged, Elmer."

When Lone stood to leave, Dalrymple said, "When do you figure on riding out with Peg's body?"

"Day after tomorrow, is the way I'm thinkin' now," Lone told him. "I plan on going out to the cabin this afternoon, camp the night there. I want to look things over before too much more time passes. Not implyin' you and Keith or anybody missed anything, I just want to put my own eyes on what they left."

"I understand."

"Also, Peg had his old war bag stowed out there in a sort of out-of-the-way spot. I'm hoping those curs didn't find it as part of their rummaging. It's got some things in it I know he'd like to have with him when he goes over."

Dalrymple tipped his head. "Good luck with finding it intact. Try to touch base again before you head for the mountains, hear?"

CHAPTER 3

The cabin where Peg had been attacked and left for dead wasn't much more than just another soddy of the type common to the Nebraska plains in the late 1880s. This was particularly true hereabouts along the southern reaches of the massive, rolling, treeless expanse known as the Sandhills that reached north and west for thousands of square miles. Having a few distinctions of its own, though, this soddy was built into the side of a hill with a reinforcing log frame around the front and a hammered tin roof over the part that extended out away from the hill. As a place for a couple of roaming adventurers like Lone and Peg to finally put down roots, it was plenty suitable. More than just a home, it was also the centerpiece of the horse ranching operation the two had begun together.

As he rode out of North Platte early that afternoon, awash in late March sunshine that was nice and bright but didn't carry quite enough heat to take a leftover bit of winter chill out of the air, Lone tried to picture the ranch as he'd last seen it. The Busted Spur, he and Peg had decided to call it; a reverse "C" with three prongs sticking out of the curve was their brand.

Lone had been away for over four months, leaving Peg behind to tend and build the meager herd they had started. Which wasn't to say that the purpose for Lone's leaving wasn't also to benefit the ranch. He'd left at the summons of a lady lawyer out of nearby Ogallala who offered payment too good to pass up. Payment that would substantially help build the Busted Spur's herd as well as make some added general improvements to the place. In the end, Lone was indeed well paid; but earning it, which involved rescuing and then helping to prove the innocence of a female fugitive corruptly convicted of murder, had been a complex, grueling ordeal that took considerably longer than expected. Long enough for Peg to have fallen victim to the prowling pack of human wolves who'd left him for dead, burned the cabin and stole the horse herd.

Lone didn't bother heaping blame on himself for not being there. That would have been wasted emotion. *Had* he been there, sure, maybe he could have intervened somehow, maybe the outcome would have been different, or maybe he would have been left lying in the dirt along with Peg. There was no way of ever knowing. Life on the frontier—especially the kind Peg had always led, as well as Lone—held countless dangers and just as many ways for it to end. It was merely a matter of time before your number came up. Peg's had. But that didn't mean there wasn't *any* blame to be laid. When the time came, Lone had every intention of placing it heavily at the feet of the bastards who'd turned over Peg's number.

For the time being, though, as he'd told Marshal Dalrymple, Lone's most immediate thoughts were on satisfying Peg's last request as far as laying him to rest. The instructions were straightforward enough, though the journey up into the mountains would be difficult, especially this time of the year. The story behind the request, though, as revealed by Peg on his death bed, had come as quite a surprise to Lone.

Though he'd never spoken of it before, it turned out the old mountain man had at one time been married. His bride was an Arapaho Indian maiden called Silver Moon. They'd spent two and a half years together in a region of the Rockies above Poudre Canyon, eventually building a cabin in the Never Summer Mountains near a spot called Weeping Hawk Peak. Silver Moon had called it their "Forever Mountain" and when she died at the start of what would have been their third winter together, Peg had buried her there. Before she breathed her last, he made her a promise that, when it was his time, he would return and finish spending forever with her. Which was where Lone now came in; taking Peg to Silver Moon in order for that promise to be fulfilled.

Dalrymple had called such a request peculiar. And, in some ways, maybe it was. All Lone knew was that Peg O'Malley, for all his outwardly gregarious ways, kept mighty tight with his deepest personal feelings. He didn't open up to just anybody and had an even greater reluctance to be beholden to anyone. So being the recipient of this "peculiar" request meant that Peg saw him as being outside both of those reservations and, for that, Lone felt honored and all the more determined to carry out what had been asked of him.

Topping a low rise and coming in sight of the Busted Spur spread—his first real look at the damage that had previously only been described to him—sent a mix of anger and sadness surging suddenly through Lone. All the work, all the hope he and Peg had invested here now lay before him as a barely recognizable sprawl of empty, blackened wreckage. At its best, the ranch would have charitably been called "humble" by most folks. But to a couple of long-wandering souls—an aging former mountain man and sometimes teamster partnered with an orphan who'd grown to make his way as a soldier, Indian scout, prospector, guide and sometimes wrangler—it was a castle at the end of a hard, twisting trail; a spot to settle their bones and bring their restless ways to an end.

But now it was all gone. The spot was still here but the castle and the dream, at least the way they had existed before, were just charred rubble. And the ultimate end to Peg's wandering and the settling of his bones would soon take place somewhere else. Would Lone then return here on his own? He shrugged away the question as soon as it touched his thoughts. There was too much to do before he'd have to come up with the answer to that. First get Peg to his and Silver Moon's Forever Mountain; then track down the killers and thieves who'd caused so much disruption. What would come after that—providing Lone's own number didn't get turned up somewhere along the way—was too far off to worry about.

As these thoughts swirled through Lone's head, he realized he had absently reined Ironsides, his big gray gelding, to a halt. He was hesitating to proceed on down the slope to the scene that was tormenting his thoughts and twisting his gut. As if holding back long enough would somehow make it change, maybe fade away. It was the same feeling he'd had earlier that morning standing outside Peg's room at Ma's boarding house, knowing that once he went on in something bad was gong to happen. Only in this case, the bad had already happened. Him going the rest of the way down wasn't going to make it any worse and sure as hell nothing was going to make it any better.

He dug his heels into Ironsides and said softly, "Come on, boy. Let's get this over with."

They had descended the slope and were plodding across the flat area leading up to the cabin when the crack of a rifle report shattered the scene's otherwise ghostly silence. Lone caught a fleeting glimpse of the rifle's barrel being thrust out of one of the blackened windows, a tongue of yellow flame licking from its muzzle. In the same instant came the unmistakable sound of a bullet slicing the air only inches above his right shoulder!

CHAPTER 4

Lone had been shot at before. He knew not to panic. He also knew not to wait around for the shooter's aim to improve.

Reacting immediately, he pitched himself from Ironsides' saddle and hit the ground rolling. Luckily, the well he and Peg had dug last summer was only a few feet away and the sandstone housing they'd built around it made good cover for him to scramble behind. He had barely accomplished that before a second shot from the cabin window sent a slug plowing harmlessly into one of the sandstone slabs.

Pushing up onto his feet but staying squatted low behind the four foot height of the well housing, Lone drew the Colt Peacemaker from its holster on his right hip and held it at the ready. He wished he'd had time to grab his Winchester Yellowboy from Ironsides' saddle boot, but it was too late for that now. The big gray, also no stranger to gunfire, had galloped off to safety. He was savvy enough not to go far, though, knowing that Lone might need him again in a hurry.

The seconds ticked by, nearing a full minute. Everything was quiet again. Lone could discern no sign or sound of movement, and no more shots were fired. He was about to holler out, asking what the hell kind of burr was digging into the shooter, when a voice calling from the cabin beat him to it.

"I told you what would happen if you came around again. Now you have seen that I meant it! Those were warning shots—if you do not gather up your horse and leave immediately, next time I will not shoot to miss!"

The words were puzzling enough in and of themselves. They were made even more disconcerting by the fact that the voice speaking them—in an odd, lilting accent—was that of a woman.

Frowning, Lone called back, "I don't know what this is about, but you're way off kilter in your claims. You ain't ever told me nothing before, because I ain't been around here for months. This is my property, though, so you're trespassin' on top of whatever other trouble you got! If you want to lay down your gun and step out in the open so we can talk, I'm willin' to forget those first two shots at least long enough to hear some kind of explanation."

The gal with the lilting accent came back sharply. "You insult me by believing I would be that big a fool! This place is obviously deserted. Whoever may have once owned it is either dead or moved away."

"You're half right on both counts," Lone told her. "My partner, the other fella who owned this place, got killed a few weeks back by some varmints who wrecked and burned everything then stole our horse herd. Like I already told you, I've been away for a spell and only just got back to learn all of that. But whether you buy any of it or not, what makes you think you've got the right to be here chasin' folks off with a rifle?"

"I use the rifle to protect myself, not this forsaken piece

of property. You should have learned that the last time!"

Lone gritted his teeth. "Lady, you're tryin' my patience! There *was* no last time—not with me there wasn't! Whatever happened, I was no part of it."

"Then why have you returned?" the female voice insisted. "You were all drunken pigs, maybe your senses were dulled. But you nevertheless found your way back, didn't you? And you know why, know what you came for!"

Lone leaned against the sun-warmed sandstones and expelled an exasperated sigh. Whoever she was and however she'd gotten here, the girl wasn't making any sense. Maybe she was touched in the head. But whatever had happened to her, even if she *was* touched and it was all in her imagination, it was clear that to her it had been very real and had left her frightened and, as long as she had the rifle, dangerous. How accurate she truly was with the weapon, Lone didn't know. But he'd seen enough to plan on continuing to be careful about finding out.

Before he could formulate what to say next, something to try and convince her he wasn't there with harmful intentions, the girl called out again. "Look behind you. It appears your friends are arriving late. Or am I to believe that they also are co-owners of this property?"

Glancing around, Lone saw that, sure enough, two riders were approaching from the northwest. Leaned forward in their saddles, whipping their reins, coming hard. Something about the pair—their hellbent intensity, the way they were pushing their mounts—immediately raised Lone's hackles. Through narrowed eyes, he continued to track their rapid approach.

They most likely were wranglers from one of the handful of cattle spreads that surrounded the Busted Spur, Lone thought. It wasn't uncommon for such men, out rounding up strays, to swing by seeking some fresh water for themselves and their horses; it had in fact been cowboys from one such outfit, the Circle L, who'd happened by for that reason and found Peg's near lifeless body. But those raised hackles, a prickling in the short hairs on the back of his neck, gave Lone a sense that the intentions of the men riding up now were something different.

These feelings, combined with some of the things the unseen girl in the cabin had been running on about, caused a sudden hunch to knot up in Lone's stomach. All at once he had a pretty good idea what was taking shape here.

Turning himself around but remaining in his squatted position, he called back over his shoulder toward the cabin. "I don't know these gents, but I'm going to stand up in a minute and face them. I'll trust you not to shoot me in the back when I do. Give me a chance to talk to them, try to get to the bottom of this."

Lone gave it a beat. Then, setting his jaw, taking a half breath and holding it, he straightened his legs and stood up full just as the riders closed and checked down their mounts in a swirl of dust. Gradually, the tightness between his shoulder blades eased as no shot came from the cabin window. He held the Colt straight down at his side and held his expression flat, showing nothing as he looked up at the two horsemen now before him. Both indeed had the look of hardscrabble wranglers. Dusty, weary, overworked and underpaid, carrying around sour attitudes.

"We heard shooting," one of the men announced. "Is there trouble here?"

Lone shook his head. "No trouble. My name's McGantry, I own this property. You're trespassin'. What business do you have here?"

The man who'd spoken first frowned heavily. He

was a long, lean number, unshaven, weak-chinned and stoop-shouldered, with the beginning of a pot belly bulging above his belt buckle. "I told you, we heard shooting and came to see if there was trouble," he said. "You're acting awful unfriendly toward a couple of fellas trying to be neighborly."

"What neighboring outfit you ride for?" Lone wanted to know.

"The Box 50," came the answer.

Lone's eyebrows pinched together. "Box 50, eh? That puts you pretty far off your range, the 50 being so far to the north. You must have already been well across your boundary to have heard those shots. How do you explain that?"

"Explain?" echoed Weak Chin. "Who the hell are you that I need to explain anything to? And don't try to give me no business about you ownin' the place. The old timer who ran this spread got hisself gunned down a few weeks back and nobody's come around since to lay any claim to it."

"I'm here now," Lone said. "And I've had half claim to the Busted Spur all along. Me and the old timer were partners, I've just been away for a spell. Now if you two swung by to water your horses and yourselves, you're welcome to draw a bucket up out of the well. Otherwise, like I said, you're trespassin' and I'd be obliged if you went ahead on your way."

The second rider, older and huskier, with gray-shot whiskers and beady eyes squeezed in too close on either side of a flat, thick nose that looked to have been broken a time or two, said in a gravelly voice, "What about the girl? You figure on layin' claim to her too?"

There it was. The hackles these two had raised on Lone and the hunch that had knotted in his gut came grinding together and formed for him a pretty clear picture now of how the situation stood.

Canting his head to one side and locking his gaze on those beady eyes of Gray Whiskers, he said mildly, "Who said anything about any girl?"

"You know damn well what my partner is talking about," Weak Chin snarled. "The Chink gal who's been hiding out in that burned-out shithole of a cabin. Don't pretend you don't know who we mean and don't think for a minute you're gonna ride in and keep her all to yourself!"

Lone spent a couple tense beats eyeing the pair more closely. Both wore sidearms holstered on gunbelts around their middles—Weak Chin's rigged for a standard draw on his right hip, Gray Whiskers packing his positioned for the cross-draw on his left. Each man looked to have endured some hard miles in their time and conveyed a certain air of ruggedness that would have logically come from such. Yet neither struck Lone as having relied much on the hardware they carried to make it this far. They could probably draw reasonably fast and even hit what they aimed at. But he nevertheless judged that, though they could no doubt be dangerous in their own way, doing gun work wasn't their regular line.

Still holding the Colt down at his side, Lone shifted it slightly in order to make sure Weak Chin and Gray Whiskers saw it there, then he said, "I withdraw my offer from before. You're welcome to nothing here. Only to wheel your horses and clear off my property as fast or faster than you rode in."

Weak Chin didn't like the sound of that at all. "You're makin' a big mistake, mister," he protested.

"Not as big a one as you'll be makin' if you don't light a shuck out of here and do it quick," Lone told him.

Gray Whiskers took another turn, saying, "Whether you're trying to be some kind of hero or, like I said before, anglin' to have the slant-eye all to yourself, you flat ain't bein' reasonable. Everybody knows those celestial gals are only good for three things; cookin', doin' laundry, and bein' belly-warmers. And for the last, it's only good while they're still young, before they turn into dried-up old crones. Until then, though, I hear tell they're practically born with real man-pleasin' skills. So, seein's how this one *is* still young, there's enough there to go around if you'd just be willin' to not be so plumb greedy and—"

His words were halted by Lone suddenly raising the Colt, extending it to arm's length and aiming it square at Gray Whiskers' face. Thumbing back the hammer, he said, "Shut your filthy mouth! Say another word, I'll feed you one of Sam Colt's .44 caliber pills that will cure you of your disgustin' ways permanent-like. So turn those nags around and make dust the hell out of here. Now!"

Except for pinning Lone with matching hate-filled glares, the two wranglers wasted no time doing as ordered. It wasn't long before they'd disappeared in a haze of dust headed back the way they had come.

Lone watched them go for a good stretch. Then, lowering the Colt once more, he turned slowly to face the cabin and spoke to the blackened, empty window. "You satisfied I got nothing to do with that double dose of scum who, I take it, caused you some recent grief? If not and you figure to commence shootin' at me some more, I warn you that I'm in a prime mood to this time do some shootin' back."

CHAPTER 5

It took awhile before there was any response to Lone's challenge. Then, gradually, a figure emerged out of the shadows filling the cabin's doorway. Coming as no surprise, it was a young woman. She was clad in a shapeless, long-sleeved blue shirt that hung loosely about her hips, baggy trousers of the same color, rope sandals on her feet. Her head was bare, revealing a cap of silky, lustrous black hair that ended just above her shoulders and framed an almond-eyed oval of a face that was quite pretty. A Henry repeating rifle was gripped purposefully in her two fists, held across her body at waist height with the muzzle angled slightly upward.

"I recognized the voices of those two men," she declared. "Earlier, the same was not true of yours. But I expected the worst and so I acted based on that. It is clear now that my judgment was in error."

It wasn't exactly an apology, but right at the moment Lone was less interested in that than he was in hearing more of the girl's story, who she was and how she'd come to be here. Though the answer to his first question seemed obvious, he went ahead and asked it anyway.

"Are you out here all alone?"

"Yes. I am. Now."

The girl answered that much readily enough but then didn't seem very eager to provide more. Lone decided that if he primed the pump with some more of the lowdown on himself then maybe he could get her to loosen up the rest of the way. "Look," he prompted, "everything I've said about myself—both to you as well as that pair of jackasses who just left—has been on the level. My name is McGantry, Lone McGantry, and I've just returned after a long absence. Returned only to learn that my friend and partner, who'd stayed behind to run things here while I was gone, ended up getting robbed and burnt out and killed by a gang of horse thieves. That happened several weeks ago, though my partner hung on until just recently before he died. I rode out this afternoon to have my first look at what was left of the place. Needless to say, I didn't expect to find anybody livin' here."

The girl's almond eyes met Lone's with a very direct gaze. "I have been staying here for four days. I only remained because it clearly looked deserted and offered some welcome shelter after a series of misfortunes befell me."

Lone nodded. "Wasn't hard to guess you'd met with some bad luck. And I never meant to say you wasn't welcome to any shelter you could find here under whatever circumstances left you stranded. What's more, now that I've come along and found you in this fix and you need to be sure and understand I ain't lookin' to force myself on you in no way like those other owlhoots, maybe I can be of some help with whatever your predicament is."

"Predicament?" The girl echoed the word, frowning, not understanding what it meant.

Lone gestured with his hands. "This. this fix you're in,

whatever trouble you had. The, uh, *misfortune* you said fell on you."

The girl's expression turned somber, sad. "Yes, much misfortune. But why would you be willing to help me?"

Now it was Lone's turn to frown. "Well, mostly I guess because you and your trouble sorta landed in my lap. I mean, I repeat, this *is* my place. So here you are and here I am and, if you look around, reckon you oughta be able to see I ain't exactly short on a touch of my own misfortune. Who knows, maybe we can lend each other a hand."

The girl regarded him. Her somberness seemed to have lifted, replaced now by a troubled, quizzical look. "I think I understand and speak very good American," she said. "But you keep confusing me with the way you put things. I certainly have never come near to sitting in your lap and what possible benefit would it be for either of us to borrow one another's hand?"

Lone responded with a hearty laugh. Not letting it last too long, he held up his free hand, palm out, and said, "Beg your pardon for laughin', ma'am. Believe me, I'm not laughin' at you. Your speech and understanding are fine. The problem is me and my backwoods way of butcherin' the English lingo. Comes from a spotty upbringin' and too much time hangin' around rugged sorts with even less proper learning than me. But it's nothing we can't overcome, you and me, though probably with a few more stumbles along the way. Just gonna take a little patience, that's all."

The girl eyed him skeptically, yet also with a spark of interest.

"Let's back up and start with something simple," Lone suggested. "You know my name. What's yours?"

"Tru. Tru Min Chang."

Lone smiled. "That's real pretty. Now we got some

groundwork to build on." He paused, sweeping his gaze in a wide, slow scan of their surroundings, lingering for just an extra beat in the direction the two wranglers, Weak Chin and Gray Whiskers, had gone, before adding, "But I'm wondering if maybe we should step on inside for a while to do our further chin wag—er, I mean discussing."

Tru didn't miss what was behind his suggestion. "You believe those men might return?"

"Not right away, I don't think," Lone told her. "But you never know. After they ride off a ways and maybe stop to try and work up their courage again, especially if they got a bottle of the liquid kind to help 'em along, there's a chance they might swing around for another try. They seemed powerful determined when they was here before."

"I was determined, too. To kill them if I had to."

By the look on her face, Lone didn't doubt her a bit. He said, "Let's hope it don't come to that. No matter what, though, it's probably smartest for us not to keep standin' out here in the open."

"Yes, that seems sensible," Tru agreed.

"Especially since I even got a sentry to put on duty," Lone said. He then turned his head and gave a short whistle. Moments later, Ironsides came trotting around the corner of the cabin.

Tru watched, eyes widening, as the sleek animal moved up and lowered his head for Lone to pat his neck and rub his velvety snout. "What a magnificent animal," she said.

"Yeah, me and him sorta look out for each other," Lone allowed. "I need to draw him a pail of water so he can get a drink, then I'll ground rein him out front here where he can graze and be on hand to let us know if anybody comes lurkin' around. He's best at sniffing out Injuns, but he saw and heard enough of those hombres from earlier to know that if he catches scent of them again it won't be a good sign. He'll do some chuffing and pawing to give us warning."

A few minutes later, after taking care of Ironsides, Lone followed Tru on into the cabin, stepping through the doorway to see what was left of what was supposed to be home.

CHAPTER 6

———

To Lone's considerable surprise, after hearing Elmer Dalrymple's description of how he'd found things when he and his deputy rode out to check, the interior was far from the ransacked wreckage he reported. In fact, except for the fire damage that was contained mostly to the framing logs and the immediate front area, the place was more tidily arranged than the way Lone and Peg usually kept it. There were quite a few things that didn't belong, a pile of crates, bundles, and a few odds and ends all stacked neatly off to one side, but most of the sparse furnishings that had been in place when Lone was last there appeared still present, all very orderly.

"I did some cleaning and re-arranging, partly to make room for these items that I brought from our wagon," Tru explained. "There was some wreckage that I had no choice but to throw away or burn in the fireplace, but otherwise I left things mostly as they appeared to have been."

Lone grinned a little. "No, you did more than that. Wasn't too often this joint ever looked so good. I'm afraid that a couple old trail rats like me and Peg weren't much as tidy housekeepers. Not that I'm complainin' about how you've dressed it up, mind you, but if you thought this place was deserted, why go to so much bother?"

"I didn't know for sure how long I would be staying here," Tru replied. "For however long it was, I did not wish to live in the midst of shambles."

"Reckon that makes sense," Lone allowed.

Tru made a gesture toward the cook stove. "I was preparing some tea just before I saw you riding up. Would you like some?"

"Don't mind if I do," Lone said. "But, while we're drinkin' it, what I'd really like is to hear the rest of your story. This pile of stuff here, for instance. Did I understand you to say it came from a wagon?"

It took a while for Tru to get into it. But gradually, steadily, after she had finished fixing and serving the tea and especially after she took a seat across from Lone at the sturdy, rough-hewn table built by him and Peg, she opened up with increasing candor. Like that of most folks, her tale had its share of hardship and tragedy, as foreshadowed, but also contained some good times and the love of close family.

Following the deaths of both parents by a fever epidemic shortly after their arrival in this country, Tru had been raised since infancy by her aunt and uncle, her late father's brother. They lived in Council Bluffs, Iowa, where Uncle Pao (though he went by the Americanized "Paul") ran a modestly successful tailor shop. After Tru's aunt, Pao's wife, passed away the previous summer, Uncle Pao decided to proceed with a plan he'd already been toying with for some time—to sell his Council Bluffs shop and relocate to Fort Collins, Colorado, where a third brother, Hai, also a widower, had his own thriving tailoring service and clothing store. He had been urging Pao to move west, buy in with him, and together grow the business into an even bigger success.

Once Pao made up his mind and set things in motion, all had gone as good or maybe even a little better than Tru and her uncle could have hoped for. Until just five days ago. Initially, Uncle Pao had gotten a fair price for his Council Bluff business, they'd outfitted themselves well for their journey, loaded essentials and some personal items into a rugged wagon pulled by a sturdy mule and were well on their way. Yes, the days of wagon travel were long and arduous and they perhaps should have waited another two or three weeks for the last lingering touches of winter to have passed more completely. But they were propelled by a dream and both were already used to hard work and long days at Uncle Pao's shop. Plus, they had provisioned a generous supply of warm blankets and water-resistant tarps to endure the cold nights and brief snow squalls they encountered.

Then, on that fateful day, just a short ways north and a bit east from the Busted Spur, all the careful planning and good luck that had gotten them this far had gone suddenly, terribly wrong in the span of just a few horrible minutes.

"We were moving along a low, grassy ridge with some flat rock outcroppings along one side," Tru related. "All of a sudden our mule reared up and shrieked as if in great pain and only then did I hear the strange buzzing, rattling sound coming from the high grass. I had the reins and my uncle was on the seat next to me, his arms folded and his chin tipped onto his chest, napping, I think, the way he did sometimes when it was slow and quiet. When the mule bolted forward, my uncle was jarred off balance and pitched to the ground. Luckily, he fell and rolled clear of the wagon wheels.

"I was able to get the mule under control after only a short distance. Once I had him stopped and the wagon brake set, I could hear my uncle also crying out in pain and fear. I seized the rifle and jumped down from the wagon to go back to him. That was when I saw him writhing and flailing on the ground where he had fallen, with buzzing, rattling snakes twisted around his feet and legs."

"Rattler nest," Lone said grimly. "They must have just come out from their winter sleep, were probably warmin' themselves in the sun on those flat rocks when your mule passed too close and riled 'em."

Tru continued on, almost as if she hadn't heard him. "My uncle struggled free and made it to his feet, came running to meet me. We quickly saw where he had been bitten several times and when we made it back to the mule we discovered that he, too, had been struck often. My uncle told me, as calmly as he could, that there was little hope for either of them but the worst thing we could do was panic."

"Sounds like your uncle had plenty of savvy."

"If you mean he had wisdom, then yes, he did. He was widely read, far beyond anything applicable to merely his skill with a needle. Unfortunately," Tru said with a dejected sigh, "he knew of no way to stop the poison flooding through either himself or the mule. While he was still able, he helped me unharness the animal to prevent it from going into a seizure or thrashing about in pain to a degree that might damage the wagon. He then led it off a ways, intending to shoot it in order to put it out of its misery. But, by then, his hands had begun trembling so badly he could not manage the rifle. So I had to put the poor beast down."

The anguish for having had to perform that act was still evident in her voice, though she tried to downplay it. What followed next, Lone knew as he listened to her tell it, was certainly even more trying.

"I got my uncle back to the wagon," Tru continued, "and positioned him underneath, making him as comfortable as I could. I propped him up and covered him with thick blankets. Built a small fire close by. He began experiencing bouts of shivering as if in a great chill and then moments later would be pouring sweat. His legs swelled badly and the skin all around the bite marks grew discolored and very sore and tender. I tried getting him to take some tea and bread, thinking maybe the bread would soak up some of the poison on his insides. But he couldn't keep anything down. By nightfall he was out of his head, thankfully unconscious much of the time, yet groaning in pain the whole while. All I could do was watch over him, and by turns beg or pray. Until he was gone."

"You did all that you or anybody could have done under the circumstances," Lone told her. "Multiple rattler bites, each one loaded with a pretty powerful dose of venom by the sound of it, way out here so far from any kind of help or treatment. Mighty tough thing to go through and not no picnic to have to see, either."

Tru went on to describe how she had buried her uncle the next day, covering the grave with stones both as a means to mark it and also to prevent scavengers from digging it up. This left her to face the prospect of being alone, on foot, with only a vague sense of where she might find another living soul who possibly could and would provide some assistance. The only thing she knew for sure, from the route they' been following on the rather crude map Uncle Pao's brother had sent him, was that she was now stranded somewhere in between the towns of North Platte and Ogallala, but with no clear sense of which was closer. She also knew she was about a mile and a half above the

South Platte River, though purposely separated from any regularly traveled trail or road running through the area.

This separation had been intentional on Uncle Pao's part the farther they traveled beyond the larger towns of eastern Nebraska and across the more sparsely populated middle and western reaches of the state. The fact they were Chinese neither stood out nor mattered all that much amidst heavier concentrations of people. But Pao, partly spurred by a cautionary comment in one of his brother's letters, had concern over the possibility that he and Tru *would* stand out in more remote settings and that the attention thus drawn might lead to remarks or behavior that would result in trouble. To avoid any chance of this, Pao elected to follow the course of the south tributary of the Platte River after it made its split—a route that would lead them practically to the doorstep of Fort Collins—but to do so at a distance meant to keep him and his niece apart from towns and other travelers along the famed "Platte River Road". On occasions when they needed to add to their supplies, Pao would venture into a town alone, after dark, then slip quickly and quietly back out again after purchasing the necessary goods.

Even as she was digging her uncle's grave, Tru recognized that avoiding other people would no longer be an option for her. At the very least, she needed to seek out someone willing to sell her a replacement mule. The thought of not continuing on to Fort Collins, even though now alone, never entered her mind. In order to pursue this, her plan was to walk south toward the river, hoping to either run into someone on the way who might prove helpful or, upon reaching the South Platte, follow it west into Ogallala and make her necessary transactions there.

That plan was altered when, shortly after starting out,

she spotted the deserted Busted Spur spread. This caused her delay striking out for Ogallala until after she had transported all off the goods from the wagon to better shelter in the unoccupied soddy.

Gesturing to the neatly arranged pile that included a couple large chests and several good-sized crates and bundles, Lone asked with a touch of admiration in his tone, "You mean you carried all of this stuff here from your wagon that's somewhere off to the northeast?"

Tru nodded. "Yes. Some I carried. Some of the larger items I wrapped in a canvas tarp and dragged. It took me the better part of two days, but I thought it worthwhile to have the goods better sheltered here rather than where they were."

"I don't know how far away your wagon is, but that was quite a feat, even over a short distance." A growing awareness was building in Lone that here was a gal whose exotic, delicate-looking outer beauty was wrapped around a plenty tough core.

"After I finally had everything here," Tru said. "I rested for another day, intending to strike out for the river on the following morning. That would have been earlier today. But last night was when the drunken men showed up. So I held off leaving today as a precaution against getting caught out in the open in case they came back looking for me."

Lone grimaced. "Turned out to be a smart precaution to take."

Tru's own expression took on some bitterness. "There were five of them to start with. I think they initially came by only to water their horses, they seemed to know this place was here. It was late twilight, not quite full dark. When they saw light from inside here, they barged in. And then, when they saw me and saw I was alone, their intentions soon turned vulgar. Two of them—the ones who just left, I believe—were very intent on having their way with me. The other three, especially one who was older, had reservations. They started to argue and that gave me the opening to get my hands on the rifle. I fired two rounds to show them I knew how to use it and that I meant business. Chased them outside and eventually away. But I strongly suspected that at least the two who were most crude would be back. I wondered if I would regret not killing them when I had the chance."

"And now I find myself wonderin' the same thing," Lone said sourly.

He drained his cup of tea, rose to his feet and walked over to the doorway. Stood there for several beats, looking out at the fading afternoon until his gaze involuntarily came to rest on where the departing Weak Chin and Gray Whiskers had disappeared in a dust haze.

Turning back, he saw Tru still sipping her tea, watching him. "You made up your mind whether or not you're ready to trust me?" he asked bluntly.

She answered without hesitation. "You have earned nothing less."

"Okay. Good. Then based on what you've told me and what I saw first-hand from that pair of skunks, I'm thinkin' now that they're almost sure to come back," said Lone. "Probably wait until dark, but not too late. They'll be smarting over getting run off a second time and that will make 'em eager to not only get at you but to also try and square things with me. Right about now they're certain to be guzzling some liquid courage, like I said before, maybe trying to scrounge some other lowlifes to bring along for backup."

Tru frowned. "How many can we expect to hold off?"

"As many as we have to," Lone told her. "Here's the thing: Way I see it, we've got a couple of options. For one, since we've got my horse we could make a run for it. There might be some risk of getting caught out in the open, same as you had concern about, but I'm pretty confident I know enough about foggin' a trail to keep them off our backs. Only that would leave all your stuff behind and unprotected. Not much doubt they're the type who would steal, wreck, or burn the whole works, not to mention finish doin' the job on my soddy, just for spite."

"What's another option?" Tru wanted to know.

"Stay and make our stand right here," Lone answered. "Get prepared, get ready—and then, when they show up, convince 'em hard and clear that the only thing we're willin' to give ain't none of what they came for."

"That is the option I prefer," Tru said.

Lone grinned. "I had a hunch that's how you'd feel."

CHAPTER 7

_____

"That Henry repeater you're so quick to reach for," Lone said, gesturing. "You as good with it as you claim?"

"I am quite proficient at hitting whatever target I aim at," Tru replied firmly.

"You don't mind my saying, that's kinda surprising."

Tru bristled a bit. "Because I am Chinese, you mean?"

"Sorta because of that, I guess," Lone admitted. "But I was thinkin' more along the lines of where you were living before you started on this journey. I ain't been back that way in quite a spell, mind you, but the last time I was, Council Bluffs—bumped up on the banks of the Missouri across from Omaha, with folks crowded in on one another and riverboats jammin' the water and railroad lines sproutin' every which way—was already a mighty busy place. My surprise comes from the thought of any young gal, Chinese or otherwise, growing up in a city like that and finding both the need and time to learn about handlin' a rifle."

"Yes, I can understand how that might seem unusual," Tru allowed. "And if not for this trip, it never would have happened for me either. But precisely because of our undertaking, Uncle Pao decided that one of us should acquire some prowess with a firearm before leaving. And since his long distance eyesight was poor, it fell to me. My uncle found a man, a former adventurer and wagon train guide, once also a mountain man such as you've described your late partner and hired him to take me out past the edge of town and teach me to shoot and care for the Henry rifle. He was very pleased with how well I learned and how accurate I became."

"I'll say again—that uncle of yours was plenty savvy," Lone declared.

"Yes, he tried to take into account every contingency." Tru paused, her expression saddening for a moment before she added, "Unfortunately, the lesson about rattlesnakes came a little too late and at a very steep price."

Lone grimaced. "Sad to say, those rattles that are supposed to give warnin' have been heard too dang late by a lot of good men."

"We could have made this trip, at least most of the way, by train. My uncle considered that," Tru said, "but in the end decided the cost—for our passage as well as for freighting the goods we wanted to bring—was too high. Uncle Pao was always very frugal. Plus, in this instance, he wanted to retain as much of the profit he got from selling his Council Bluffs shop so that he could invest in a bigger share of the joint business with his brother once we got to Fort Collins. Ironically, the alternative he chose cost him far more dearly than the train expenses he sought to avoid."

"Do you believe in fate? Is there a Chinese word for that?" Lone asked.

Tru considered. "*Mingyun*, I guess, would be the closest. Fate, destiny. Are you saying you think it was my uncle's fate to die from a snake bite?"

"Not exactly," Lone said, scrunching up his face, trying to come up with the right words. "More like Fate had in store for this to be his *time*. How or where a person meets their fate sorta depends on the lives they lead, the choices they make. But there's a Bigger Hand somewhere rollin' the dice on when. So if it's your time, it's your time and ain't a whole lot a body can do about it."

Tru regarded him. "I'm not sure I followed all of that. But I believe your words were meant to comfort me and for that I am grateful. I have done the immediate grieving for my uncle and will do more, in a personal way, over time to come. But, apart from that, the best thing I can do for him now is to continue on to Fort Collins and join Uncle Hai in growing the family business there."

"And my money's on you plumb succeeding," Lone said with a nod. "Leaving the first step toward makin' that come true a little matter of clearin' your path of some foul-minded rannies we expect to be comin' around to try and get in the way. So let's commence gettin' ready to deal with 'em."

******

As anticipated, they returned in the murkiness of late dusk. The sun was gone, the moon hadn't yet appeared and the glimmer of stars was beginning to show only weakly in the pale charcoal sky. The bellies of a few clouds far to the west were tinted pinkish purple by the last stubborn rays of sunlight reaching up over the horizon.

The recognizable shapes of the same two riders approached slowly, spread about a dozen feet apart. Each had a rifle drawn, butt propped on his hip, muzzle angled upward. From Lone's point of view—peering out through a gap between the boards he had nailed over the empty, charred-edged window through which Tru had previously taken a couple shots at him—Weak Chin was off to his left, Gray Whiskers to the right.

A little over ten yards out, they reined up their horses and Weak Chin called ahead. "You in the soddy! We know you're in there. We been watchin' and know you ain't went nowhere, plus we see some light leakin' out through the boarding-up you done on the windows."

"That's right. No secret we got a light burnin' in here," Lone called back. "It ain't a very bright one, but I guess it Mangyan might seem like it to you—seein's how what you got between your ears is provin' to be almighty dim. Didn't I warn you not to come around here again?"

"You huffed out some gut wind, if that's what you mean," snarled Gray Whiskers. "But that was when you already had a drawed gun on us and we didn't have no reasonable chance at ours. Only, as you can see, this time we came better prepared to do some huffin' and snortin' right back at you."

Lone chuckled tauntingly. "There's more sign of that dimness between your ears. You're perched out there in the open while I'm tucked behind solid cover—yet somehow you got the bulge on me?"

"That's the way we see it," Weak Chin came back. "We figure we're far enough back and dark is settlin' in fast enough so's if you decide to start throwin' lead, ain't no guarantee you'll hit your mark with the first shot. And any after that first one ain't gonna come so easy. 'Cause we'll hit the dirt and start throwin' back. And, just so you know, we made sure to bring along plenty of cartridges so's we can riddle that sod shack to nothing but a pile of crumbled dirt and grass tufts."

"What's more," added Gray Whiskers, "we also brung along a jug of coal oil. Meanin', if we take a mind to, we can finish the half-assed job somebody else did and set that whole hill afire!"

If that was supposed to rattle Lone, his sarcastic reply quickly showed otherwise. "So you're gonna accomplish what you set out for by killin' me and roastin' the girl. That what you're saying?"

"We're saying it'll keep you from hornin' in and claimin' the slant-eye all to yourself, you cocky bastard," Weak Chin snarled. "We'll by-God accomplish that much!"

"Are you that hard up to force yourselves on a woman?" Lone goaded some more. "I been away for awhile, like I told you—but did all the whores suddenly move out of North Platte and Ogallala?"

"Whores cost money. And the ones hereabouts are gettin' snootier and more expensive all the time," said Gray Whiskers.

"That's right. Free is free, and that's always too good to pass up," declared Weak Chin. "Besides, I've always had a hankerin' to dally with a slant-eye. Which makes this one all the more reason not to pass up."

"What about that Chink they had in Ogallala for a while? I thought you took yourself a turn with her?" Gray Whiskers asked, sounding genuinely curious.

"Haw! She wasn't no Chink at all," Weak Chin scoffed. "They made her out to be so's they could charge extra for her being all exotic and special. When the truth came out, she wasn't nothing but a scrawny Tennessee hillbilly gal with squinty eyes. What's more, she couldn't even—"

"Excuse me, gents," Lone interrupted. "Much as I'd like to spend the evening listenin' to your tales of unrequited love and heartbreak. How about givin' some thought to turning our situation here into something that maybe wouldn't be so disappointing?"

"What's that supposed to mean?" Weak Chin demanded. "We ain't fixin' to ride away from here disappointed. Not entirely. We're aimin' to get us some satisfaction, one way or another."

Lone said, "How about money? Would that satisfy you? Enough to afford several visits to some of those snooty, higher-priced whores? Hell, enough so's you could afford a trip to Lincoln or maybe even Denver—somewhere they'd be certain to have some *genuine* Chink gals to dally with."

There was a long pause before Weak Chin replied. "You're layin' it on mighty thick, mister. And the smell is about equal as thick. But, at the same time, I gotta say you've caught our interest. So let's hear some more. What are you drivin' at?"

"The thing is," Lone responded, "when you and the others first came 'round the other night, you was too boozed up and hump-backed to notice anything more than a pretty gal you figured was yours for the takin'. You found out quick enough that you missed the rifle she got her hands on and ran you off with. But what else you missed was all the trappings stacked in here with her—things that should have been a sign that she was more than just some cast-off left for your easy pickings."

"So what?" said Gray Whiskers. "I saw some boxes and bundles of stuff piled in there, but what difference is that supposed to make?"

"If you took time to think about it, it might have given you a clue that here was a woman of substance, of means. Which happens to be the case." Lone paused to let that much sink in, then went ahead with the lie he and Tru had concocted with the aim of trying to throw the two troublemakers off course. "You see, Miss Chang—that's her name—is the niece of a successful businessman in the Denver area. She was on her way to join him after her father passed away back east. But the men her uncle hired to bring her to him turned out to be lowlife skunks. They got this far and then cut out on her—took the money they'd been paid, plus what more she had with her for traveling expenses along with some valuable jewelry and left her here to fend for herself."

"That sounds like hard luck," Weak Chin said somewhat thoughtfully. But then, showing he wasn't quite drunk enough or gullible enough to swallow the bait whole, he added, "Only what sense did it make to bring her this far before doing her like that? Where did they start out from? Wasn't there plenty of chances before this for them scoundrels to pull their double-cross?"

"Those are some reasonable questions," Lone allowed. "For the answers, I reckon you'd have to ask 'em of the scoundrels who did the dirty dealin'. All I know is that Miss Chang has told me her tale and I believe her. I also believe her when she says that anybody who helps her out of her fix by gettin' her somewhere so's she can wire her uncle to let him know what happened, she will make sure they get a fitting reward."

"That sounds to me like a big, fat, hot-air story meant to stall us from what we came for," growled Gray Whiskers. "The onliest reward I want from Miss Chinky Chang she has got ready to hand over right now and I'm plumb sick of holdin' off to get at it."

"Now hang on, cousin. Hang on," Weak Chin urged him. "I'm stoked up, same as you and I ain't sayin' I buy that yarn whole. But just think on it a minute and remember the old story about the goose what laid the golden eggs."

"What in blazes do geese and golden eggs have to do with anything?"

"I said *think* on it a minute!" Weak Chin barked. "We go for the kind of reward you want, we get it and it's over. Done with. But if there's any truth to that yarn they're spinnin', then we might be lookin' at a bigger reward that will make for a *whole bunch* of those them other, quicker kind. Don't you see? That's why I'm sayin' we take a little minute to think on it."

Sensing the time was right, Lone called out, "Sounds to me like it might be useful for you to hear some of this from Miss Chang herself. Can you keep civil tongues in your heads long enough have a palaver with her?"

"She don't try to lay on the lies too thick, we'll do our part," Weak Chin said. "But she'd better be convincin' and be quick about it—this is draggin' out too long."

"Oh, I got a feeling this is gonna take a better turn before much longer," Lone told him. Then, pushing away from the window, he gave a go-ahead nod to Tru before turning the rest of the way around and gliding silently toward the back wall of the soddy. Ducking down and entering into a black, barely discernible opening there, immediately off one end of the fireplace, he heard Tru's lilting voice start to speak behind him, "Hello. I am Tru Min Chang. And everything Mr. McGantry told you is true."

CHAPTER 8

The opening at the base of the rear wall was an escape tunnel that Lone and Peg had dug when first cutting into the hill, even before building the rest of the outward-extending soddy cabin. "A couple old Injun fighters like me and Peg weren't about to put ourselves in a box without a back door," Lone explained to Tru upon revealing it to her as part of formulating their plan for dealing with the expected return of Weak Chin and Gray Whiskers.

The passage, about four feet in diameter, extended back a hundred feet at a slight upward angle, exiting in a stand of tangled brush on a slope at the far side of the hill. Other than Lone crawling through once or twice to make sure it stayed clear of cave-ins or blockage from root growth, it had never been used. The description of how Peg's body had been found lying outside in front of the cabin seemed to indicate he'd been caught by surprise and ambushed before he realized he was in danger, therefore giving him no chance to try and gain cover inside and possibly utilize the escape route.

But such was not the case tonight. With time to think

and plan, Lone had struck on the idea of using the tunnel not as a means of escape but rather as a tool to help gain an advantage over the upcoming confrontation. If Weak Chin and Gray Whiskers could be lured to the front of the cabin and made to think they had Lone and Tru trapped inside, which was how things now stood, then a sudden and unexpected flanking maneuver would not only catch the pair by surprise but would turn *them* into the ones who were trapped, out in the open, by a potential crossfire.

All that was needed for it to work, Lone told himself as he squirmed and scrambled frantically though the tunnel (into which he had earlier made another precautionary trip to make sure the way was clear), was for Tru to be able to keep talking long enough to allow him the time he needed and to not let the men out front grow suspicious.

After Lone had gone just a few feet, the only sound he could hear was that of his body scraping along and the grunts of his effort. This blotting out of other surrounding noise also seemed to distort his sense of time. He felt like he was crawling steadily but at the same time anxiety gripped him that maybe he was taking too long. Dragging his Winchester Yellowboy along with him made moving in the cramped space more difficult, but having the weapon was important for the upcoming confrontation once he made it outside. Writhing through the tight space, that had at first seemed so cool and dry, quickly had him dripping with sweat.

And then he could feel and smell a stirring of fresher air and abruptly his head was poking out of the tunnel and up through the tangled underbrush. He forced himself to refrain from clambering out eagerly and sucking in great mouthfuls of the chill night air. Instead he withdrew slowly and quietly, though nevertheless drawing in plenty of deep, grateful inhalations.

Easing out of the brush, Lone crouched and listened intently in order to hear how the exchange between Tru and the two surly wranglers was going. He was relieved to discover that it sounded to be continuing okay in measured, albeit somewhat tense tones.

"Seems to me," Weak Chin was saying, "that what you're askin' amounts to expectin' me and my cousin to buy a pig in a poke."

"I do not understand," Tru came back. "I am not offering to sell you any pigs. No animals are part of the transaction we are discussing."

Lone couldn't suppress a grin. He wasn't sure if he was listening to another case of Tru being genuinely perplexed by some slang phrasing or if she was merely pretending to be for the sake of eating up time, dragging out the conversation.

"Jesus Christ," Weak Chin growled in frustration. "How can you use such big, fancy words one second and then turn around and not understand plain lingo! Look, 'pig in a poke' ain't really got nothing to do with pigs, see? It's what you call, uh, an expression. uh, sort of like."

Lone put away his grin and set himself in motion once again. He had time to neither wonder about nor admire Tru's tactics; what he needed to concentrate on now was making sure he got in position to have the crossfire set up when the time was right, either when the confab between Tru and the wranglers broke down, or as soon as Lone decided he was ready to make the call.

Circling out wide away from the back side of the hill, remaining in a half crouch, Lone ghosted to a section of three-rail corral fence and slipped to its opposite side. When the bunch who'd gunned down Peg had then stole the Busted Spur horse herd, they'd knocked down a long stretch of the corral's front railing. It remained mostly collapsed. But this side section was still intact, providing Lone some bands of shadowy cover as he glided along toward where the gap was.

He could have wished for brighter conditions but, at the same time, the lack of moon- or starlight eliminated the risk of being given away by any glint off the barrel of the Yellowboy swinging at his side. Besides, his vision was well adjusted to the dark by now, heightened even more by emerging from the pitch black of the tunnel. What was more, the peripheral night vision of Weak Chin and Gray Whiskers would be dulled by their attention to the cabin and the bars of illumination seeping out from between its boarded-over door and windows. As he catfooted along the corral railing, Lone made sure not to affect his own sight by glancing over at the lighted cabin.

When he reached the break in the railing, Lone froze in place. He was almost perfectly in line with Weak Chin and Gray Whiskers. He could see both of their murky shapes silhouetted against the pale charcoal sky. The only problem was the distance. Considering the murkiness, he wanted to move up closer on them if at all possible. A bulky old wooden wheelbarrow offered that opportunity. Tipped over on its side with its wheel broken off, it lay in a patch of weeds eight or ten yards nearer to the two mounted men from where Lone currently knelt. Reaching that 'barrow would not only achieve the closer proximity Lone desired but would also provide better cover in the likelihood lead started flying. The risk posed by crossing the open space in between, Lone decided, would be worth it.

He slipped around to the front side of the rail then dropped a little lower in his crouch, holding very still once again. He wondered if Tru had spotted him from her vantage point.

The back-and-forth between her and the wranglers was starting to grow a little frazzled.

"If you refuse to believe the things I have told you," Tru was saying, "what other explanation can there be for why a young woman would be stranded in such a remote place, as I am, along with a large assortment of personal items?"

"It ain't up to us to explain nothing or to give a damn how or why you ended up in the fix you're in," Gray Whiskers hollered back. "All we care about is that we're the ones who found you and that gives us dibs on what we want. All you got to do is show us a little friendliness up front, then we'd be happy to deliver you somewhere you can send your wire. How about we end all this jabberin' and just cut to it?"

The coarse proposition was too much. It pushed Tru past being able to hold her temper in check any longer. Tone dripping with disgust, she responded, "I would have to be dead and infested with maggots before I would be friendly with the likes of you in the filthy manner you are suggesting!"

This, in turn, riled Gray Whiskers to where he could barely sputter out his next words. "Why, you treacherous little slant-eye! Did you think we were ever gonna agree to anything without *that* bein' part of the bargain?"

"How about it, McGantry?" demanded Weak Chin. "Who's stringin' who along here? You had to've understood we always figured on gettin' ourselves a turn at the gal as part of any deal. Didn't you? Speak up, man—quit lettin' this sharp-tongued Chink do you talkin' for you!"

There it was. Tru had bought Lone the time he needed, but nothing extra. The basketful of eggs had just been dropped and the contents were busting wide open.

Staying in his crouch and jacking a shell into the Yellowboy's chamber—the sound of the action snapping in the stillness almost as sharply as if he'd pulled the trigger—Lone pressed the butt stock to his shoulder then called out, "Over here, coyote brain! You bet I'll speak up and unless you two freeze right like you are, I'll do my talkin' with lead!"

The entire scene seemed to freeze.

One tense second ticked by. Then another.

The two riders sat perfectly motionless in their saddles. Lone could *feel* their eyes rolling toward the sound of his voice, searching to try and pinpoint where he was.

He spoke again, rasping out, "I got a Winchester set dead on you. One wrong twitch, I'll cut you down like plinkin' bottles lined up in a carnival shoot. Now start by pitchin' your own rifles to the ground."

"Like hell we will," growled Gray Whiskers, the one nearest to Lone. "You ain't gonna chase us off so easy this time."

"You're right about that," Lone told him. "I don't intend to go as easy on you as before. This time you'll hobble away from here on shank's mare, stripped down to your long handles and socks. Or, if you play it dumb, belly down over a saddle."

"I don't think he can get us both, cuz. Not in the dark," said Weak Chin. "I say if we clear these saddles and hit the ground blazin', we got a chance to take him. But you're the one closest, the one most at risk. You make the call."

Lone tried one last warning. "It'd be a fool's play, no matter who calls it. Don't forget, there's also a rifle in the cabin trained on you. You've already had a taste of what it serves up."

"Nuts to that," sneered Gray Whiskers. "The slant-eye may know how to make noise with a gun, but I'm bettin' she can't hit shit. Go for broke, Isaac!"

Everything that had been holding still suddenly broke into a flurry of frantic activity. The two horsemen twisted at the waist, turning in opposite directions from one another, and hurled themselves from their saddles. This meant that Gray Whiskers was facing in Lone's general direction as he left his stirrups. At the same time, he was swinging his rifle around and triggering a shot blindly out ahead of himself. With no clear idea of Lone's actual position, however, the shot went harmlessly high and wide.

But the same wasn't true for the round issued almost simultaneously by Lone. A fraction of a second after feeling the kick and hearing the roar of the Yellowboy in his hands, Lone also heard the grunt of pain coming from Gray Whiskers as the slug punched into him on his way to the ground. A moment later, though, it became evident that the strike hadn't been a finisher. Immediately upon landing heavily, Gray Whiskers kicked himself into a pair of side rolls, all the while maintaining a grip on his rifle. As soon as he was done rolling, he shoved the rifle snout forward and got off another shot, this one targeted on Lone's muzzle flash.

For Weak Chin's part, he too had fired a shot on his way out of the saddle. The bullet smacked dully against the reinforcing boards nailed over the front door of the soddy. Before he could fire again, Tru—overcoming a slight touch of hesitation before pulling a trigger on a human target—cut loose with her Henry and began sizzling the air all around him with lead. Cursing, snapping off return fire with little or no aim, Weak Chin clambered to his feet and made a dash for the same well housing Lone had used for cover earlier in the day.

Panicked by all the shooting and cursing and the rib-gouging departure of the riders from their backs, the horses belonging to Weak Chin and Gray Whiskers reacted in confusion and fear. They reared up, wheeled aimlessly and shrieked in terror. This shifting of massive bodies and the dust cloud kicked up by their pawing, stamping hooves immediately added to the murkiness of twilight.

Nevertheless, even with the dust thickening, the red flame of Gray Whiskers' rifle as he poured more shots at Lone continued to mark his position despite his distinct outline becoming more blurred. That was all Lone needed. Dropping flat onto his belly, letting Gray Whiskers' bullets slice the air above his head, Lone stroked his trigger calmly and again heard the wrangler issue a grunt of pain as the slug pounded into him.

Gray Whiskers had gone into another roll and then rose up on a knee before commencing the volley he'd been sending Lone's way. The second bullet strike jolted him and dropped him onto one hip. But the stubborn bastard kept on still trying to make a fight of it. From his half-prone position he thrust out his rifle and triggered another erratic round. By then, Lone had jacked a fresh round into his Yellowboy and was ready with a response. The third bullet he sank in Gray Whiskers elicited no grunt of pain this time—but the manner in which the heavyset man's body finally sagged as loose and lifeless as a lumpy pile of clothes told the story silently but plainly.

By the same token, there was nothing silent about the rest of the scene. The horses were still wheeling and shrieking and Tru and Weak Chin were continuing to trade a fierce barrage of lead.

Lone's attention was drawn fully to this immediately after putting Gray Whiskers down. A piercingly shrill screech from one of the horses made it particularly demanding. Squinting in order to peer through the dust haze, Lone saw that the cause for the poor beast's mournful cry was having been caught by an errant round. Throwing its head high, the animal made a drunken sideways stagger and then collapsed. The remaining horse reacted by breaking away and galloping off in a thunderous clamor of pounding hooves.

All of this brought about a slight break in the shooting. Weak Chin, who hadn't yet made it to the well housing because he'd been busy dodging the panicked horses, trying to keep from getting knocked down and trampled, now used the lag in gunfire as an opportunity to instead find cover by throwing himself in behind the body of the fallen horse. "You slant-eyed bitch," he hollered in the direction of the cabin, "you killed my horse!" and then promptly resumed pouring more lead as a follow-up to the words.

Lone also spotted a slice of opportunity in the moment. Shoving to his feet, he lunged forward and made the dash to the old wrecked wheelbarrow he'd wanted to reach earlier. Scarcely had he skidded in behind it, though, than Weak Chin seemed suddenly struck by an awareness that there was no longer any shooting taking place off to his side. Whether or not catching Lone's movement out the corner of his eye accounted for some of this realization, there was no way to know.

But it really didn't matter. What it came down to was that Weak Chin's position, even with the cover he'd gained, had just turned a lot more desperate.

"Jerome?" he wailed, a quaver in his voice. "You over there, cuz? Talk to me, man—let me know you're okay!"

Lone responded, "Jerome's a little busy right now. Busy bein' dead! So no, he ain't okay and neither are you gonna be—not unless you throw down your guns and be mighty quick about it."

But, like his cousin, Weak Chin showed a determination to carry the fight all the way to the end. He twisted around behind the horse carcass and thrust his rifle barrel in Lone's direction, bellowing, "Damn you! I won't be okay until I've blasted you to hell and gone!"

There followed a flurry of shots that battered the old wheelbarrow mercilessly, splintering the weathered wood and knocking loose a year and more's accumulation of dust that puffed out in gritty tan clouds. Lone stayed hunkered low and safe and let the enraged fool burn powder uselessly.

Then came the sound Lone had been waiting for, the dull click of the firing pin on Weak Chin's rifle hitting an empty chamber. It quickly sounded again, and then again. In his rage, Weak Chin had spent all off his bullets.

Now Lone rose up and took his time aiming the Yellowboy that still had plenty of rounds left in it. Weak Chin glared hatefully at him, his eyes glowing like hot coals in the murky light. Lone didn't waste time with another warning; either the man in his sights saw the hopelessness of his situation or he didn't.

The answer came in the form of Weak Chin flinging away his emptied rifle and then desperately, defiantly clawing at his right hip, trying to yank free the revolver holstered there.

Lone once more stroked the trigger and felt the Yellowboy buck against his shoulder. In the same instant, there came the roar of Tru's Henry from the cabin window.

The double impact hit Weak Chin, jerking his upper body into a quarter spin and then pitching him out away from the horse carcass to leave him lying flat on his back, dead fingers closed on the grips of the revolver still in its holster.

CHAPTER 9

"Ho-lee blazes, Lone," wailed Elmer Dalrymple. "You out to set some kind of record or something? You been back in the area not even two whole days and you already got three bodies piled up around you."

Lone frowned. "I'll thank you not to include any mention of Peg in with the likes of these two varmints. For one thing, I had nothing to do with him checkin' out, I just happened to be there when he did. But I'm plenty willing to take credit for helpin' to snuff the wicks of this pair. You happen to recognize either one of 'em?"

From where he was leaning over the travois attached to Ironsides, Deputy Keith Overstreet replaced the corner of the blanket he had peeled back in order to examine the faces of the two dead men loaded on the litter, then straightened up. "Yeah, we know 'em both," he announced. "The huskier one of the two is Jerome Greer. The other is Isaac Halsey. Cousins. Or, reckon I should say, that's who they *was*."

Overstreet was a tall, leanly muscled specimen with pale blue eyes and curly, reddish blond hair, part of which was displayed in thick sideburns reaching down from under his hat and running along the sides of his face. He'd been Dalrymple's deputy for a good many years, loyal and competent in the performance of his duties, though with a leaning toward intolerance, even hot-tempered at times.

"They claimed they rode for the Box 50," Lone said.

"Yeah, they did," confirmed Dalrymple.

"And on account of that, all things considered," added Overstreet, "I'd say the reaction to their deaths ain't gonna go over very smooth."

Lone nodded. "I figured as much, knowin' how thick riders for the same brand can be. That's why we didn't waste any time loadin' this pair up and bringin' 'em here, wanting to get the whole story laid out straight before any of their fired-up pals came around lookin' to settle the score and only make things worse. The horse that took off when the shootin' started no doubt made its way back to the Box 50 spread where there are at least three other hombres who'd know about the interest these two curs had in Miss Chang. With the riderless horse showin' up as a sign of trouble, it seemed almost certain that at least one of those three would speak up and lead the rest to the Busted Spur as a likely spot for the trouble to have took place. I decided I didn't want to risk puttin' me and Miss Chang through another shootout, especially not against probably even greater odds."

It was that line of reasoning that had led to Lone and Tru, with their grisly cargo, showing up here in North Platte just after sun-up. Being inclined neither to break a sweat burying the two dead men nor to merely leave them laying for the other Box 50 riders to find and stoke their thirst for vengeance all the more, Lone had built the drag litter out of blankets and a couple of corral poles. With this then attached to Ironsides and the bodies piled on, they'd traveled through the night to reach the town. Lone had walked and had put Tru up in the saddle to begin with; but after a short ways, insisting she did not want to over tax the big gray, she got down and strode step for step alongside Lone.

They had rousted the two lawmen immediately upon arrival and the four of them now stood in front of the jail building with the rest of the town just coming awake and starting to show loading signs of activity around them.

"Keith," Dalrymple addressed his deputy, "how about you get these bodies on over to the undertaker? Go around the back way and try to draw the least amount of attention you can before everybody gets fully woke up. Meanwhile, I'll take Lone and Miss Chang inside and get their official statements on how all this happened."

"Will do," Overstreet said. He cut his gaze to Lone. "Where you want me to bring your horse after I get shed of the bodies?"

"Ma Sharples keeps that little stable out behind her place," Lone replied. "I'm hoping Ma has got a couple rooms where me and Tru—er, Miss Chang—can stay until we get this business sorted out. Even if she don't, Woodrow, the old gent who looks after her stable, knows how to care for Ironsides."

"That's where I'll drop him off then." Now the deputy turned his attention back to Dalrymple. "After I get that taken care of, Marshal, you want me to ride out to the Box 50 and notify 'em about Isaac and Jerome?"

Dalrymple seemed to consider for a minute. Then, twisting his mouth wryly, he said, "I think you can hold off on that. At least for a little while. Based on what he's told us so far, I think Lone is right. I expect we'll be seeing some representatives from the Box 50 soon enough, without the need to go out there and notify anybody."

******

"Isaac and Jerome are—or were, I guess I should say," Marshal Dalrymple was explaining, "the kind of fellas my sainted old mother would have called ne'er-do-wells. You probably know, or have known, the type. Not really bad in a criminal way—leastways not until how these ones were trying to force themselves on Miss Chang—but at the same never headed for any good without somebody herding 'em in line and looking out for them."

"The difference with Isaac and Jerome, though, was that they belonged to some relatives who were a cut above. There were four Halsey brothers and Jerome, their cousin, who all showed up in this area not long after the war. Isaac was the youngest and I think him and Jerome were about the same age—then there's Cliff, Royce and Granger. They all signed on for ranch work at first until some eventually branched out. Cliff became a deputy marshal over in Ogallala. Royce he sort of drifts around, never too far, doing some shotgun guard work or the like until he gets a poke and then goes on the gambling circuit until he's cashed out again. Granger, the oldest, he stuck with cattle and now is the ramrod out at the Box 50. He's the one who's been holding Isaac and Jerome most in line, leastways in line enough to keep them—though just barely, at times—employed as part of his crew."

"So now," summed up Lone, "by us killin' those two low rungs of the family ladder, you figure the higher rungs will be looking to make us pay?"

"I'm afraid they might, yeah."

"Even though the other three brothers are supposed to be upstandin' citizens? Even though me and Tru were actin' only in defense of ourselves and our property? And no matter if the law—namely you—buys our story of how and why it happened?"

"I do buy your story, Lone. Ain't no 'if' about it," Dalrymple said. "I know you, know you wouldn't have killed those two jackasses without good reason. And you sure wouldn't have brung in their bodies if there was something dodgy about you gunning 'em. But me believing you may not mean a hill of beans to the Halseys. I got a bad feeling they're going to see responding to those shootings as an obligation—a matter of blood. And then there's the jurisdiction thing. The shooting happened outside my official jurisdiction in the first place and if they decide to retaliate outside my jurisdiction. well, you've heard that song before."

This conversation had moved inside, into the marshal's office where Lone and Tru were seated in wooden chairs hitched up before the desk while Dalrymple fussed at the stove getting a pot of coffee brewed.

For practically the first time since arriving in town, Tru spoke, "I do not understand this talk about a song and, and jurisdiction?"

Lone smiled tolerantly. "The song thing, that's just some more American lingo. It's a way of talking about something that gets said over and over again. But jurisdiction, that means what it says. It's a kind of legal thing. It's the, uh, boundaries of an area that somebody like Marshal Dalrymple here has control over. Inside of town, within the city limits, see, he makes arrests or does whatever he needs to do to enforce the law. But outside of town, like out at my ranch, he don't have any official authority. That's outside his jurisdiction."

Tru frowned. "But a wrong deed—hurting or killing someone, or one person forcing their will on another—is wrong wherever it happens, is it not? Those are basic rules of decency that should apply anywhere. Laws, if you choose to call them that. Shouldn't a law *enforcer* be able to act against such misdeeds no matter where they are encountered?"

Lone, his grin widening, shifted his gaze over to the marshal. "How about it, Elmer? Sounds to me like what the gal is suggestin' makes some pretty good sense."

"Can't say I disagree," Dalrymple replied. "But until the state legislature puts laws on the books that officially read that way, I'm bound by the way it is. To do otherwise, would make *me* a rule breaker."

Tru looked appealingly at Lone. "Legislature?"

"You don't want to know, kid," Lone told her with a wag of his head. "It's what they call a pack of mostly musty-headed old geezers back at the state capitol who get elected to dream up rules and laws that the rest of us have to abide by, whether they make good sense or not."

"That's about as good a description as you're likely to get from common folk like me or Lone, miss," Dalrymple told Tru. "Don't try to make sense out of it, especially since you're on your way to Colorado. They've got their own set of rules and laws you can confuse yourself with once you settle there. In the meantime, this coffee is ready. You two want a cup?"

Anyone who'd ever tasted the wretched brew Dalrymple called coffee, as Lone had on a few occasions, was unlikely to be in a hurry for more. So, for his own sake as well as Tru's, Lone said rather hurriedly, "Thanks, but I think we'll go ahead and pass, Elmer. If I can speak for Miss Chang, what me and her need most is some place to get off our feet and find some rest. We put in a mighty long night."

"Somewhere to wash up and rest, yes. That would be most desirable," agreed Tru.

"Like I already said, I'm hopin' Ma Sharples has a couple spare rooms to put us up in. If not," said Lone, "we'll check in to the Platte River Hotel. If and when some Box 50 men come around. Well, you'll find me one place or the other."

Dalrymple made a sour face. "I'm afraid there ain't no if about it. But when they do, I'll get word to you right away."

CHAPTER 10

"Oh, man. Oh, man, this don't look good. not good at all."

Rob "Cully" Cullen groaned out these words as he stood gazing down at the dead horse out front of the Busted Spur sod cabin. Cully was a lean, narrow-shouldered young man in his middle twenties, a ranch hand and cow puncher for over half of that time. Only marginally competent in the performance of his duties, his awareness of this left him with a perpetually uncertain, somewhat anxious expression. But seldom more anxious than it was at the moment.

"This is Isaac's horse sure enough. Shot deader than a stone," Cully went on. "And there's enough spent cartridges scattered around to make it look like somebody fought a war."

"Well, a-course it's Isaac's horse," said a frowning Buck Telford from where he stood a few feet off to one side of Cully. He was about the same age, a bit stockier though still trim, his facial features somber-looking and weathered some by the elements though retaining a trace of boyish handsomeness. "Seein's how it was Jerome's nag that showed up back at the ranch," he added, "you had to figure Isaac's was still out here somewhere and, since it didn't come back too, most likely hurt or dead."

Cully's forehead puckered. "But that still don't tell us where Isaac or Jerome are. Though the fact neither of 'em are laying around also dead is maybe a good sign, don't you think?"

"You can hope for that, but I wouldn't take it as too strong a sign those boys are necessarily in good shape," said Virgil Sweeney, a third man who was standing a bit apart from the other two. Though he had no way of knowing the spot's full significance, his feet were planted astraddle the bloody patch of ground where Jerome had bled out. Sweeney was tall and solid of build, twenty years older than either Cully or Buck, with every day of those years showing on his weathered, deeply-seamed, squinty-eyed face; but his back was as straight as his shoulders were wide and it was a grudgingly accepted fact all through the Box 50 outfit that in his methodical, never-a-wasted-motion manner of doing things he could outwork any of the younger pups on the crew any day of the week.

"There's a powerful amount of blood been spilled here," Sweeney noted, "and plenty more spent cartridges to go with it."

"Oh, hey!" Buck suddenly exclaimed, craning his neck to look down at the ground between him and Cully. "Oh lord, there's a big patch of blood here, too and it ain't from the horse."

Cully groaned even louder than before. "Aw, Jesus, you don't suppose that Chinee gal opened up on Isaac and Jerome and cut 'em down in a shootout, do you?"

"I don't know what to think," replied Buck. "But if that's where all this blood and everything came from, where are their bodies?"

Sweeney pulled his worn old Colt from an equally worn holster rigged for the cross-draw on his left hip. "Could be," he drawled, "they got shot up and crawled into the cabin to tend their wounds. By the look of all the bullet holes on that door and those boarded-over windows, whoever was in the cabin got a healthy or un-healthy, I reckon you could say, dose of lead fed right back to 'em. Maybe everybody's in there now. Either healin' up or…"

As the old cowpoke's words trailed off ominously, Cully and Buck swung their own gazes to the front of the cabin. Eyes widening, they drew their own sidearms.

"Fan out and keep a sharp eye peeled," advised Sweeney as he started toward the front door.

A handful of minutes later, after Sweeney had shoved the door open while standing cautiously off to one side, all three Box 50 men were milling inside the cabin. It smelled faintly of powder smoke and a few nicks where bullets had slammed their way inside could be spotted, but otherwise there were no signs of trouble or disarray.

"No blood, no hint of a struggle. no nothing," declared Buck. "What the hell gives?"

"I don't know, but this is getting crazier by the minute," replied Cully, for some reason feeling the need to speak in a hushed whisper.

Sweeney's only response was to turn and walk back outside. The two younger men followed him, halting abruptly to stand back and watch as he shuffled a few slow steps back and forth in front of the cabin, studying the ground closely as he did.

"What is it, old timer? What do you see?" Buck wanted to know.

"Fresh horse tracks, in closer to the cabin. But not from Isaac or Jerome. And looky here" —Sweeney pointed— "at these other marks, too."

Buck and Cully studied what he was indicating—straight lines gouged into the dirt about three feet apart.

"What are those? From the wheels of a cart or something?" asked Cully.

"Drag litter. A travois. Like Indians sometimes use to haul their belongings or sick behind a horse," Sweeney said. "Leastways, that's my guess."

Buck looked puzzled. "So you're saying that Chinee gal shot Isaac and Jerome and then drug their bodies off behind a horse?"

"All I'm sayin' is that it looks to me—and I don't pretend to be no great shakes at readin' ground sign—like somebody dragged away *something* behind a horse." Sweeney released an annoyed sigh. "Who did the draggin' and what they was haulin', I got no clue."

"But that Chinee gal didn't have no horse or nothing," said Cully. "We made sure of that the other night when, well, when we was here before."

"Maybe it was somewhere we didn't see. Maybe somebody else came by. I can't say. What I can say," Sweeney insisted, "is that these hoof prints ain't from Isaac or Jerome. And these other marks, I'm pretty sure, are from a drag litter."

"Looks like they're headed south and east," Buck observed. "The Sarben settlement is due south, and Ogallala is away off to the west. That makes it whoever left these tracks appears to've been headed for North Platte."

"Makes sense," Sweeney allowed. "If they're haulin' hurt and wounded, there's where they'd be sure to find a doctor."

Cully's expression grew deeply anguished. "Man, oh man. Do I ever wish Granger and Mr. Denton wasn't off on that bull-buying trip. Especially Granger. If he was here, Isaac and Jerome wouldn't have ever got in this fix."

"Don't count on it," Buck replied. "Not even Granger could keep those two in line all the time. Not when they decided to go on one of their benders and particularly not when they got all snorty and hump-backed like they did at the sight of that doggone Chinee gal. Maybe we'd've been better off to let 'em have their way with her that first night and been done with it."

"I don't want to hear that kind of talk," snarled Sweeney. "I'll take the blame for not keepin' 'em closer to the ranch yesterday instead of sendin' 'em out to round up strays. And I'll lay some blame on you two for not tellin' me sooner that you knew they'd shirked ever even startin' that duty. But, by God, we ain't packin' no blame for standin' by and purposely lettin' 'em have their way with that gal. That's something."

"Maybe so," Cully said sullenly. "But if anything bad has happened to 'em, then the only blame I'm worried about is the kind Granger might heap on us for not holding 'em better in check."

Sweeney's mouth pulled into a tight, grim line. Then he said, "We'll have to face that if and when the time comes. But first, we need to follow these tracks on into North Platte and find out just how bad things are. Let's saddle up."

CHAPTER 11

The way it turned out, Ma Sharples had only one room available at her boarding house when Lone went in search of a place for him and Tru to stay. But, in spite of what he'd told Dalrymple, Lone elected not to seek out alternative accommodations at the hotel. Instead, he arranged for Tru to take the room while he settled for some sleeping space in a clean stall of the livery barn out back. When Tru tried to protest, he explained how it really wasn't that much of a hardship on him.

"You gotta understand, kid," he told her, "that in my life I've spent far more nights sleepin' on the hard ground under the stars and sometimes minus the stars, but instead storm clouds sending down rain or even snow, than I have in a bed under a roof. So my bedroll blanket spread over a pile of soft, fresh straw is practically a luxury for me. Heck, I might even take a notion to hop in one of the horse troughs and have me a bath."

"No sense arguing with him, dear," Ma encouraged Tru. "He ain't apt to change his mind and if it happens he *does* soak his stubborn hide in a bath, that will be a victory all its own. The main thing for you to worry about, after the rugged night you've had, you poor thing, is getting your own self cleaned up and then laid down for some much needed rest."

Reluctantly, Tru allowed Ma to lead her off to her room and Lone made his own way out to the stable. He really did intend to make good on his promise to take a bath or at the very least scrub down thoroughly, but after spreading his blanket on the dry, clean-smelling straw Woodrow had pitched into an empty stall for him, he couldn't resist pulling off his boots and stretching out to cool his heels and relax some of the sore muscles in his legs from riding too many miles on shank's mare. He'd lay here for just a minute, he told himself.

The next thing Lone knew he was being wakened by somebody calling his name while poking a booted toe against the bottom of one sock-encased foot. Even before his eyes were open, Lone's right hand was reaching for the sixgun holstered on his right hip.

"Take it easy. It's only me," said a familiar voice.

Lone found himself squinting up at the lanky form of Keith Overstreet hovering over him. There was a moment of disorientation, until a darting glance to either side reminded him where he was and brought him the rest of the way awake.

Easing his hand off the grips of the Colt, Lone pushed to a sitting position and said, "Jesus. What time is it? Reckon I fell asleep a lot harder than I meant to."

"'Bout an hour past noon," the deputy told him. "And, yeah, you were sawing logs pretty good when I came in."

After pulling on his boots, Lone rose to his feet. Slapping loose straw off the seat of his pants, "What brings you around, Keith? Anything wrong?"

"The marshal sent me to fetch you. Don't know that anything's wrong, leastways not any more than already was. But some Box 50 riders showed up in town a little bit ago. They're over at the jail now. Elmer's giving 'em the lowdown on things, but he thought it'd be best if they heard some direct from you."

"The Halsey brother, the Box 50 ramrod, he with them?" Lone asked.

"No. He's out of town on a stock buying trip," came the answer.

Lone frowned. "Maybe that's good, maybe it'd be better to face him and get it over with." His frown deepened as something occurred to him. "You didn't drag Miss Chang over there, did you?"

Overstreet shook his head. "Elmer said to let you make the call on that."

"We'll leave her out of it, then. At least for now. She's been through enough," Lone declared. He brushed past the deputy and walked over to where a hand pump was mounted on a low platform at one end of a watering trough. As he began working the handle of the pump, he said, "Give me a chance to slosh away some sleep and leftover trail dust, then we'll head for the jail."

******

Three men, all obvious wrangler types, sat in wooden chairs before the marshal's desk. Their eyes tracked Lone's entrance with a mix of curiosity, sadness and smoldering anger. As Overstreet ushered him into the office area and closed the door behind them, Lone returned the looks he was getting with cool indifference. Then he slowly cut his gaze to Dalrymple, seated behind the desk.

"Lone," the marshal said, "these fellas ride for the Box

50 brand. In the order they're seated from where you're standing, you got Virgil Sweeney, Buck Telford and Cully Culbertson. Gents, this is the man I was telling you about—Lone McGantry."

A fresh round of looks were exchanged. Nobody made any move to stand or shake hands.

Dalrymple went on, "They came by the Busted Spur earlier this morning, looking for Jerome and Isaac. Spotted the dead horse and other signs of where there'd been trouble, came on into town to see if I'd heard anything. I told 'em the unfortunate news about their friends, told 'em how you brought in the bodies and came straight to me with the details of how it happened."

With no more chairs left to sit in, Lone edged around a bit more to the front of the Box 50 men. Continuing to meet their gazes, he said, "If the marshal told you everything I told him, then I don't rightly know what else I can add. I expect you probably got some questions anyway, though."

"You damn betcha we do!" blurted Cully.

"Just take it easy," Sweeney said out the side of his mouth to the younger man.

"That's right," Dalrymple emphasized. "I understand tensions are raw. But I'm warning everybody here and now, we're gonna keep this civil. Is that clear?"

"It's hard to think about bein' civil, marshal," said Burt, "when we just learned two of our friends are dead and the man who killed 'em is standing right here in front of us."

"I was standin' in front of your friends, too," Lone told him in low, flat tone, "when I gave 'em every chance to ride away without things turnin' no worse. They wouldn't listen to reason. When it came to gunfire, I did what I had to."

Burt's eyes narrowed. "You faced 'em straight up, two on one, yet you're standing here without a scratch while they're cut down cold and dead—that what you expect us to buy?"

"Buy or not, that's up to you. All I can do is tell you how it was," Lone stated. "It was near dark, I confronted 'em with a leveled rifle while they were still on their horses. We'd had words earlier in the day and that time they left. But they came back again, liquored up, havin' sucked some added orneriness and courage from a bottle. This time there wasn't no discouraging 'em from den makin' a harder try for what they was after—the girl. They figured they could pitch out of their saddles and take me, once on the ground, before I was able to do both of them. They made a scrap of it for a little while, but in the end it didn't work."

"Boy, you're a regular gun-blazin' Wild Bill Hickock, ain't you?" sneered Cully.

Lone fought to keep his temper and his voice under control. "Right now I'm just somebody tellin' you how it was. But if you don't wipe that smirk off your face when you're talkin' to me, I'm gonna be the hombre who wipes it off for you."

Simultaneously, in warning tones, Dalrymple said "Lone!" and Sweeney said "Cully!" The two men thus spoken to continued glaring at one another, but nothing more.

Sweeney gave it a beat and then addressed Lone, saying, "You mentioned the girl. What became of her?"

"She's okay, if that's what you mean," Lone answered. He purposely didn't want to mention that Tru had had any part in the shooting of Isaac. "She's here in town, resting, being looked after by a friend. She was inside the cabin during the shootout."

Sweeney nodded. "For what it's worth, I'm glad she wasn't harmed."

"In that case, let me ask you a question," said Lone. "You three. Are you the ones who were with that pair the first night when they came by and bothered the girl?"

Sweeney suddenly had trouble meeting his eyes and even Cully and Buck appeared somewhat more mollified.

"Yeah. That was us," Sweeney admitted quietly.

"But you didn't know they were coming back around again yesterday?"

"They was sent out to round up strays at the start of the new day. When they didn't show up for grub at suppertime, I figured they'd snuck off to town again to do some more drinkin'. The rascals had a bad habit of goin' on benders like that, especially when our foreman wasn't around." Sweeney scowled. "It didn't occur to me they'd make another try for that Chinee gal again. I thought they'd got that out of their system after she put the run on us the first time. Only when we found Isaac's horse, still saddled but without no sign of him or Jerome, did it hit me what they might've been up to."

"So that's why you went straight to my ranch."

"*Your* ranch?" Cully echoed. "That place has been deserted for—"

"If you've been around these parts for any amount of time," Lone cut him off, "you'd know the only reason it got deserted was because my partner was gunned down and left to die while I was away on other business."

"I know you. Seen you around before, when you and the old mountain man was first startin' up your spread there. You fellas made your well welcome to any of our boys wantin' a drink of fresh, cold water when they was travelin' back and forth from town," said Sweeney. "Hard luck about your partner, the old mountain man. Knew you'd been gone for a spell, never heard if you were comin' back again."

"Well, I did," Lone told him. "Call it timing or luck whatever you want, but I got there yesterday just ahead of your two men. Like I said, I managed to convince 'em to aim their attention somewhere else that first time. But I had a hunch they'd be back. So I forted up the cabin some and waited to see what the night would bring. Like I already explained, it worked out to their misfortune."

Cully's face reddened with a new flush of anger. "So you ambushed 'em! That's how you were able to cut down both Isaac and Jerome."

Lone could feel streaks of heat crawling up the sides of his neck. "You got a real careless way with words, pup," he said in a tight voice. "Watch out they don't splatter back and get you hurt."

Marshal Dalrymple stood up behind his desk. "All right," he announced. "I think we've covered this sufficient for the time being." He let his gaze settle on Sweeney. "I've known Lone here for a long time, Virgil. Long as you and then some. He ain't no ambusher or back shooter. He's killed before, but never without justification. I've listened and considered his story and the girl's and I think they're telling it straight."

"I know how hard it is to lose men who ride for your same brand—especially, in this case, when they're kin to Granger and he ain't around to shoulder it himself. But let's face the hard truth. If you do some thinking and considering of your own, you'll have to admit that Isaac and Jerome both had a real unpleasant side. Particularly when Granger wasn't right there to keep 'em in line. And what they was out to do if they'd cornered that Chinee gal alone, was way the hell over the line."

Sweeney looked back at him. "You saying they got what they deserved, Elmer?"

"I'm just a lawman, not a judge. I just call it when somebody crosses over, I don't hand out deserves."

"Would you say those same words if Granger was here?" challenged Buck.

Dalrymple's mouth pulled a little tighter. "I expect we'll be finding that out soon enough. If you fellas get on with tending to the matters you ought to, that is—like sending out wires, notifying Granger and the other brothers. And getting with the undertaker to start some preliminary funeral arrangements for when they get here."

A dour-faced Sweeney rose from his chair. "He's right, boys. We're done here for now. We need to look after those other matters."

Cully and Buck shoved to their feet also. Overstreet stepped over and held the door open for them. They filed out sullenly, silently.

Except for Cully, who paused in the doorway long enough to half-turn and glare at Lone. "We're done for now, mister. But you'd better believe you ain't heard the last of this."

CHAPTER 12

Lone sat at the food prep table in Ma's kitchen, wolfing down a couple of roast beef on sourdough sandwiches she had made for him. He chased the fare with gulps of cold buttermilk and couldn't remember any meal ever tasting better.

"I almost lost track of how long—since before I headed out to the ranch yesterday—that I'd gone without eatin' anything," he was saying around a mouthful of bread and tender meat. "With everything going on, I plumb never got around to it."

"Hmph. That ain't all you never got around to," Ma said as she placed a slice of cherry pie in front of him and then shuffled around the corner of the table and took a seat for herself.

"What's that supposed to mean?" Lone wanted to know.

Ma arched a gray-streaked brow. "That bath you promised—I make it you never got around to that neither. And don't claim that pumping a couple strokes of soapless water over your head counts for anything."

"It was all I had time for. The marshal and those Box 50 men were waitin' for me at the jail. Besides," Lone protested, "I never exactly *promised* I was gonna take a bath. I said I had me a notion I *might*. But when I stretched out on that pile of straw Woodrow forked up all fluffy for me, meaning to relax for just a minute. well, I was more bushed than I realized. Next thing I knew, Deputy Overstreet was pestering me to wake up."

Ma failed to show much sympathy. "Excuses, I say. That poor girl you dragged in here was plenty bushed too. What did you expect, after making her walk all through the night? But she still took time to clean up proper before laying herself down to rest."

"Her name is Tru. Tru Min Chang." Lone scowled. "Everybody keeps calling her 'that girl' or 'that Chinee' or 'Chink' or 'slant-eye'. I'm getting blasted tired of it and am about to start settin' folks straight on calling her by her proper name."

"You don't have to bark at me. I know her name well," Ma countered. "She and I had a nice talk while she was getting cleaned up and settled in."

"How is she doing?" Lone asked sincerely.

"Fine. Tuckered out, like I said, but sleeping like a baby the last time I looked in on her. She's tougher than that tiny little frame might suggest."

Lone took another drink of buttermilk and then said, "Just so you understand, the only reason she walked most of the way was because she insisted on it. She didn't want to make it too hard on Ironsides, she said, dragging that litter and carrying her on his back too—as if her little bit of weight was going to make a whisker's difference."

Ma smiled a strange little smile. "Her reasons had to do with more than just Ironsides."

Lone had never seen Ma smile quite that way. He said, "Now what's *that* supposed to mean?"

"It means, you lunkhead, that she was trying to impress you."

"Impress me?" Lone echoed. "Did she tell you that the first time she laid eyes on me she took a couple shots at me with that Henry rifle of hers?"

Ma's smile turned into a surprisingly girlish little laugh. "No. She somehow didn't get around to mentioning that part."

"Well, it's true. She mistook me for one of those other skunks, thought I was one of 'em comin' back around to bother her some more." Lone's eyes narrowed, thinking back. "Luckily or unluckily, I guess I should say, leastways seein' how it ended up for them, I was able to convince her I was cut from a different bolt of cloth."

"Oh, she's convinced of that now. Trust me," Ma said. "In fact, she thinks you're cut from a bolt of cloth she finds mighty appealing."

Lone had forked up what was going to be his first bite of pie. He paused with it raised part way to his mouth. "I don't know where you picked up this habit of sayin' things half way or talkin' in riddles or whatever you want to call it, but it's gettin' doggone annoying, Ma. What do you mean Tru finds the cut of my cloth appealing?"

"Oh, for Christ's sake," exclaimed Ma, who forbade any foul language in her boarding house yet——having learned the full dictionary very well after nearly four decades of being married to a frontier cavalry man——could, when inclined, cuss a blue streak with the best whoever did it. "Have you got trail dust packed too tight between your ears? What I'm telling you is that the girl——Tru——has developed a huge crush on you, you ninny. Didn't you pick up a single clue?"

Lone didn't know whether to feel flattered or frightened. All he knew for sure was that he felt suddenly very uncomfortable.

He eyed Ma closely. "Are you sure?" And then, as another thought shot through him: "Or are you puttin' me on?"

"No, I wouldn't tease you about something like that," Ma said firmly. "And yes, I'm convinced the girl is totally infatuated with you. You were all she talked about right up until she fell asleep. Asking questions about you one minute, then the next telling me repeatedly how brave and strong and self-assured you were in the way you stood up to those polecats who were out to do her harm."

Lone's brow puckered. "Jeez. I only know her or her me, about twenty-four hours. Right about this time yesterday, she was taking those shots at me."

"I don't know about the shooting part. But as for the other, getting smacked by that certain feeling, I know it don't go by no calendar, not even a clock." Ma paused, her tired old eyes seeming to gaze off at something far away. Then she went on, "The first time I laid eyes on my mister was at a dance. I was out on the floor, in the arms of another fella and I saw him across the room. He was leaning on the bar, half in the bag, a cigar stub poking out one corner of his mouth. I kept glancing over at him every time I twirled. And, before the music was done playing, something inside me told me that there was the man I wanted to marry. And never for a minute of our time together, right up to when the old scalawag passed, did I ever regret having that feeling."

Lone didn't know what to say. So he went ahead and finally took that bite of the pie.

Ma's rows pinched together. "Now. Nobody's saying you have to return the girl's feelings. That's for you to work out. But the least you can do is not resort to trying to chase the poor thing away by continuing to smell like horse sweat and trail dust. There's others who would appreciate a change from that, too. So after you finish that pie, I've got a kettle of hot water on the stove and an empty tub in the back room. I think it's time to act on that *notion* of yours about taking a bath."

Lone forked up another bite of pie. "Yes, ma'am. Whatever you say."

CHAPTER SEVEN

CHAPTER 13

————

Cully Cullen hung his head low over a half-empty glass of beer and gazed down at the foamy amber liquid with a tortured, uncertain expression.

"I dunno. Maybe this ain't such a good idea after all," he muttered.

Seated beside him at a table near the back wall of the Lucky Dog Saloon, Buck Telford paused with his own glass of beer raised part way to his lips. He scowled darkly at Cully and said, "What the hell you mean it ain't a good idea? You're the one who came up with it—now you're crawfishin'?"

Cully thrust out his chin. "No, I didn't say that. I never said such. But, doggone it, this is serious shit. I mean" —here his voice lowered to a conspiratorial hush— "killin' a man ain't something to be took lightly, no matter how much he might have it comin'."

In the middle of the afternoon, the Lucky Dog wasn't very crowded. The lunch crowd had come and gone and the evening drinkers and card players hadn't started to gather yet. Aside from Cully and Buck, the only other customers in the joint were three men leaning on the bar—a couple old soldiers with their bony shoulders jammed together, gray-whiskered chins wagging over shots of cheap redeye as they swapped embellishments of past battles and glories; and down at the end, as far away from the two old timers as he could get, a pudgy, derby-hatted drummer of some kind sat pouring over his inventory ledgers. Behind the bar, the bored-looking stick man was shuffling back and forth, clinking glassware and occasionally rolling his eyes at a whopper being spouted by one of the old soldiers.

With the shutters and the storm door outside the batwings all closed against the dust blowing in from the street, the interior was dim and stuffy. The smell of stale cigarette and cigar smoke hung thick in the air, mixing with the tang of a handful of low-burning coal oil lanterns placed about. A shaggy-looking, half-crippled old swamper clumped in and out of the shadows around the edges of the room, dragging his bad leg after him as he sprinkled fresh sawdust on the floor and gathered up full spittoons that he took somewhere out back and then returned with, presumably cleaned.

Appearing oblivious to any of this, Burt went ahead and took a long pull of his beer. Then, leaning in closer to Cully, he said, "Okay. I see what you're saying. Anybody would. But your notion to settle the hash of this McGantry fella was a good one. Not just for the sake of squarin' things for what he done to Isaac and Jerome, but also as a way to put ourselves in a better light with Granger and Mr. Benton. If we're the ones who make sure Isaac and Jerome get proper avenged, then that'd certain clear of us from any blame for not doin' a good enough job of lookin' after 'em. And don't tell me that wasn't part of your thinkin' when you brought the idea up."

Cully gulped down most of what was left in his glass. "Yeah. Yeah, it was." He paused to burp, then went on.

"But, dang it all, why should that even be a concern for us? All we did was let ourselves get hoorahed into comin' into town for a bout of drinkin' with 'em. Everybody knows how pushy Jerome and Isaac could be when they made up their minds they wanted some drinkin' company. They were bound and determined to go, one way or t'other. Sweeney was the one Granger left in charge, it shoulda been up to him to hold those two guzzlers in line and that would've left us off the hook altogether."

"Well, it *was* Sweeney who showed up, right here at this very place and hauled us back to the Box 50," Buck pointed out.

"But not before we stopped to water our horses along the way," Cully said, looking more dejected than ever. "Stopped at that burnt-out, godforsaken, supposedly deserted soddy where we ended up discovering the girl. There's where everything really started going to hell."

"But nothing bad happened there. Not then," Buck insisted. "That Chinee gal got scared and got talked to a mite rough, yeah, but Sweeney herded us out of there, along with her poking that rifle gun in our faces, before any serious harm came of it."

Cully's eyes shone bright as he stared across the table. "But Isaac and Jerome wasn't ready to call it quits with her. They might have let Sweeney steer them away for the time bein', but they full intended to go back the first chance they got. I could tell that, and so could you. I'm surprised Sweeney didn't see it, too."

"Maybe he didn't *want* to see it," Buck suggested. "Maybe he was tired of tryin' to keep those two rannies in line while Granger was away and just wanted a reasonable excuse to be busy with something else when they went back and did what they was bound to do."

The notion caused Cully's brow to pucker furiously. "You really think so? That Sweeney would just turn his back on something like that?"

"Look. All I know is that it seemed awful accommoda-tin' for Sweeney to have sent them rascals out roundin' up strays right away the next morning." Buck shrugged. "If you and me was savvy enough to spot how hump-backed they still was, how could Sweeney miss it?"

Cully's expression turned deeply thoughtful and his gaze seemed to drift off somewhere.

"Now what's the matter? Now what's churnin' around inside that noggin of yours?" Buck wanted to know.

"I was just thinkin' about that Chinee gal. How we all crowded around her at first that night, cornerin' her like. like some frightened wild animal caught in a snare." Now Cully's gaze came back into focus and fixed tightly on Buck. "That was what I thought about right off, what ran through my mind seein' her like that. But then Isaac and Jerome started in, makin' it plenty clear what they saw when they looked at the girl, what was on their minds to do with her. And pretty quick I got to feelin'. I mean, if Sweeney hadn't been there. Aw Jesus, Buck, don't you see what I'm sayin'? I was damn near ready—"

"Knock it off," Buck snapped. "So you was drunk, you saw this snared celestial before you who was vul-nerable-lookin' and mighty easy on the eyes and the talk around you fanned the flames low in your gut to build up some steamy thoughts. You see that as some kind of problem? As something bein' wrong with you?"

Cully's brow remained puckered. "It would have been wrong if I'd gone ahead and done like Isaac and Jerome was encouragin'. And I was damn near ready to, Buck. So help me I was."

"But you *didn't*. That's all that counts," Buck declared. "And even if Sweeney hadn't been there to break up what might have happened otherwise, you likely would've thought better of goin' through with it anyway. What's more, you didn't wake up the next morning still full of steam and immediately start anglin' for a way to charge out and to act on it, did you? Like Isaac and Jerome did. That's what makes you a smarter and better person than they were ever bound to be."

Cully still looked ill at ease. "But if they were such louses," he wondered out loud, "then why are we talkin' about killin' a man in order to try and settle the score for them?"

Buck heaved an exasperated sigh. "Because that's how hombres who ride for the same brand are supposed to think. But mainly we're countin' on it to benefit ourselves in the eyes of Mr. Benton and Granger. Ain't that what we just agreed on?"

Cully made a sour face. "Why the hell couldn't Sweeney have just left us here to drink until all we would've had to deal with was a round of head-bustin', gut-crawlin' hangovers?"

Buck lifted the quarter-full pitcher of beer that stood on the table between them and emptied it, equal amounts into their glasses. Setting the pitcher aside, he next reached for the bottle of whiskey that also occupied the table and from it filled each of the shot glasses that stood before him and Cully.

Setting down the bottle, Buck lifted his shot glass and gestured in a choppy toast, saying, "The thing now, acting on your idea, is to try and come out of this better than just survivin' a hangover."

Buck threw down his whiskey and Cully did likewise. After he'd chased his with another gulp of beer, Cully said, "You're right. It's up to us. We ain't got no choice but to do what we got to—for Isaac and Jerome and, like we keep sayin', for our own sake."

Buck smiled. "That's more like it. So now that it's settled once and for all, there's only a couple things holdin' us back."

"What's that?" Cully asked.

"First, we need to lay low and give Sweeney time to finish sending his wires and such. He thinks we already headed back to the ranch, like he sent us to. Before we make our move on McGantry, I want to know for sure that Sweeney's headed back too, so's we can be certain he won't be around to do any more interfering when we set things in motion."

"Makes sense. What else?"

Still smiling, Buck hefted the empty beer pitcher. "In the meantime, I'm gonna get this refilled. No more hard stuff. We can't afford to brace McGantry with muddled brains."

Cully nodded his approval. "Not hardly. If he managed to cut down both Isaac and Jerome ambush or not, he can't be no slouch when it comes to gun work."

"That's why, as we take our time nursing down a fresh pitcher of suds, we also take our time formulatin' a careful plan for how to best go about callin' that damn murderer to account."

So saying, Buck shoved his chair back away from the table and started to stand up. But before the chair slid as far as he meant for it to, it bumped hard against something and came to a stop, nearly tipping over. This caused Buck to stagger off balance himself, forcing him to grab the table for support. The pitcher he'd been holding crashed to the floor, joining the metallic clang of other objects hitting the hardwood.

"What the hell's going on over there?" demanded bartender Shorty Harper.

"That's what I'd like to know!" Buck snapped back, looking around.

The stooped, shabby form of the crippled swamper reverse-melted out of the shadows along the back wall. "It was my fault," he said meekly. "I was distributing some clean spittoons, being real quiet so as not to disturb these gents in their talk, when this fella pushed his chair back unexpected-like and—"

"Bein' quiet so as not to disturb us?" Buck cut him off. "You damn near caused me to trip and break my neck, you clumsy old rum pot!"

The slump-shouldered swamper looked deeply contrite. "I'm sorry, mister. I was trying to stay out of the way, truly I was."

"Well, you didn't try hard enough," growled Buck, flinging aside the chair that had nearly tripped him and then taking a menacing step toward the swamper. "So maybe I ought to throw your raggedy old ass across the room a couple of times to *show* you how to get out of the way!"

"That's enough, Buck! There's no need for anything like that," said Shorty from behind his bar. "It was an accident, plain and simple. To show there's no hard feelings, I'll draw you a fresh pitcher of beer—on the house."

Buck reluctantly halted his advance on the swamper.

"I'll get this broken pitcher cleaned up right away," said the swamper.

"Never mind that for right now," Shorty told him. "Pick up those other spittoons you dropped, then go on in the back and clean some more. Get some extra ready for tonight. Here, I'll give you a short beer to take with you, settle your jitters. Stay back there out of sight for a while, let things cool down."

CHAPTER 14

"Like the old saying goes, I feel like I'm caught between a rock and a hard place."

Lone made this declaration from where he sat in one of a half dozen high-backed, deeply cushioned armchairs situated around the parlor of Ma Sharples' boarding house. To his left, occupying a nearly identical chair, was Elmer Dalrymple. Across from them, separated by a low coffee table and seated side by side on a colorfully-patterned couch, sat Ma and Tru Chang. Atop the table was an oval serving tray set with a pitcher of lemonade, glasses and a bowl of oatmeal cookies. There was no one else in the spacious room, Ma's other guests either up in their rooms or out and about conducting some late afternoon business.

In response to Lone's words, the marshal said, "I full understand you got some things facing you. But exactly what is it you feel is squeezing you so?"

"Should be plain enough," Lone said, frowning. "The undertaker is telling me he has Peg all prepared and bundled for the trip I agreed to take him on. In addition to me wanting to get started on that, there's the matter of Tru—Miss

Chang—and her need to also get on with her interrupted journey. Since Fort Collins, her destination, is right at the foot of Poudre Canyon, the first leg of my route up into the mountains, it only seems logical for us to share a team and wagon to haul our individual cargo and make the trip that far together."

"When Mrs. Sharples told me how Mr. McGantry had cause to also be traveling toward Fort Collins," Tru explained, "I'm afraid I was bold enough to suggest we pool our resources. In truth, I was imposing on him to act as my escort and he, of course, was too gallant to refuse."

"Yeah, that's our Lone. Gallant," said Ma with a twinkle in her eye.

Lone shot her a guarded look, fully aware that she'd gone out of her way to tell Tru about his planned trip as a way to nudge the two of them closer together. But, at the same time, he had to admit he hadn't fought too hard against the idea once it had been brought up.

"That sounds like a kind of convenient thing," said Dalrymple, hearing it for the first time. "I still don't quite see where the squeeze comes in, Lone."

"Aw, come on, Elmer," Lone snapped back irritably. "The squeeze is from the hombres who are milling around out there with a grudge against me for shootin' those two jackass cousins. You saw those Bar 50 hombres in your office this morning, all lookin' at me with fire in their eyes, especially the young pups wantin' to tear into me. And they wasn't even kin not like the three brothers still expected to show up."

The marshal sighed. "I already told you. Those brothers ain't expected to show up for days. Granger, the oldest and the ramrod of the Bar 50, is somewhere up in the Dakotas with the ranch owner, Angus Denton, on a bull buying trip; I don't even know for sure if any of the telegrams me or Virgil Sweeney sent out have reached him yet. Same for Royce, the gambler brother—nobody seems certain where he is. That leaves Cliff, the second youngest, the one who's a deputy marshal over in Ogallala. No doubt he's gotten word by now but I can't picture him doing anything on his own, at least not until Granger shows up. And the same is true for any of the Bar 50 hands, no matter how much snortin' they do or stink eye they aim your way in the meantime."

"So, you see, it'll be days—maybe near a week—before the brothers are all collected here. And, even then, it ain't for certain they'll be looking to answer lead for lead. Especially not if you and Miss Chang are already gone off on the trail."

Lone's mouth pulled into a grimace. "But that's the whole thing. Don't you see? I can't have it look like I'm runnin' away—like I'm afraid to face 'em!"

Ma slammed one meaty fist down on the arm rest of the couch where she sat. "Lone McGantry, you prideful fool! How you talk! Did your brains turn to mush while you been away, or can you truly sit there and say you think anybody who knows even a whisker about you would believe for a minute that you'd turn tail 'cause you was yellow? And any varmint who *did* let a thought like that pass through their reptile brain would be too low of a belly-crawler to be worth the sweat off your tally whacker!"

Tru gave a little start when Ma's fist first came down, but otherwise appeared unphased by the tirade that followed. Had her understanding of slang been stronger, however, there was little doubt that the colorful anatomical reference, especially coming from the elderly woman, would have drawn a more shocked reaction.

While Lone understood the reference plainly enough, it neither shocked him nor was it the part of what Ma said that he took exception to. "Dang it," he replied, "I don't care what kind of lowdown critter might think it, I don't want it on the mind of nobody—especially not the Halsey brothers themselves, whenever they finally come around."

"So you're bound and determined to wait for 'em and make sure that the sight of you as soon as they get here helps goad them into doing something—is that what you're angling for?" Ma demanded.

"That ain't it at all," Lone insisted. "Do you really think I *want* more trouble?"

"Ma makes a valid point," Dalrymple interjected. "It's like I tried to say, too. When the Halseys get here, they're going to have burying and grieving to tend to. If you ain't right here in their faces—sort of crowding them into re-acting against you, the way they might see it—there's a chance it won't go no farther. It ain't as if they're a bunch of proddies who go around looking for trouble either. And it should make a difference, too, once I'm able to explain more about how Isaac and Jerome, neither of who were strangers at getting out of line, stepped way over this time and that's what got 'em killed."

"You didn't seem so sure about all of that before," Lone reminded him.

The marshal wagged his head. "I ain't sure about any of it now. I'm just speculatin' how it *could* go. When I woke this morning to the sight of those two bodies piled on that drag litter, my first reaction was kinda raw, fearing the worst about what might come next. But having had some time to think it through more, I can see how and I'll admit maybe this is just wishful thinking, it could go a tamer way."

"But only," Lone said stubbornly, "if I was to light out and not be here when the Halseys arrive. Right?"

"That'd help, yeah. I ain't denying it," conceded Dalrymple.

"As far as lighting out," said Ma, "doing so wouldn't be simply for the sake of you avoiding the Halsey brothers. Don't forget, you got more and better reasons totally apart from them. For starters, you got the promise you made Peg. He hung on long past his time to die, just to give you his last wishes. Now you gonna make him wait some more, in a box at the undertaker's, while you stick around for the sake of keeping your pride or ego from getting bruised? And what if the Halseys *do* come at you hard and you find out that this time around you ain't indestructible—the same as Peg found out. What then? Who will honor your commitment to take him to his rest up in the mountains? And who'll be around to help Tru reclaim her belongings and make it the rest of the way to Fort Collins?"

For the first time, Lone felt and displayed, signs of wavering.

"Another thing to consider," said Dalrymple, "is that you leaving ain't hardly no guarantee that the Halseys, if they decide they want blood for blood, won't come after you anyway. You traveling by wagon, even with a three or four day head start, wouldn't be hard for them to catch up with. The risk of facing them out on the trail don't exactly stack up as no picnic."

Half of Lone's mouth cured wolfishly. "Me out in open country against a tally whacker cow puncher, a town-fattened deputy and a gambler. Excuse me if I don't find those odds overly frightening."

"If they came at you like that, there'd likely be more than just them three," Ma said, sounding thoughtful and suddenly looking less confident than she had with her earlier comments. "And if Tru ended caught in the middle."

Speaking abruptly, Tru said, "It seems to me that everyone is suddenly caught up in worry about risks. As if that is something new to what has already gone before and what will surely be part of whatever lies ahead, no matter the course taken. My uncle and I took risks every inch of the way after leaving Council Bluffs. And Lone, from everything I've heard, is no stranger to risk—up to and including his decision to stay and help me, a complete stranger, against those evil men with most foul intentions. For that, he has earned the right to face those who may be coming for him as a result in whatever manner he chooses. And have no doubt that *I* am fully prepared to stand with *him*—be it here in town, or out on the trail."

Nobody spoke for several clicks of the clock on the parlor wall.

Until, grinning, Lone said, "Best get your travelin' duds laid out, kid. If you need anything before leavin' town, have Ma show you where to get it. In the meantime, I'll go pick us out a good team and a sturdy wagon and get Peg loaded aboard. After that, we'll trouble Ma for a supper meal and a place to lay our heads tonight. Then, first thing in the morning, we'll hit the trail."

CHAPTER 15

"Look out! On your right!"

The shouted warning momentarily froze Lone—his reflexes torn between turning toward the voice issuing the warning, which came from behind and off to his left, or looking to the right as urged. His indecision caused him to inadvertently lean back on the wagon seat where he was perched and that was enough to save him. Just barely.

The bullet, hurled by the crack of a pistol about ten yards to his right, passed barely an inch from his chin. Even without the accompanying gunshot, the sound of the slug slicing so close was unmistakable. Lone had heard that sound too many times before, and it was something you only had to experience once to have it etched crystal clear in your mind.

Survival instincts kicked in immediately. If leaning back a little bit had proven beneficial, Lone reasoned, then more of the same seemed like a good course of action. So he wasted no time twisting at the waist and pitching back off the seat, tumbling down into the wagon bed that stretched behind him. Landing on his left shoulder, his right hand instantly clawed for his Colt as he continued to twist and squirm until he'd worked around onto his stomach with the .44 gripped tight in his fist . By then, more shots, coming from both his right *and* left now, were ripping through the air and hammering into the three-foot-high sideboards of the wagon.

One of the rounds penetrated through and tore a chip off the top edge of the rectangular crate bolted to the floor of the wagon—the temporary resting place for the remains of Peg O'Malley.

Lone swore under his breath. "Rest easy, old pard," he said, patting the crate with his free hand. "I'll figure a way out of this fix in no time."

"This fix" was busting loose at the mouth of a narrow, cluttered alley that ran along one side of the long, unassuming building that housed the Farthing Funeral Home up front and a rear area where the undertaker embalmed and otherwise prepared the dearly departed for their send-offs. Aided by Undertaker Farthing, Lone had just finished loading up Peg's traveling casket back in the rear and was starting to emerge from the alley at the reins of the team and wagon he'd acquired for the upcoming trip, when the warning shout and the first shot had forced a sudden change of plans.

It was early dusk. The last of the sun had sunk out of sight mere minutes ago, leaving still plenty of light left in the cloudless sky. The street lamps along North Platte's main drag, most of its length reaching off to the right of where Lone's wagon was coming out of the alley, hadn't begun to be lighted yet for the darker hours of the night. Everything was quiet and still down this way and activity farther up the street, even in the heart of the business district, was getting sparse as the day wore to a close.

But now, suddenly, things in the immediate vicinity had turned anything but peaceful and quiet!

Lone's mind raced, trying to figure out what this was all about. The most obvious likelihood, of course, was that it had to do with the Box 50 bunch and the prior shootings of Isaac and Jerome. But who was it pulling the triggers and why now? There was at least two of them, blazing away at the wagon from either side of the alley. Based on what Dalrymple had learned from the telegrams he'd sent out, Lone reminded himself, it seemed too early for Granger or either of the other Halsey brothers to have shown up. And, based on what he'd heard about the brothers, they sounded more like the type who would conduct at least an initial face-to-face confrontation ahead of resorting to gunplay.

But the ambushing polecats currently blasting hell out of his wagon and keeping him pinned down clearly lacked the guts to show their faces before cutting loose. Lone did some more hard, fast churning inside his head. There was the wild, outside chance that this attack *didn't* have to do with the Box 50 business. It wasn't like he had a shortage of enemies from his past, and there were plenty of those who wouldn't hesitate to go the dry-gulch route.

Not that it would really matter who was behind a bullet if it turned out to be the final one but while the lead was still flying, Lone had a hankering to know who was burning the powder to keep it in motion. It might make a difference how he conducted himself, what maneuvers or risks he'd consider based on who he was up against.

At the moment, unfortunately, no matter *what* he knew or didn't know about his ambushers, there wasn't anything he could do but press himself tight against the floor of the wagon and hope to hell none of the incoming slugs punched through to him. Lone squeezed the grips of his Colt tighter and felt the frustration and rage building inside him, willing himself not to let it pull him into doing something too reckless.

And then he got an unexpected break. Up until now, the matched pair of deep-chested grays he had purchased along with the wagon had only been fidgeting and shuffling a minimal amount in their traces—showing amazing restraint, considering all the shooting and whizzing bullets. Lone laid this to the fact that the liveryman who sold him the team had mentioned they were former army property once used to haul around heavy artillery; thus explaining their relative calm in the face of booming guns. But while the sound of close gunfire was one thing, the burn of a ricocheting bullet gouging deep across the rump of one of the mares was quite another. And when that happened, it sent the stricken animal bolting forward with a shriek of protest that caused her pulling partner to surge right along with her.

The wagon jolted into motion.

At first, since he was flattened tight to the floor of the wagon bed, this had little affect on Lone except to make sure his face didn't get mashed by the suddenly bouncing surface on which he lay. But then, as the team rumbled out into the middle of the street, gaining speed and continuing to do so as they decided to make a wild turn and head for uptown, Lone's position suddenly became more precarious. The wagon was whipped like a long tail by the frantic swing of the bolting horses, sending Lone half-skidding, half-rolling, until he slammed to a hard stop against the crate that held Peg.

Luckily, Peg's crate was bolted in place, meaning it didn't get likewise tossed about. But, at the same time, this presented a different problem. The crate was fastened all the way to one side of the wagon bed, tight against the sideboard. This happened to be the *out*side of arc the wagon was whipped into as the pulling team made its frantic turn. With Lone's weight also slamming against the crate, this seriously over-balanced the otherwise empty wagon. And when the sideways-skidding wheels dropped into and got caught by the numerous wagon ruts running the length of the street, it was too much—the wagon shuddered, tipped, and then flipped all the way over onto its side.

Lone was tossed across Peg's crate and sent sailing through the air. The instant he hit the ground on the opposite side of the dusty street, even as it pounded the breath out of him, he forced himself into a series to side rolls in order to make sure he got clear of the toppling wagon. He bumped to a halt against the edge of a weathered boardwalk that ran in front of a farm and ranch equipment store. Through the high, boiling clouds of thick dust, he could barely discern the outline of the wagon but it was enough to tell him it had come to rest on its side and showed no signs of tipping over the rest of the way. Even the pawing, blowing team of horses appeared to be ceasing to strain in their harnesses as a sign of accepting this and knowing they were done pulling the rig any farther for the time being.

But that still left the lowdown ambushing skunks who had caused all of this.

The shooting had stopped at some point when the wagon went rumbling out into the street and was remaining silent now. The swirling wall of dust thrown up by the uncontrolled sweep of the wagon left visibility now blurred for a block-long stretch. Gripping the Colt he'd drawn before getting flung clear, Lone knew he had to try and take advantage of this condition that temporarily hid him from those gunning for him. Still fighting to get sufficient breath sucked back into his lungs, he edged back onto the sagging boardwalk and then moved down the front of the implement building until he came to the corner where it ended and gave way to another alley.

This alley was even narrower than the one beside the undertaker's building and its mouth was tally whacker choked with a stack of fence posts and some rolls of barbed wire. Lone slipped around and dropped into a crouch behind these as the slowly eddying haze of dust began to dissipate. No sooner had he settled there than the front door of the store opened a crack and the wide-eyed face of an elderly man peered out.

"What' going on?" the old man whispered harshly.

Lone waved him frantically back inside but stayed low and said nothing, not wanting to give away his new position. The old man got the message and ducked back, re-closing the door.

Faintly, from farther up the street, other questioning voices also started calling out. The shooting and the wreck of the wagon had naturally drawn attention. But some cautious common sense was bound to be shown, Lone figured, so it would be a while before anyone—most likely in the form of the marshal or his deputy—advanced closer to try and find out what was behind it. That meant if the ambushers remained in place across the street, bent on trying to finish him, they still had time to get the job done.

As if in response to that thought, a vaguely familiar voice called out. "Hey, Buck! Can you see what became of that McGantry varmint? Did we get the sonofabitch?"

After a slight hesitation, another voice said. "Can't tell for sure, Cully. I think he might be pinned under that overturned wagon."

Lone grimaced. Buck and Cully. the surly young pups

from the Box 50. So that *was* at the heart of this whole thing. That surprised him a little; he had the pups pegged as being the type more likely to just run their mouths rather than work up the gumption to actually take action. Unless there was a third gun over there on the other side of the dust haze—the old wrangler Sweeney, maybe—egging them on. Lone waited, thinking Sweeney might speak up too. But if he was involved, he kept quiet.

The dust haze hanging in the air began to dissolve rapidly now.

From where he crouched behind the posts and wire rolls, Lone saw that his vantage point was at an angle about a quarter block down from the undertaker's alley he had emerged from a few minutes ago. This gave him a wide view to either side of the alley across the street. What had been on his right before—the direction the first shot came from—was to his left; what had been on his left when he was over there was now to his right.

His gaze swept involuntarily in search of the source for that first shot. It didn't take long to spot him. There he was, still hunkered low and peeking around the corner of Farthing's building on the side opposite the alley. Cully. The narrow-faced little bastard.

Lone's eyes darted the other way, looking for Buck, the second shooter. He was almost directly across the street, crouched in the bed of a high-wheeled, thick-walled freight wagon parked empty and unhitched in front of a deserted-looking shack with busted-out windows and weeds growing tall all around.

Before Lone could act on an impulse to take the sure shot and cut down the lousy bushwhacker right then and there, Buck called out to his partner. "I'm closest to that tipped wagon, Cully. Ain't nothing stirrin' there but the nags hitched to it. I think our man's a goner. You keep me covered, though, just in case, and I'll slip over to make sure."

"Okay. I just finished reloadin', I got a fresh six in the wheel. I'll cover you real good," Cully told him. "Just hurry up, there's a crowd formin' up the street. We're gonna have to hightail it outta here pretty quick."

Buck hopped down, brandishing a long-barreled sixgun. "Yeah, yeah, I can see. This ain't gonna take long, I'm pretty sure that hombre who was supposed to be so tough is mashed under the wreck like a hen's egg."

"If that's the case, I guess we'll settle for it," said Cully, straightening up and stepping around to the front of the undertaker's building, also holding a drawn pistol before him. "But I hope at least one of us planted some lead in him. Hey! If it happens he's still breathin', let me come over and plunk in the finisher, you hear?"

Buck, who had by now nearly reached the overturned wagon, chuckled nastily. "Boy, a little trigger pullin' really brings out the blood thirstiness in you, don't it?" He paused abruptly and looked over at his partner, frowning. "Say, speakin' of trigger pullin'—who was it hollered out over there just before you first cut loose on McGantry?"

Cully shook his head. "Heck if I know. Must've been that spooky ol' undertaker nosin' around. But he disappeared quick enough when the gunsmoke started rollin'. Never mind him now, just make sure McGantry is in line for his next dose of embalmin' juice."

Buck took the remaining steps that brought him to the end of the tipped wagon. Then, poking his gun ahead of him, he leaned cautiously around the tailgate and peered into the bed.

"Whatya see?" called Cully. "Tell me he's layin' in

there with his yellow guts ripped wide open."

"I can't tell you nothing," Buck replied dully, leaning forward for a closer look. "I don't see him anywhere."

"Maybe because you're lookin' in the wrong place," Lone grated, emphasizing the words by thumbing the hammer of his Colt to full cock.

CHAPTER 16

Buck froze in his bent forward pose. Lone could only see one side of his face, but his eye appeared to bulge big and bright.

From over in front of Farthing's, Cully said, "What'd you say? I didn't quite catch—"

"For Christ's sake, shoot him!" Buck blurted. "He's still alive—don't you see him?"

"Wrong answer, Buck," Lone muttered, triggering his Colt and sending a .44 slug straight to the side of Buck's head, just behind that bulging eye. The impact knocked the Box 50 man sideways against the tailgate then left him to crumple forward and sprawl in a lifeless heap partly on top of Peg's casket.

Rising up to make that shot finally exposed Lone to Cully on the other side of the street. Still, it took a moment for the startled, sagging-mouthed ambusher to react. That gave Lone enough time to adjust his own aim and the two of them ended up firing simultaneously.

Lone's shot was more accurate, blowing off the tip of Cully's right collar bone and spinning him half around with a yelp of pain. Cully's bullet came sizzling high and about six inches wide of Lone's head. It was nevertheless enough to cause Lone to duck involuntarily and, when he did, lean too much weight against the stack of fence posts he was half-crouched behind. This resulted in the top three or four posts being dislodged and rolling away in a loud clatter, throwing Lone momentarily off balance.

Once he'd righted himself and again swung the muzzle of his Colt back in line, Lone could only watch as a half-staggering Cully once again ducked away around the corner of the undertaker's building. Lone cursed in frustration and squeezed off a round anyway, but all the good it did was to gouge a fist-sized chunk from the corner of the structure.

Lone thumbed a fresh round into the cylinder and held his pose, gun aimed steady at the spot where Cully had disappeared, ready in case he might poke back into sight and attempt some return fire. When seconds passed with no fresh sign of the pup, Lone stepped wide around the end of the post pile and made a dash to the overturned wagon. He halted there, using the upended tailgate for cover while he continued to watch (and hope) for a reappearance of Cully. But there was nothing.

After taking a moment to reach down and drag Buck's limp body to one side, so no part of it was any longer touching Peg's casket, Lone straightened up and braced himself, meaning to run the rest of the way across the street, to the corner of the Farthing building.

Before he broke into motion, however, he was stopped by a voice calling out from that very spot.

"Hold your fire, mister. Don't shoot no more—I'm a friend!"

The voice wasn't one Lone recognized, certainly not that of Cully. With his Colt raised and ready, Lone eyed the corner tighter than ever.

"I'm gonna step out where you can see me," the voice called again. "Cully's back here with me, but you got no worry about him now. He ain't dead but, trust me, he ain't a threat to nobody no more, neither."

"Step on out, then. Slow and careful," Lone ordered whoever was doing the talking.

There was an uncertain hesitation before—slow and careful, like Lone had urged—a figure edged into view out past the end of the building. It was a man of some years, though exactly how many it was hard to guess. His hair was long and tangled, his pale, worn face badly in need of a shave and his clothing, frayed and torn and amounting to little more than a collection of rags, hung loose on his slump-shouldered stick frame. When he stepped up onto the boardwalk he dragged one limp, twisted leg after him.

Lone couldn't keep from gawking. It ran through his mind that here was the sorriest looking individual he had ever laid eyes on.

Before he could say anything more to this apparition, the crowd from up the street—which had been growing larger and noisier—now came tramping too close to ignore. Lone turned his head to give them a hard look. When he did, he saw to his relief that Marshal Dalrymple was in their midst and working to crowd his way up to the front. Deputy Overstreet wasn't far behind him.

The crowd slowed their advance under Lone's glare and this allowed the marshal to shoulder the rest of the way up to the fore. He was puffing hard from hurrying the length of the street.

"Jesus Christ, Lone," Dalrymple huffed, throwing a glare of his own, "what have you got yourself into now?"

Lone gritted his teeth. "That might be a question better

suited to Buck Telford, one of the skunks who opened up on me from ambush a couple minutes ago. You'll find him laying over behind this tipped up wagon. Don't reckon you'll get much of an answer out of him, though, on account of he's dead."

"Oh Jesus Christ," Dalrymple said again.

An excited murmur ran through the crowd gathered close behind him.

"His partner, on the other hand, that weasel Cully," Lone drawled, "might be a little more talkative. From what I understand, even though I put a bullet in him, too, he's still breathing somewhere around the corner of that building over there."

All eyes swung to Farthing's place and the shabby man standing in front of it.

"Boone!" barked Deputy Overstreet. "What the hell are you doing here?"

"Never mind him for right now," said the marshal. "Get around there and see what kind of shape Cully is in." Then, scowling with agitation, he turned on the crowd. "Somebody go fetch Doc Hurlbert. On the double! The rest of you find some place else to be. Go on about your business, go home to your suppers. There's nothing more to see here for now. The bloodstains will still be in the street tomorrow. Get going. Scat!"

CHAPTER 17

——

Lone sat once again before Dalrymple's desk in the marshal's office. On his right was seated Tru, who'd insisted on being here after receiving news of the latest shooting. On his left slumped the shabby individual who by this point had been introduced as one Ira Boone.

It was Boone who was at present doing the talking. "Like I keep telling you," he was relating, "I first heard 'em jawing about it earlier this afternoon in the Lucky Dog Saloon. Saying how they aimed to get even with Mr. McGantry for killing those other two Box 50 men and embalming how they figured taking care of him would make 'em look good in the eyes of Granger Halsey and Denton, the big ranch owner."

"They said all this right in front of you?" The marshal's tone was dubious.

"Not in front of me, no. They said it while I was sorta working around the edges of the room, cleaning spittoons and laying down fresh sawdust and such." Boone slitted his eyes and regarded the marshal with a kind of bleary bitterness. "In other words, Marshal, they flat out wasn't paying no never mind to me. Just like most everybody don't. You remember—I lurk around town like a scraggly old alley cat nobody wants to look at. I swamp saloons and clean spittoons and do other scut work, all to earn a plate of beans and maybe a slice of cornbread at the end of each day to take back to the wood shed where I'm allowed to sleep on a straw pallet in the corner. Oh and I almost forgot, I also get the bonus of slurping the last few drops out of all the whiskey bottles I can lay my hands on, that others have cast aside in the wasteful belief they were empty."

Dalrymple set his mouth in a tight, straight line before saying, "I know your story, Ira. I'm sorry, but I ain't the one who cast your lot in life."

"I wish I knew who did," Boone muttered quietly, wistfully.

Lone looked over at the hapless man. "I don't know about any that and I sure don't mean to sound ungrateful. But I don't recall us ever meeting before. So what made you feel the need to come around and shout the warning that helped keep me from getting ambushed?"

"I did it on account of Peg," came the answer.

Lone frowned. "You knew Peg?"

"You bet I did. And pleased and proud to say so." For a moment, Boone's murky eyes shone a bit brighter. "Ol' Peg was one of the few who, for a long time now, ever treated me, decent. Whenever he came to town, he'd look me up and you can bet we'd have more than a few snorts together. Never knew for sure what caused him to ever take a second look at me, other than kinda figuring it was on account of us both being crips. He lost his pin to a griz, I lost mine—leastways the use of it—to a Reb basket ball. But no matter the cause, the cost was the same." Boone issued a quick, dry laugh. "We called ourselves the Brotherhood of the Bum Leg!"

Tru leaned forward to look past Lone and said, "It must have been very sad for you to hear he had been shot and left so gravely injured."

Boone hung his head. "It was hard news, that's for sure. I tried to go see him after they brung him to town and put him in that boarding house, but. No, that ain't exactly true. I never really *tried*. I started out a half dozen different times, but always turned back. I knew that hatchet-faced old Sharples woman would never let me past the front door."

"But getting back to your involvement with the ambush attempt on Lone," said Dalrymple. "You're saying you took an interest in that because Lone was a friend and partner to Peg?"

"That's exactly what I'm saying," Boone told him. "I couldn't do nothing to help my friend Peg when he got gunned down, but all of a sudden it seemed like I maybe could do something to help *his* friend McGantry from getting the same."

"Why didn't you come to me about the things you'd overheard, Ira?" Dalrymple wanted to know.

Boone just looked at him. "No offense, Marshal, but how much attention would you have paid me?"

Before anything more was said, the front door opened and Keith Overstreet came in. Outside, past his shoulder, darkness had settled over the town, offset slightly by intermittent pools of illumination thrown by the street lamps.

"I thought you were going to stay at the doc's in order to keep an eye on Cully," Dalrymple said by way of greeting.

"Cully ain't going nowhere, not no time soon," his deputy replied. "Doc had to put him under with some chloroform to work on that busted up shoulder. He's out cold and gonna stay that way for a spell. I had to get away and breathe some fresh air before it knocked me out too."

"He say anything before he went under?"

Overstreet walked over to the stove and poured himself a cup of coffee. "Oh, he was jabbering plenty there for a while. Between moaning and groaning and wailing in pain, that is."

"Well? What did he jabber?" Dalrymple said impatiently.

"Mostly he kept saying how sorry he was he got Buck killed. Sorry, see, on account of it was his idea to go after Lone. Just like Boone has been telling us" —Overstreet tipped his head toward the old swamper— "those two chowderheads had the notion if they gunned Lone it not only would square thing for Isaac and Jerome but would also gain them high appreciation from Granger and old man Denton."

Dalrymple wagged his head. "Chowderheads don't begin to say it."

"Didn't take spending a whole lot of time with those two," remarked Lone dryly, "to see they weren't packin' around an overload of brains."

"How about Virgil Sweeney? Did Cully say whether or not he was in on this idiot notion?" asked Dalrymple.

"No, he wasn't. Matter of fact, Cully told how him and Buck purposely dodged Virgil, waited for him to leave town and head back to the ranch so's he wouldn't be around to interfere."

"Yeah, I heard 'em discussing that part, too," said Boone.

Dalrymple scowled at him. "Okay, I guess I can understand why you didn't come running to me with what you overheard. But why didn't you try to at least warn Lone ahead of time instead of waiting until the last second before Cully opened fire on hm?"

"Because I lost track of where to find him," Boone explained with a shrug of his bony shoulders. "He was going all around town trying to make a deal on a wagon and team and then getting ol' Peg loaded up. I was always a step behind. In the end, when I saw Cully and Buck leave the Lucky Dog, I followed after them and all of a sudden they was taking positions on either side of that alley next to Farthing's, getting ready to catch Lone in a crossfire."

"It was very brave of you to remain and expose yourself to danger—calling out as you did, and saving Lone's life," declared Tru.

Boone actually blushed. "Well, I don't know about that. I didn't have no gun or nothing, wasn't much else I could do but give a holler."

"No, there was something else you *did* manage to do," corrected Overstreet. "What happened when Cully came tearing back around that corner after he'd been wounded?"

"Boy, I sure wasn't expecting that." Boone squirmed uncomfortably in his chair. "I was trying to slip up for a closer look at what was going on and, boom, all of sudden there he was! I could see he'd been hit but I could also see he was still holding on to his six-shooter. So I grabbed a length of two-by-four that was leaning against the side of the building and chunked him over the head with it."

Overstreet's eyebrows lifted. "Oh, you chunked him alright. Doc says, in addition to the bullet damage Lone gave him, Cully also has a whale of a concussion that's likely to leave him seeing double for a month of Sundays."

Boone seemed to consider this for a minute and then, setting his jaw firm, he proclaimed, "That's too blasted bad. I ain't sorry I done it, not nohow."

"And no right-thinking person could ever say you should be," allowed Dalrymple. "But that don't mean the incident won't still bring you plenty of regret before it's over, Ira."

Lone didn't like the sound of that. "What's that supposed to mean?"

The marshal spread his hands. "Stop and think. Another shooting involving more Box 50 men. Another one of 'em dead, a second one badly wounded, no doubt the full use of his arm ruined for the rest of his days. You think that ain't gonna do anything but fan the flames of the situation already set smoldering by the deaths of Isaac and Jerome?"

"So that sends the flames lickin' a little hotter in my direction," Lone responded. "I'm the one who killed Buck and messed up Cully—who I gladly would have killed, too, if I'd gotten the chance. No matter, me and Tru are still ready to roll out of here tomorrow and still ready to deal with any trouble that tries to follow us on the trail. But what does that have to do with heapin' added regret on this poor devil Boone?"

It was Tru who answered. "Because he will be left behind and there are those who will take it out on him because he helped you. Not only warned you of the attempt on your life, but then actually struck one of your assailants. He will not be treated well for that."

"I'm used to that kind of thing, ma'am," Boone said meekly. "When the cowboys from different ranches around come into town and get liquored up, some of the ornerier ones take it out on me regular-like. Sorta the way you might kick a dog that don't get outta your way quick enough."

"I'm afraid Miss Chang is right," Dalrymple said somberly. "This is likely to get a lot rougher than the usual stuff, Ira. With Lone and Miss Chang gone from town but Cully still around to keep wailing and stirring the pot about Box 50 mistreatment—which you know he blamed well will do, no matter what Granger or his brothers make of it—there's them who'll be bound to see you as a handy whipping boy. And I mean that literally."

"In that case, ain't it your job to protect him?" Lone demanded.

Dalrymple glared defensively. "In case you haven't noticed, mister, I got a whole town to look out for. There's just me and Keith to do it, and we do a pretty damned good job, all things considered. But we can't be everywhere at once. That means we can't babysit Ira—or anybody else—twenty-four hours a day."

Several tense clock ticks went by.

Until, with absolute resolve, Tru said, "The only solution, then, is for Mr. Boone to come with Lone and I."

CHAPTER 18

Noon of the following day found Lone's newly acquired team and wagon pulled up in front of the Busted Spur soddy. Lone, Tru, and Ira Boone were busy transferring Tru's belongings from their temporary storage inside the cabin and packing them snugly and securely around Peg's bolted-down casket already occupying the wagon bed.

Though limited by his bum leg, Ira worked steadily and earnestly at performing his share of the task at hand. A bath, a shave, and some clean duds availed to him from the left-behind assortment of clothing Ma Sharples kept in a trunk at her boarding house had transformed the outer appearance of the shaggy, unwashed ex swamper an almost startling degree. Up closer, his inner torments—all the past misfortunes and the unending craving for the next shot of busthead, as particularly evident in his bleary, bloodshot eyes—took off much of the sheen. But he was fighting it hard, and so far holding his own. Lone had made it clear he could come along on this trip with the understanding it meant laying off the booze; and as long as Ira kept moving and kept busy, his shakes were only minimally noticeable.

Tru, again with some help from Ma, had also undergone a few changes. Absent were the baggy trousers and sandals, replaced by snug, durable corduroy pants and a pair of sensible though still ladylike high-laced shoes. Once again a loose-fitting blouse completed her attire. It was long enough and loose enough at the waist to effectively hide the money belt (formerly belonging to her uncle) that only Lone knew she wore underneath. But at the same time, the material of the garment was a silk-like weave that clung to her breasts and hips in a way that made no secret of the fact it was draped over trim, womanly curves. Lone caught himself noticing this more than he wanted to admit and it didn't help that, some of the times when he was noticing, he found Tru gazing back. He mentally cursed Ma Sharples on two fronts: One, for planting in the former scout's head a notion that the girl was infatuated with him; and Two, for how she (Ma) had likely had a hand in selecting the clinging blouse to try and ensure the responsive attention it was getting.

Once the wagon was loaded the rest of the way and its added cargo tied securely in place, they took time for a lunch of sandwiches and fresh fruit that Ma had sent with them. After rolling out of North Platte at sunrise, they had stopped along the way at the spot where Tru and her uncle had had their rattlesnake encounter and where Uncle Pao was buried. Lone took time to make sure the immediate area was currently clear of vipers, then he and Ira helped add some more stones over the grave to dissuade any attempts by scavengers to dig up the remains lying below the surface. Tru also added a small marker she had arranged a North Platte stone mason to fashion for her, and then the two men had left her alone for a while to say her final goodbyes to her uncle.

During this hiatus, Lone also took a few minutes to examine the wagon that had carried Tru and her uncle from Council Bluffs. But it showed no advantage over his, in fact was smaller and lighter in build. The wagon Lone had bought in town proved durable enough so that, once righted again by him and a handful of helpers following its tip-over in the middle of the street, it remained basically undamaged. Just to make doubly sure, he'd asked Woodrow, Ma's handyman, to give it a good looking over and his report came back all satisfactory. But the one thing Lone did take from Tru's abandoned wagon was some sections of harnessing, to be used for rigging repair in case it was needed at some point farther on.

With lunch out of the way and all of Tru's belongings now loaded—in addition to Peg's war bag which Lone had found intact in its hiding place—it was time to get rolling again. Ira had already demonstrated a good touch at handling the team and wagon, so he once more took the reins. Tru sat quietly on the seat beside him. Lone, astride Ironsides, rode either alongside or slightly ahead of the wagon. Before leaving North Platte, he'd decided to purchase a second saddle mount, a wiry, sand-colored mustang that trotted along behind the wagon on a tether. Tru had spoken up for wanting to do some riding on this animal, but at the moment was showing no interest in doing so. The visit to her uncle's grave had left her somewhat melancholy, though she seemed to be coming out of it as they resumed travel.

"We'll basically stick to Uncle Pao's plan of followin' the South Platte, but at a distance to the north," Lone had announced when they first started out. "The going won't be that much harder, but keepin' off the more commonly traveled path closer to the river might help confuse anybody comin' along behind on the lookout for us. And we'll for sure swing wide of Ogallala when we get that far. I don't know if the Halsey brother who's a deputy marshal there has yet been notified we've started his way. Even if he has, Dalrymple don't think he's likely to try anything without any of the others—but we're just as well not temptin' him."

"Sounds like a sensible idea to me," allowed Ira.

Before leaving the Busted Spur, Lone had dug out a flask from his saddlebags and gave the ex swamper a swig from it. He recognized how hard it was to break the grip of the whiskey demon when its claws were sunk deep in a wretch, and he wanted to help wean Ira off a little easy as long as he was putting the effort he was showing. The short nip, coming on the heels of the poisons he'd sweated out loading the wagon, seemed to strike a helpful balance going into the afternoon.

"How far is Ogallala?" Tru asked.

"As the crow flies, a little over fifty miles from North Platte," Lone told her. "We're part way there but won't come close tonight. I expect we'll be on past sometime late tomorrow afternoon."

"How far to Fort Collins after that?"

"Barring no trouble, I'm reckoning we should make it in about ten days."

"But we'll come in sight of the mountains before then, won't we?" Tru asked anxiously. "I am so looking forward to seeing real mountains."

Lone chuckled. "Oh, you'll be seeing mountains alright. Well ahead of reaching Fort Collins. The Rockies. One of the biggest, grandest mountain ranges anywhere. And once you're settled in your new home, in the foothills below Poudre Canyon, you'll have 'em loomin' up practically right out of your back yard."

******

They made good progress through the balance of the day.

The southern reaches of Nebraska's fabled Sandhills over which they were passing consisted of little else but treeless, rolling hills—minor undulations in the land compared to the massive mountains that lay ahead to the west or even the great, steeper-sloped grassy dunes reaching farther to the north—dotted infrequently by modest sandstone outcrops and occasional deep gully wash-outs. Amidst the tall, yellowed stands of last year's leftover grass, hints of early spring green was starting to show and stubborn clumps of yucca sprouted everywhere.

When the sun went down, they made night camp on the flat of a hollow between two low, blunted hills. While Lone was tending the horses, Ira took care of setting up the campsite and getting a cooking fire going. Over the flames, Tru made coffee and prepared a meal of rice and beans mixed with chunks of canned pork, served with sourdough biscuits from a sackful sent along by Ma.

"Boy, this sure beats a daily ration of dry cornbread crusts and a scoop of overcooked mush," Ira declared as he ate. "I ain't feasted like this since. well, not for an awful long time."

Starting the prior evening (after Lone had grudgingly given in to the notion of the hardluck soul tagging along with them) and on through the course of the day, Ira had proven to be quite open and talkative, with flashes of a wry sense of humor. It was evident that the time he'd spent shunned and shoved aside had bottled up an affability longing for some kind of outlet. He and Tru hit it off quickly, so that the two of them sharing a wagon seat together presented no problem. In fact, other than Tru's brief period of quiet melancholy following the stop at her uncle's grave, they chattered nearly as steady as a couple of old washerwomen trading gossip while hanging up clothes in neighboring back yards.

While Lone didn't engage directly in much of the conversation, he overheard enough of it to learn the story behind how Ira had fallen to the sorry condition he'd reached back in North Platte. After the war, the way he told it, he'd found work uninhibited by his bad leg as a successful whiskey drummer out of Wichita, covering a territory that included a sizable chunk of middle and northern Kansas and a portion of southern Nebraska. This enabled him to afford a nice house for his wife back in Wichita and gave him a welcome home base to return to after his long stretches on the road.

But, gradually, those long stretches started to take their toll. Ira began "sampling" his own product too strongly and his wife proved unfaithful during his absences. This led to an ugly divorce that drove Ira deeper into the bottle. In time, he lost his job with the whiskey distributor and began to drift, stopping here and there to do menial work that could buy him cheaper and cheaper brands of rotgut and space on the floor of some drafty back room where he could spread his bedroll.

A serious attempt to crawl out of the downward spiral he was on gained him a job with a freighting outfit hauling mining equipment to Deadwood. That lasted until the outfit laid over one night in North Platte. Ira ended up going on a drunken bender that left him passed out in a whore's crib when the freight wagons rolled away the next morning. That was last fall and Ira had been wallowing in despair and self-pity in North Platte ever since. Shorty Harper at the Lucky Dog Saloon, a former customer from back in his drummer days, had helped him survive by offering swamper and other scut work for a meal a day, another back room floor to sleep on and whatever whiskey dregs he could slurp out of cast aside customer bottles.

"That's quite an elaborate lifestyle to leave behind," Ira had summed up with wry wistfulness. "But, seeing how Box 50 avengers in one form or other were almost certainly bound to bring it to an end anyway, abandoning it to present company and present conditions ain't all that bad."

"What you ought to be abandoning above all," Tru told him sternly, "is your enslavement to the bottle and your own self-loathing. I am seeking a fresh start, a new life in Fort Collins. You have even greater reason to do the same. All you have to do is want it bad enough."

"I do want it. Want it bad," Ira had responded. "It's time and past time that I quit living in the gutter. I just need…"

When his words trailed off, Tru said, "You just need to quit feeling sorry for yourself and planning to fail. When you get to Fort Collins, you will have a friend willing to help you. Me. And another you called friend lies behind us in a wooden box. In short order, he will be looking down, watching from high up in the mountains. If you allow yourself to fail and return to the gutter again, you will be letting down more than just yourself."

Listening to this exchange, Lone smiled ruefully. Based on his own experience with the powerful force of will contained in the deceptively delicate package that was Tru, he was inclined to think that if all Ira needed to straighten his life out was a firm hand to keep shoving him in the right direction, then he may have met his salvation. On the other hand and here Lone's expression clouded darkly at the thought, causing him to turn away so the others couldn't see, if some combination of Box 50 riders and/or Halsey kin came after them with vengeful intentions stoked hot enough, then the journey to salvation might be cut brutally short, no matter what.

CHAPTER 19

The following day, their first full day on the trail together, went without incident and once more added up to a span of solid progress. The weather remained clear, sunny and fairly warm but still with a touch of winter crispness in the air. Overnight it had grown quite chill, but they were outfitted with plenty of warm blankets to offset that. Lone and Ira slept in bedrolls under the wagon while Tru occupied a well cushioned space in the middle of the hauling bed left purposely open for her slumber and a degree of privacy. She'd objected to this special treatment though not too strenuously but the men had insisted.

After breakfast, Lone had offered Ira another swig from his flask as a bracer to help start the day. He was well aware of how the miseries of alcohol withdrawal had caused the poor wretch to toss and turn most of the night, even though Lone had given him a nip to help settle him down before turning in.

But this time, in spite of the torment on his face and the trembling in his hands, Ira hadn't reached to accept the flask. Instead, he stared at it for a long count, then licked his lips and lifted his bleary eyes to meet Lone's gaze before saying, "Tru's right. If I'm going to crawl out of the gutter and make it stick this time, then it starts with ending the booze. I appreciate you trying to help wean me off kinda slow, but that's only prolonging the inevitable. If I'm going to stop, then I might as well do it and get it over with. You can put the flask away and there'll be no need to bring it out, at least not for me, again."

Lone couldn't help but admire the turn-down. Knowing how hard the craving for a drink was raging inside Ira, he even felt a little guilty for having offered the temptation. Resisting it was a step, a big one. But, at the same time, Lone also knew that resisting temptation once was a long ways from being able to do it over and over again going forward.

Nevertheless, as the balance of the day unfolded, Ira had seemed to grow firmer and steadier even without the bracer. His pallid face took on some color from the sun and his initially shaky grip on the reins grew stronger and surer, working the pulling team smartly at his command. After their noon stop, when Tru offered to take over for a while, Ira had assured her he was fine to continue.

This then freed Tru to spend the afternoon hours in the saddle of the wiry mustang Lone had purchased as a spare mount back in North Platte. Her limited riding experience and a touch of greenness still left on the mustang had given the undertaking some challenging moments. Overall, though, it was still highly enjoyable for Tru and not surprising, by the end she was handling the mustang just fine.

And so it was that Lone's signal to stop for night camp came as a most welcome call to his two weary (though uncomplaining) companions. The spot Lone chose was a flat patch of green bordered on one side by a nameless, trickling tributary of Lodgepole Creek. It provided particularly lush graze for the animals and even had a handful of trees—birch and cottonwood—grouped near the creek.

"Come morning, before we head out," Ira announced as they relaxed around the campfire after their supper meal, "I'll make up a couple bundles of deadfall and branches from those trees to take with us. There's bound to be upcoming stretches where fuel will be mighty sparse."

Lone gave an approving nod. "Good thinking. You've traveled this area before, I take it—to know about the scarcity of firewood?"

"Yeah, my circuit brought me up through here as far west as Julesburg," Ira answered. "Even made it as far as Denver a time or two. Though I've seen those big ol' Rockies, I can't say they ever thrilled me the way Tru is looking forward to."

"But there *will* be trees when we get to the mountains, won't there?" Tru asked.

"Oh, yeah. Plenty of 'em," Lone told her. "But, between here and there, we might have to resort to the old pioneers' trick of burning buffalo chips to do our cooking."

"Yeah, we probably better start being on the lookout for some of those, too, while we're rolling along," said Ira. "They've grown plenty scarce these days as well."

Tru looked puzzled. "Buffalo chips?"

Lone and Ira exchanged uncomfortable glances.

A corner of Ira's mouth lifted in a grin. "You're the one who brought it up. I'll leave it to you to explain."

Tru's gaze probed Lone's face, waiting for an explanation.

Lone frowned, trying to think of how to delicately describe the practice of using dried buffalo droppings as fuel for a cook fire. Before he was able to find the words, his attention was suddenly diverted by something else, a sound, coming faintly from a distance. A sound unfortunately all too familiar to Lone.

The way he cocked his head and the change in his expression immediately altered and heightened the attention he got from both Tru and Ira.

"What is it? What's wrong?" Ira wanted to know.

Lone's frown deepened. "Don't you hear it? Listen. Somebody out there is—"

"Shooting!" Ira blurted. "Yeah, now I hear it—the sound of gunfire."

Tru's eyes widened. "What does it mean? Who is it?"

"Don't know who it is, but the sound of gunfire seldom means anything but trouble," Lone grunted, rising up from where he'd been sitting cross-legged beside the fire.

Ira stood up too. "Sounds pretty far off, don't it?"

"Seems like," Lone allowed, shifting his gunbelt, adjusting the way the holster hung down over his hip. "But sound can travel funny, tumbling in and out of these hills. Best kill that fire and then you and Tru pull in tight around the wagon while I go have a look-see."

Ira began kicking dirt over the flames as instructed, but over his shoulder he questioned, "Don't you think it'd be safest if we held here and all stuck together?"

Lone leaned over his saddle where it was propped against one of the wagon's front wheels. After giving his Yellowboy a shove to make sure it was seated tight and secure in its scabbard, he straightened up and hoisted the rig onto one shoulder. Before starting toward where Ironsides and the other horses were picketed, he said, "The safest thing, I think, is for me to go find out who's out there and what they're up to. In case it's somebody with an interest in us, it'd be good to know. If it is, I might have the chance to prevent 'em from showin' up to surprise us either yet tonight or maybe on the trail tomorrow."

"But if it's somebody interested in us, who are they shooting at *now*?" Tru asked.

"I don't know. They may *not* have any interest in us. Could be some ranchers catching rustlers in the act. Could be some drunk cowboys shooting at the moon. What exactly it means is what I aim to find out, kid," Lone told her.

He strode over and started saddling Ironsides. Tru and Ira followed along and stood close as he worked. Once he had the cinch pulled tight and the mounting stirrup dropped back in place, Lone turned to face them. "On second thought, I got a better idea," he said. "Instead of you two stickin' close to the wagon, take some blankets and the rifles, Tru's Henry and the Winchester from under the wagon seat and go nest in among those trees over there. That way, in case it *is* somebody who means us trouble and they get by me or come around before I get back, they'll be drawn to the wagon and you'll see them before they know you're anywhere around. The moon's nearly up, your eyes will adjust and you'll have good visibility even without the fire."

A scowling Ira said, "Are you trying to put us at ease or scare the hell out of us?"

Lone responded, "I'm trying to keep us all safe. Remember that."

A moment later he was up in the saddle, wheeling Ironsides, and pointing the big gray northwest, toward the sound of the distant gunfire. Over his shoulder, he called, "Do as I said. I'll be back before you know it."

CHAPTER 20

For a time, as Lone rode away from the camp, the thump of Ironsides' hooves pounding the grassy earth was loud enough to drown out the sound of the gunfire up ahead. A couple times Lone slowed the big gray down to make sure the shooting was still going on. It was, though sporadically. There would be a rapid burst of shots, then a pause, then more shots. An occasional lone pop would sound during some of the pauses. Once or twice, Lone thought he might have heard some shouting but the words were in-decipherable.

Lone hadn't gone far before the ground began to rise, eventually flattening to a broad table with few of the un-dulations that marked the surrounding terrain. The ascent to this flat expanse had been up through several slanted ridges separated by wide wash-outs, like the splayed fingers of a giant hand. Up on the flat, illumination from the now fully risen moon and a wash of stars growing individually brighter by the minute, gave Lone a silver-tinted visibility nearly as clear as daylight. And the sound of the gunfire was sharper and clearer, too, coming from closer than he had previously judged.

Lone slowed Ironsides and proceeded cautiously. He had ascended the table on its southern edge and continued keeping close to that lip as he moved along in a westerly direction. Ahead, he could see where the flat surface flared out gradually wider, still to the south. The night air was cooling rapidly and up here on this higher elevation a faint breeze was stirring, rustling softly through the high, dry grass. Good, Lone thought; that would help mask the sound of his approach to the shooters up ahead during the quiet of the lull periods.

Lone followed the flare-out of the tabletop, sticking close to the lip, eyes peeled sharp for any actual sign of the shooters. When the next burst of gunfire shattered the air, it sounded alarmingly close. Lone decided it was time to quit the saddle and proceed on foot. Pulling his Yellowboy from its scabbard, he did just that. He ground-reined Ironsides, gave him a departing pat for reassurance, then advanced without him.

After about fifty yards, Lone saw, just ahead, where the edge of the flat broke suddenly away into the wide gouge of a wash-out that slanted sharply to the base of the elevated ground dozens of feet below. Lone halted, dropping to one knee, and scanned ahead even more closely. He saw where the flare-out of the tabletop started to curve back in after another thirty or forty yards. But between there and where he was, its edge was notched by three more break-aways falling into deep, ragged wash-out gullies.

And a short ways down into the maw of the middle of these, the second one in line from Lone's position, he spotted his first sign of movement directly connected to the shooting that had down him here. Twenty feet down from the rim of the tabletop, two men were wedged into the cover of ragged, twisty notches worn into one sloping wall of a wide wash-out trough. They were brandishing pistols with which they periodically leaned out and fired down at somebody at the base of the wash-out.

Lone's quick assessment was that the pair holding the high ground had the cover to pull back and withdraw up over the rim if they wanted, meaning whoever they were trading lead with down below likely was pinned in place. He further judged, based on the pacing of the shots, that there was only one shooter in the pinned-down position. The set-up and the odds immediately inclined Lone toward favoring whoever it was caught farther down in the wash-out.

But he had to be careful. There could be a solid explanation for how things were stacked up and maybe the hombre down below deserved what he was getting. Before he threw in with one side or the other, Lone would have to try and make certain which was the *right* side, based on more than just his gut inclination. Or. since whatever was going on here pretty clearly had nothing to do with him or his party (who already had enough concerns of their own), he could just back away and leave this little fracas play out however fate decided.

But that just flat wasn't in him. Lone knew that even before the thought was done tumbling in and out of his head.

He edged forward, low and slow. He worked his way around the inner point of the first wash-out and moved toward the next one. When he got close, he dropped down and bellied to the edge, cradling his Yellowboy in his arms. This middle wash-out was half again as wide as the first, its walls sloping at fifty degree angles, their surfaces burnished by the wind and hard-baked by the sun. Marring these walls were irregular seams, gouged-out pockets, and a few short ledge-like sections.

The two high level shooters were now in full view of Lone, perched a half dozen feet apart on the opposite wall, each occupying a deep, crooked seam that gave him cover from down below and at the same time provided purchase back up to the lip of the rim. Even though the moon- and starlight were brightening the night pretty thoroughly, it wasn't enough for Lone to make out any distinct features of the two shooters. Only that they were lean, hard-looking sorts who appeared mighty comfortable handling a six-gun.

What Lone really wanted to get a better look at—try to get a better *sense* of—was the hombre down below. He bellied closer to the edge of the rim and parted a screen of tall grass to peer down. Like he figured, there was only one man down there and he was trapped in amidst a cluster of boulders, rubble tumbled down from the sides of the wash-out.

The trapped man was able to pop up long enough to throw a shot or two, but then had to duck quickly back to keep from getting his head blown off. Exposing himself long enough to try and make a run for it would have amounted to a form of suicide. What was more, even if he did break free from the boulders he'd only be running into another kind of trap. Just beyond the boulders, Lone could see the sprawled, motionless body of a dead horse—the man's mount, killed by bullets from above. In other words, if the man got away on foot, his attackers—assuming they had their own horses tied somewhere close by—could give pursuit out into the open and easily ride him down.

Lone grimaced, a silent curse running through his head. The poor bastard was in bad shape, no two ways about it. His chances for survival stretched only as far as his ammunition lasted.

What that left Lone to decide was what he could or

should do to help. No matter how much the one-sidedness of the situation rankled him, he still didn't know for sure who was in the right here.

And then, unexpectedly, he got some help making up his mind.

After pouring a quick three-round burst of lead down into the boulder cluster, one of the men in the high rocks leaned back in the safety of his notch and issued a nasty laugh. "How about it, law dog?" he cackled. "You enjoyin' your diet of boulder dust and lead chips? They whettin' your appetite for the full course—one of our slugs catchin' you square one of these times when you ain't so quick to duck back? You know it's just a matter of time before that's gonna happen."

"No better than you sorry asses shoot," the man down below responded, "I'll die of starvation or old age before either of you hit what you're aiming at."

"Maybe you're right. Then again, maybe you plain ain't worth wastin' no more lead on," said the second man up on the wash-out wall. "Maybe we should leave you thinkin' about what we warned you would happen if anybody gave chase too soon and explainin' it to the others who'll eventually show up and see how you didn't listen and how it turned out."

"You go ahead and do that, you dirty bastard," called the man in the boulders, his voice quavering. "You harm that boy and leave one piece of me alive, I'll stalk you to the ends of the earth!"

The men in the high rocks cackled some more at his impotent rage.

Lone had heard enough. He still didn't know all the circumstances behind this, but the fact the man in the boulders had been referred to as "law dog"—a lawman,

in other words—told him all he needed to know about
which side to come down on.

He shifted his position, turning the Yellowboy in his
hands and slowly, quietly levering a round into the chamber. He refocused his attention fully on the two men fitted
into notches on the opposite wall of the wash-out.

And then, suddenly, the world fell out from underneath
him!

CHAPTER 21

One minute Lone was belly down on the rim of the wash-out, getting set to draw a bead on the two skunks across the gap—a second later a huge slice of the rim immediately around him broke away and tore loose from the tabletop, spilling him forward and down and dropping him into the gap with a smothering cloud of dust, dirt clods, and rocks raining down with him. Lone was instantly stunned, barely comprehending what was happening. All he could do was flail and grab wildly, blindly, hoping to seize something that might break his fall and try to keep from getting buried in the landslide threatening to swallow him.

It was to no avail until, abruptly, he crashed onto something solid enough to hold him in place even as earthen debris from the break-away continued to pour over him. Lone curled as best he could into a fetal position, feeling crushed and hammered by a hundred blunted fists that pounded every inch of him and drove the air out of his lungs. He managed to get his arms up, wrapping his head protectively and at the same time creating an enclosed little pocket around his face that allowed him to try and regain some breath without sucking in choking mouthfuls of dust.

His head swam and he nearly blacked out. As clarity returned, Lone realized the landslide had stopped, at least for the time being. Nothing more was spilling onto him, though he could still feel the weight of what had previously accumulated. It wasn't crushing, however, he sensed he could shake it off without too much difficulty. Before he did, however, the sound of voices caused him to remain still.

The voices were coming from the other side of the gap, choppy and somewhat muffled to Lone by the dirt covering his head and filling the cavity of one ear. He was able to make out this much:

"Never mind that law dog ... in no shape to give chase no more."

". say we get the hell out of here before we get caught by a damn landslide over on this side."

There was more muttering but it was unintelligible as the voices seemed to be fading, departing. Getting "the hell out of here".

Lone continued to lay very still. He was keen to the fact that, from what he'd overheard, there was no mention of him. Could it be that the two ambushers were unaware of his presence, of how he'd been caught in the landslide— hell, how he had probably inadvertently *caused* the damn thing by resting for too long too close to the rim? Or maybe they simply figured he'd been crushed by it. In any event, they seemed to be leaving with either no concern or no awareness regarding him.

To make sure he did nothing to cause any re-assessment by the pair, Lone remained still for several more minutes. And then he thought he heard, very faintly, the sound of hoofbeats riding away up on the tabletop. Maybe it was only his imagination or wishful thinking, but it was enough to finally stir him into motion. First he straightened out of his fetal tuck, then pushed up on one elbow, then hitched around and sat up. All the while, a layer of dirt and sand and various-sized chunks of rock was being dislodged and sent pouring off him.

From his sitting position, Lone brushed dirt from his face, blinked it out of his eyes, and tipped his head from side to try and clear his ears. The taste of dirt was on his tongue but when he tried to spit it out he found his mouth was too dry to work up any saliva. He was certainly battered and bruised and scraped in numerous places, but there didn't seem to be any serious bleeding and it didn't feel like he had any broken bones.

After he was done taking stock of himself physically, Lone looked around to see where he'd ended up that left him in no worse shape than he was. He'd gotten hung up, he saw, on a ledge-like outcrop jutting away from the sloping wash-out wall about a quarter of the way down from the top. This had saved him from tumbling all the way to the bottom and likely getting buried under more of the 'slide than he ever would have crawled out of. In other words, all things considered, he was damn lucky to be sitting there counting his cuts and bruises.

Further evaluation by Lone was interrupted by a voice calling from the boulder cluster below. "Hey, you up there! I can see you're surprisingly still alive. You hurt very bad?"

Lone hadn't forgot about the man the ambushers had had pinned down in those rocks, but the shout from him came unexpectedly all the same. Lone responded, calling back, "Far as I can tell, I'm still in one piece. That's more than I would have bet on a few minutes ago."

"I can only imagine," the man returned. "When I saw

you disappear in that mass of dust and dirt, I thought for sure you were a goner."

"Those hombres who were throwing all that lead must have thought the same. Lucky for me they didn't stick around to make sure."

"I don't think they even knew you were over there. They never spotted you in all the tumbling dust and rubble. I wouldn't have either if I hadn't caught sight of your rifle barrel poking out over the rim just before it gave way under you. When that happened, those polecats thought it was a natural thing and got worried it might happen over on their side, too. That's what put 'em in such a hurry to light out without finishing me all the way—they figured they'd already put me in bad enough shape as it was."

"How bad a shape *are* you in?" Lone asked.

There was a pause. Then: "Been better. Those bush-whacking bastards shot my horse out from under me. When I fell, I landed hard on my shoulder and busted it up pretty good. I can move some, but I don't think I can make it up there where you are."

Lone rose to his feet on the ledge, leaning against the wash-out wall for support. It was painful, his legs were stiff and sore, threatening to cramp. But once he was upright, he felt reasonably sturdy and strong. "You stay put," he called down. "I've got a horse up on top. I'll fetch him, we'll find a way down to you."

CHAPTER 22

Ira had the fire going again, burning bright and hot, with the pot of leftover coffee from supper bubbling on the edge coals. Lone, Tru, Ira, and the injured man Lone had brought back to camp were circled in close around the crackling flames, seated on folded blankets. The new addition looked to be a man in his early thirties, even-featured and clean-shaven, with a thick head of reddish brown hair. His wide mouth was presently pulled tight by the pain of his injury and his eyes had a faraway, somewhat forlorn cast to them.

Ira and the injured man each held a cup of steaming mud. Tru gripped a shawl that she had pulled around her shoulders against the chill air. The night was growing steadily colder and the stars in the sky now seemed to have taken on the glint of ice chips.

Lone sat with his prized Winchester Yellowboy lying across his folded legs. To his great relief—fearing the weapon had probably been hopelessly buried in the landslide that tore it from his grip when the section of rim had broken away underneath him—he'd been able to retrieve it from the rubble at the bottom of the wash-out once he'd

made it down that far. As he and the others conversed now
in the flickering light of the fire, his hands (almost as if of
their own accord) were busy slowly, methodically stripping
down, cleaning, oiling, and re-assembling the rifle. To the
touch and to the examination of his frequent downward
glances, there appeared to be no damage.

"So you're convinced the owlhoots who had your ears
pinned back were part of the Gemsil gang—as in Three
Finger Jack Gemsil?" This query came from a frowning Ira.

With a solemn nod, the injured man replied, "Not a
doubt in my mind. Neither Jack nor his brother Boyd were
part of the pair who doubled back on me, but the ones who
did were from the same crew. I'm certain of it."

Ira gave a low whistle. "Three Finger Jack and his boys.
That's a mighty rough crew for anybody to go up against.
Especially all alone."

The injured man's face clouded. "Tell me something
I don't know. But I already explained why I had to go at
it that way." He sat in a rigid, awkward manner, his right
arm folded over his stomach and secured there by the tight
wrapping of torn blanket strips that had been applied by
Lone and Tru, starting from under his left arm and angling
up to encircle his damaged right shoulder, arm and much
of his upper torso for the purpose of immobilizing said
shoulder as much as possible.

"Why do they call this bad man 'Three Finger Jack'?"
Tru asked, pulling her shawl a bit tighter about her.

"Because he's only got three fingers," Ira answered with
a shrug. "Got one of 'em—the ring finger, I believe—
chawed off in a bar fight when he was younger. Whoever
did it had the right idea, seein's how it was his gun hand, but
they made the mistake of leaving his trigger finger. Some
say that's what turned Jack so ornery, losing his finger that

way, so then he went on to use the trigger finger that got left for demonstrating his displeasure."

Lone made a sour face. "You seem awfully well versed on the subject."

"Always before, Jack's stomping ground was mainly down through Kansas. Same as mine used to be," Ira explained. "So talk of him and his exploits was a frequent topic of discussion thereabout, especially in the establishments where I did my business."

His expression still dark, the injured man said, "Well apparently just talking about Jack and his robbing, killing ways gave way to some folks deciding to try and do something about it. To our misfortune, the heat they brought to bear on him down there drove him up to our neck of the woods."

"But, the way you told it to me, it sounds like you damn near made it *his* misfortune when your marshal was sharp enough to recognize him and his boys as soon as they hit town," Lone pointed out.

The injured man's expression didn't change. With a touch of bitterness edging into his tone, he said, "If only the trap we tried too hastily to spring on 'em—the way they did on the James boys up in that Minnesota town a few years back—had been as sharp and quick. If it had worked. well, I wouldn't be sitting here now."

Tru regarded him, sadness filling her eyes. "The hostage they took in order to make their escape—the little boy, your son—are they really so vicious that they would harm him?"

The injured man hung his head. "They're animals capable of anything. They've proven as much time and again. That's why I had to risk going after them. By myself. They warned what they would do if a posse gave pursuit, said they'd release the boy safe once they were in the clear. But I knew better than to trust their word. I thought one man traveling fast and alone might have the chance to...." His words trailed off and he barely managed to choke back a sob.

"You did what any father, any man with enough guts, would have done in that case. You can't fault yourself for it," Lone said grimly.

Still with his head hung, the man responded, "But I can't deny the failure of it either. I only made things worse. Here I sit out of commission in the middle of nowhere while Marshal Stubin and others back in Ogallala have no way of knowing, so they're continuing to hold off, waiting, giving me a chance and my son remains left to the mercy of those, Those..." Again his words trailed off.

Nobody spoke for several beats. There was only the crackling voice of the fire.

Until Lone said, "Reckon there's closer help for that boy than from clear back in Ogallala."

All eyes cut to him.

"Not to brag," he went on, "but I'm one of the best trackers around. And I've even had success at snatchin' a captive away from a pack of Injuns once who were a hell of a lot savvier than this handful of rabid coyotes ever thought of being."

The injured man lifted his face, eyes widening. "You'd attempt that. For *me*?"

Lone's head moved from side to side a barely perceptive amount. "No. I'd do it for the sake of a ten year old boy somewhere out there in the hands of cutthroats who don't value human life much higher than that of a rodent or maybe even a bug. It's like I already told you, Halsey. I'm sorry you lost a brother and a cousin. But I make no apology for my part in it. They forced my hand, I did what

I had to. What I'm saying to you now ain't me seeking some kind of atonement or forgiveness for that. It's strictly about the boy."

So there was the rest of it. In an astonishing twist of coincidence and bitter irony, the injured man Lone had brought back to camp was none other than Cliff Halsey, blood relation to the men Lone had slain four nights ago in front of the Busted Spur cabin and thereby one of the kin everybody speculated would be coming after Lone for revenge. Before Deputy Halsey had left Ogallala to join up with his other two brothers in North Platte, however, an even closer and more demanding tragedy struck when the arrival of the Gemsil gang to his own town resulted in them shooting their way clear of being apprehended and grabbing the deputy's young son as a hostage.

Lone and Halsey had discovered one another's identity shortly after Lone and Ironsides were able to descend down from the high table and reach the busted-up deputy at the base of the wash-out. Whether this knowledge beforehand would have changed Lone's reaction when first arriving on the scene was hard to say and, in the end, a moot point. Once the full facts were known, it wasn't in the former scout to just turn away and ride off, leaving the injured man behind. The rest of Halsey's story, what he was doing out there as a result of the Gemsil gang and their captive, had come out during the ride back to camp.

And now another curve in this bizarre turn of events was on the table.

Halsey gazed at Lone with tormented eyes. "I don't. I'm not sure what to say."

"I do," declared Ira. "I say it's a crazy idea on your part, Lone. My heart goes out to the thought of that little fella in the hands of those lowdown skunks, too. Anybody' would. No telling what they're capable of. But one of the possibilities is that they just *might* let him go unharmed, like they said, if they ain't bothered. Seems to me that getting poked at by somebody continuing to come after 'em, in spite of what they warned, could prod 'em more the wrong way instead of it doing any good. And that ain't saying nothing about the risk you'd be taking on for yourself."

"Thanks for your concern, Ira. But it's my risk and my choice to take it," Lone told him.

"Alright. But what about the risks beyond just your own?" Ira persisted. "Anything happens to you, where will that leave Tru and me? And what about your promise to get your friend Peg up into the mountains?"

Lone's eyes flashed. "For starters, I ain't figurin' on anything happening to me. When I set out to do something, I don't make a habit of plannin' to fail at it." He paused, glancing over at Tru, softening his gaze. "If it works out different this time, you two are capable of continuing without me. You're well outfitted, it's only six or seven more days to Fort Collins, all you have to do is keep following the river to get there. Comes to worst" —here he cut his gaze back to Ira— "I count on you to do right by Peg and plant him somewhere you figure is fitting."

Ira swallowed. "You'd trust that to me?"

"Said so, didn't I?" Lone replied flatly.

Tru had been gazing at him silently for some time. Now, softly, she said, "Yes, you must do this thing. I understand. You would not be you if you did anything less."

Lone held her eyes for a long count, then had to look away. He stood up and worked the action on the Yellowboy, making sure it felt loose and properly functioning. Satisfied, he said, "I'll want to get started at first light. Once I've headed out, the rest of you should move on, too. Keep followin' the river west. By my reckoning, you're closest to the little railroad settlement of Big Springs. Last I knew they didn't have much there, not likely a doctor of any kind. But they'll have a telegraph and like I said, the train goes through there. You can get in touch with Ogallala and make some kind of arrangements with them to get the deputy taken care of."

"After that, Tru and Ira should continue on for at least as far as Julesburg across the Colorado line. There's a marshal there I've had some dealin's with, name of Tobe Crenshaw. He's kind of a hard nut, but fair. If you want to hold there for a day or so and wait for me, explain things to Crenshaw and he'll look out for you while you're in town."

Lone paused. His mouth curved in a sheepish grin. "There. Having babbled all that, I'll now note there ain't a whole lot of night left and I'd like to grab a piece of it for some shuteye before it's time to head out come sunrise. Suggest you all do the same."

Cliff Halsey also pushed to his feet, awkwardly, doing his best to keep from wincing at the pain. He stepped closer to Lone, saying, "I ... I still don't have the words, McGantry. No matter how much you protest, you can't stop me from being grateful for this, for what you're doing. But, at the same time, I want to be clear that I can't speak for my brothers—about that other business with Isaac and Jerome, I mean. Bad as I might want to, I can't give no guarantee that their minds won't still be—"

Lone cut him off. "Save your breath, Deputy. I never asked or expected any different. However they or you feel about that other, ain't got nothing to do with this. I keep telling you, this is strictly about the boy. Now, the best thing for all of us right now is to try and grab some sleep."

CHAPTER 23

"Deader'n a cigar store Injun, that's how we left him!"

So declared Hash Crawford as he swiped the back of one hand across his mouth after taking a swig of busthead from the long-necked bottle he held clenched in the fit of his other hand. He raised the bottle for another quick belt and then handed it to the man standing beside him, saying, "Ain't that right, Angel?"

Crawford was a tall man of average build whose forty years of hard life showed in the weary slump of his shoulders and the deep lines in a face that no one would have ever called handsome to begin with. His eyes were too close together, his nose too blunt and he had thick lips that seemed perpetually peeled back in a half sneer that revealed horsey, yellowed teeth.

Angel Rejos, the young Mexican he handed the bottle to, was a couple years short of thirty, trim and handsome in a sharp-featured sort of way. His expression conveyed a smugness to match Crawford's sneer and he carried himself with a swagger befitting the pair of matched, ivory-handled Remingtons that rode in silver-trimmed black holsters hung low on his hips.

"Si," agreed Angel, taking the bottle and flashing a cocky grin. "We left that dumb *bastardo* as dead as the rubble of rocks surrounding him."

The two men had just returned to camp after purposely lagging behind to check their back trail and subsequently lay the ambush for Cliff Halsey. The fabrication they were currently putting forth was something they had concocted on the way back as a more suitable report to gang leader Three Finger Jack than to admit they had hastily and perhaps prematurely quit the scene out of concern for getting caught in a landslide instead of hanging around to make certain the deputy was dead. After all, they convinced themselves, he was as good as. What with a dead horse and the man himself lying injured at the bottom of a wash-out in the middle of nowhere, was there really much difference? The answer lay in the difference of how Jack might react if he viewed the job as being left only half-assed done. With Jack, it was always safest to figure he was in a bloody mood preferring anyone who went against the gang to be left thoroughly dead in their wake.

So the pair was playing it safe and giving him a report he was least likely to find any fault with.

Crawford and Angel had ridden most of the balance of the night to catch up to where the rest of the gang had stopped to make camp. It was now only an hour or so short of daybreak. Jack was on watch and so was there to greet them when they rode in. The other two members of the gang, Jack's older brother Boyd and Harlan Bigbee, a seasoned roughneck with a criminal record that stretched from Galveston to Denver and a wide swath to either side—lay asleep in their bedrolls. Wrapped in blankets between the two of them was the smaller lump of their hostage, Ethan Halsey.

Jack (woe be to anyone who used the "Three Finger" nickname anywhere he could hear it) regarded Crawford and Angel in the muted light of the fading moon and stars and the smoldering campfire. A few months past thirty, Jack was average height, solidly built, with chiseled facial features, a pencil mustache, and startlingly intense eyes. In moments of calm, those eyes were faded blue in color yet with a piercing quality that made it seem as if they could stare right through someone; in moments of anger, the faded blue would deepen to brilliant cobalt and there was seldom any doubt about the violence that would follow.

"So who was this character who showed up on your trail?" Jack wanted to know.

"One of the law dogs from that town, Ogallala. We seen his badge. But we didn't exactly get around to exchangin' introductions," replied Crawford, his sneer on fine display.

"That's right. We only bothered to introduce ourselves with lead," confirmed Angel.

Jack frowned. "But only one man? That's all they sent after us?"

"Ain't that one too many?" Crawford came back. "I mean, considerin' how you hollered out what we'd do to the brat if anybody followed us."

"That's just it," Jack argued. "If they were going to ignore my warning, why send only one man? What chance did a single pursuer have?"

Crawford snorted derisively. "About as much a one as he got when he ran into us layin' in wait for him."

"I still don't get it," Jack said, his frown holding. "If they decided to come after us, why not come with a full posse—enough of a force to have a chance at overpowering us if they were able to catch up?"

"Maybe the lone fool wasn't *sent*," Angel suggested. "Maybe he was some loco hombre who decided to act on his own, try to prove himself a big hero while everybody else in town hung back in fear."

Jack considered. Then: "Could be. You sure this jasper you took care of was all alone? Not some kind of scout, with maybe more following behind him?"

The two faces before him turned back and forth in negative response.

"We're sure," Crawford said. "You see, we had him pinned down for a while before we was able to finish the job. Hate to admit it, but we hurried our opening shots some and only managed to wound him and put down his horse at first. He managed to crawl into some close-by rocks and make a fight of it before we finished him. Had any more been comin' up behind him, they'd've had reason enough and time enough to show themselves before the shootin' was over."

Now Angel's head switched to bobbing up and down in eager support of Crawford's assessment. "That's right, Boss Jack. Whatever his reasons, that loco hombre was there strictly on his own."

"Good thing he was, from the sound of how sloppy you two went about taking care of him," Jack muttered. Then, heaving a sigh, he added, "But I guess it fits how our whole damn day went yesterday, practically from the time we hit that lousy town of Ogallala. Bad luck and sloppiness all the way around."

Crawford pointed out, "But we still fought our way out of that shithole. All in one piece, too. Well, mostly." At the last, his eyes cut over to the largest of the three forms wrapped in bedrolls.

"Yeah. mostly," Jack said sourly, his gaze following

Crawford's.

"How's Bigbee holdin' up? How bad is he hit?"

"Seen worse. But that don't make it good by any means," Jack answered. "Bullet got him in the back, right above the belt, went all the way through at an upward angle and came out the side of his belly just under his ribs. Boyd thinks it missed any part of the intestine but might have grazed a rib. If it did that, there's a chance it might've left some of the slug behind."

"Oh, shit. Lead poisonin'?"

"No sign of it so far, but Boyd's watching close. He got the bleeding stopped, that's the main thing for right now. Still leaves Harlan in a miserable lot of pain, though."

"Bigbee is one of the toughest old buzzards I ever saw," said Angel. "Pain he can push through."

"But nobody's tough enough to push through lead poisonin'," Crawford responded. He looked over at Jack. "We gonna try to get him to a doctor?"

"We might, if I knew where to find one!" Jack snapped back. "Ain't none of us knows the territory up this way worth a damn, in case you forgot. Even if we did, between here and Lead or Deadwood, where we're aiming for, there ain't nothing but a whole lot of nothing. Boyd thinks there's a town by the name of Alliance two or three days to the north that might be big enough to have a doctor. But other than that, without going back the way we just came, chances for finding a sawbones are mighty slim."

"Lot of risk goin' back the way we came," allowed a scowling Crawford. "After that dust-up in Ogallala, word is bound to get spread that we're in the area. That means every wide spot in the trail big enough to have a doctor is likely to also have some kind of law dog who'll be on the lookout for us."

"Tell me something I don't already know," Jack growled. "That's why turning back ain't an option. We keep riding north and hope Harlan can hold on long enough for us to find some help for him. In the meantime, you two go ahead and take another belt of that" —he gestured to the bottle of whiskey now back in the grip of Crawford— "but save the rest for Harlan, he's gonna be needing it worse. Then you'd best grab some shuteye. I'll hold us here a little extra past daybreak, Harlan can use the extra rest too. But I want to get moving by mid-morning so we can eat up some miles yet today."

"No argument on a little shuteye sounding good," said Angel, reaching for his turn at the bottle after Crawford had taken another swig.

"What about the brat?" asked Crawford, jerking his chin to indicate the small bedroll lump that was their hostage. "We gonna get rid of him now?"

"I don't think so. Not just yet." Jack looked thoughtful. "Something about that lone rider showing up on our trail keeps nagging at me. I reckon we'll drag the kid along a while longer, he might still prove useful."

CHAPTER 24

The next morning, Lone rode for a long time continuing to feel the warmth of Tru's parting touch on his cheek. It had been a pleasant, though unexpected and somewhat awkward moment. With Ira and Halsey looking on, Tru had walked up to him just as he was getting ready to shove a toe into Ironsides' stirrup. Without saying anything at first, she'd stepped very close and then reached up to rest the palm of one hand on his cheek. Silently, she gazed up at him with those lovely almond eyes. He'd felt a wild urge to take her in his arms but resisted. After what seemed like a long, heart-thudding span of time, she stepped back and let the silken palm slip away, saying quietly, "I will see you again in Julesburg, Lone McGantry. I will not contemplate otherwise."

This gave Lone even greater resolve not to fail at the task he was undertaking. It was a reminder that not only was there the life of an innocent child at stake, no matter the boy's lineage or the complexities that might add later on, but there were personal obligations also hanging in the balance. Ira had rattled off several of them last night. And now Tru's quiet words and imploring gaze had driven the point home even deeper.

For most of his adult life, Lone had operated quite in keeping with his name. He wasn't cold or aloof in his manner, yet at the same time periods of solitude suited him just fine. Being autonomous neither depending on anyone nor having anyone depend on him other than for fulfilling the various jobs he took on, was how he preferred it. The only long-lasting relationship in his life was with Ma Sharples. She'd been a young army wife who, along with some of the other women at the fort, helped raise him after he was orphaned as an infant when Indians massacred his pioneer family, the McGantrys, his name derived from him being the "lone" survivor yet with no record ever found of what his parents had intended to call the child. Lone's second close relationship of any length, becoming friends and eventual partners with Peg O'Malley, hadn't developed until some years later.

And now that was over. Peg was gone.

Which meant one of the lingering obligations Lone felt weighing on him as he rode out this morning was the commitment he owed his old friend and the worry it might seem as if he was abandoning it to go after the captive boy. Though he believed Peg would understand and, in his place, likely do the same, it also left an interruption to the more recently acquired obligations Lone saw as resting on him—the ones to Tru, and to Ira. Helping her finish the journey to her surviving uncle in Fort Collins; keeping Ira safe from Box 50 retaliation while also helping him on his own journey to a fresh start.

These were the thoughts swirling through Lone's mind as he and Ironsides pushed though the brisk, bracing morning air. By the time they reached the high table area above the wash-out where Halsey had been ambushed, however, he was starting to set those concerns aside in order to focus on the more immediate task at hand—tracking the ambushers to the rest of the gang and the boy he was counting on finding still alive in their clutches.

Then would come the minor detail of snatching the kid *out* of those clutches. Lone smiled grimly at this prospect. He wasn't a man given to braggadocio but, at the same time, he knew and was confident of his skills. He had every reason to believe he was far more familiar with this country than any member of the Gemsil gang. He also was familiar with the ways of stealth and using the night against superior odds; he'd employed such tactics before. That meant if he could catch up with the gang by the time night fell again, he reckoned he'd have a good chance of finding a way to slip away with the boy and use the cover of remaining darkness to make good their escape.

The first step to all of this was to pick up the trail of the two ambushers where they departed from the high table. That turned out to be simple. The trick from there was going to be for Lone to stick with this sign until it led to those leaving it and then be able to close on them without being spotted on their back trail.

******

Granger Halsey stood on the platform out front of the train depot in North Platte and groaned aloud. He glanced once more at the telegram he held in one hand and then closed his fist and crumpled the paper savagely into a ball. "God in Heaven!" he exclaimed. "What has my family done to deserve this onslaught of tragedy and terrible fortune? When is enough going to be enough?"

Granger was a tall, heavyset man of near fifty, iron gray hair combed straight back from a rugged, weathered face that wasn't likely to be described as either handsome or homely, with deep set brown eyes and a wide, expressive mouth currently twisted into an anguished grimace.

Standing beside Granger on the platform was a second man, the two of them only recently arrived via the train whose mighty engine stood motionless, though still hissing and puffing, a few yards ahead on the tracks. The second man was roughly the same age as Granger, perhaps two or three years older, equally as tall but a bit thicker around the middle and overall softer and more pampered looking. The attire of the two was of even sharper contrast—a tailored frock coat and trousers compared to Granger's worn corduroy jacket and plain gray pants.

This second man was Angus Benton, owner of the Box 50 where Granger ramrodded the crew of wranglers. Observing the reaction of his top man, Benton looked on with genuine concern and said, "What other news did that telegram bring, Granger? What else has happened?"

Granger turned his head from side to side. "Nothing new, really. Just a more personal account of what Marshal Dalrymple already told us. This," he held up the wadded ball of paper, "was sent by my brother. Before he struck out on his own to try and get little Ethan back from those. those ruthless bastards!"

Benton scowled in the direction of Dalrymple, who'd been on hand to meet the train. He also stood on the platform, somewhat apart from the Box 50 men, squinting in the late morning sun. "What the hell has become of our world, Elmer?" The ranch owner wailed. "A rash of shootings and killings here in our own town. And now this – this notorious outlaw gang sweeping up out of Kansas and invading our neighbors in Ogallala. Are we slipping backwards, reverting to the old untamed days all over again?"

Dalrymple glanced uneasily in the direction of Granger. Choosing his words carefully, he said, "I know these recent events are mighty painful for some good, undeserving people. But a lot of it can be traced to the unfortunate decisions of only a handful of individuals. All except for the business over in Ogallala, that is. That amounts to some serious bad news if the Gemsil gang has decided to come stomping through our neck of the woods."

Granger turned to glare at him. "What do you mean *if* Three Finger Jack and his scurvy bunch decide to come here?" He shook his fist with the crumpled telegram in it. "This right here makes it pretty damn clear they've already arrived, don't it? They arrived, shot up Ogallala and killed a slew of folks, then took my nephew hostage. And now my foolishly brave brother is on their trail—alone—trying to get his boy back. For all anybody knows .. by now he may even be..." The man's words trailed off and he issued another mournful groan.

Benton placed a comforting hand on Granger's shoulder. "Take it easy, man. You've enough bad news that can' be denied. Try to hold out some hope that more isn't necessarily on the way. Cliff is no foolhardy sprout. He's proven himself a competent lawman many times over. He wouldn't be going after those owlhoots if he didn't think he had a good chance to succeed."

"I know that. You think I don't *want* to hold out hope?" Granger replied. "But I also know how crazy Cliff is about his boy. If anything happened to little Ethan or if Cliff got close enough and saw even the slimmest chance to pull him out of danger. I fear he wouldn't stop at anything."

Benton cut his eyes back to Dalrymple. "Haven't you had any further news from Ogallala?"

Dalrymple shook his head. "Not since yesterday. I got

two telegrams late in the day, one from you, telling me you and Granger would be arriving by train this morning, the other from Marshal Stubin in Ogallala, telling me how the Gemsil gang had shown up and hit 'em hard. I didn't even know the part about the boy being taken hostage until you got here and Granger found the wire from his brother waiting for him."

"Whoever came up with the old saying about telegrams never bringing good news had an unfortunate knack for accuracy," muttered Benton.

"Where's my brother Isaac? And Jerome?" Granger asked abruptly.

Virgil Sweeney, who sat his horse with two other Box 50 riders near the edge of the depot platform and up until then had been mostly quiet, spoke up now with the answers. "They're over at the funeral home. Along with Buck Telford. I traded wires with Cliff right after it happened, Granger, and he said to go ahead and have Farthing get 'em all ready but to hold off any kind of service until you and Royce were able to get here. I went ahead and did the same for Buck, too, Mr. Benton."

"When is Royce due in?" Granger wanted to know.

"That's a good question," Dalrymple told him. "Me and Virgil both sent out some wires—so far we got no response to say any of 'em caught up with him yet."

"God, what a sad, sorry mess." Granger pulled the broad palm of his free hand down over his face. Then: "Well, the funeral services are going to have to wait a while longer. And only partly because of Royce. Not meaning to sound cold, but other than taking a minute to go to Farthing's and pay my respects, there ain't a whole lot else I can do for Isaac and Jerome right now. But, like Angus said, I have to hold out hope that Cliff and little Ethan may still be alive.

So I need to get to Ogallala. At the very least, I can try to comfort Cliff's wife and I should be there if—no, make that *when*—the blame fool shows back up again."

"That's perfectly reasonable, Granger," said Benton.

Granger jabbed a thumb toward the temporarily stopped train. "The next scheduled stop for this westbound is Ogallala. Think somebody could convince the engineer to hold up here for a few extra minutes while I go pay my visit to the boys at Farthing's?"

"Consider it done. I'll make sure he waits for you," assured Benton.

One of the Box 50 riders swung down from his saddle. "Funeral home's at the other end of town, Granger. Borrow my horse, make it quicker and easier on yourself."

"Obliged, Smitty," said Granger, descending the steps of the platform and taking the reins of the offered mount.

"Go ahead. I'll stay here to guarantee the engineer doesn't set this tar bucket in motion," Benton called after him. "I'll stop by to pay my respects to the boys a little later."

Silently, a somber-faced Sweeney wheeled his horse and rode off alongside Granger.

Benton gazed after them for a minute, then turned slowly to the marshal. His expression had turned flat and hard, his eyes conveying more of the same. "Alright," he said, his tone also taking on a sharper edge. "Granger's got more pressing matters he has to focus on. So I'll be the one to ask it, Elmer. Where's this trigger-happy sonofabitch who thinks he has a right to go around gunning down men who ride for the Box 50 brand?"

CHAPTER 25

"Hey, Jack! Hey, Boyd! Hold on a minute. Harlan just fell plumb out of his saddle."

At these words, Three Finger Jack and his brother, riding stirrup to stirrup beside him, both reined up sharply and twisted around in their own saddles. Looking back at the rest of the gang strung out behind them, they saw that, sure enough, the mount of Harlan Bigbee had stopped moving and stood without a rider on its back. The wounded man who *had* been there lay on the ground five or six feet behind the animal, a motionless heap now flattening a patch of the seemingly endless grassland they were traversing.

"Damn it all," muttered Boyd Gemsil. "I was afraid too much steady riding might take more of a toll than he could stand."

Two years older than Jack, Boyd was a shade taller and notably bulkier than his brother. He had a lantern-jawed, strong-featured face with a wide mouth not shy about flashing a crooked, engaging grin. In contrast to Jack's piercing blue eyes, Boyd's were more blue-green and had a general mildness about them that was in even greater contrast to the cobalt fierceness that anger caused to flare in Jack's.

A touch of that anger flashed momentarily now as the brothers wheeled their horses and Jack said, "Well he'd better find a way to stand it and quick."

They swung their mounts wide around Hash Crawford who was riding next in line directly behind them. Perched in front him, wrists bound together and wide eyes darting anxiously in all directions, was their tow-haired young captive.

Next came the fallen form of the wounded man. Angel Rejos, who'd been bringing up the rear and who was the one who'd called out when Bigbee dropped, had already reached him and was swinging down from his saddle. Jack and Boyd got there and also dismounted.

Bigbee lay on his left side, the side the bullet had passed through and was puffing hard to try and regain some of the air that had been knocked out of him. Boyd knelt beside him and gently rolled him onto his back. The wounded man looked up at him with dazed eyes and the rugged, weathered features of his face, squeezed between bushy, reddish brown sideburns and a ledge of same-colored bushy eyebrows, was dotted with fat drops of sweat.

"Jeez, Boyd," Bigbee gasped. "I don't know what. I took a hell of a spill."

"He was going along okay," said Angel, leaning close. "But then, all of a sudden, he gave a jerk, like he had a sudden pain or something and then he fell."

Boyd pushed back the left side of Bigbee's jacket. Underneath, his shirt was soaked through with fresh, bright red blood. "Doggone it, Harlan, you've started bleeding again. Bad. Why didn't you tell me?"

"I – I didn't know. Knew I was hurtin' like sin. Didn't know bleedin' came with so much pain."

Boyd sleeved the sweat off Bigbee's forehead and then rested the back of his hand above the ledge of brows. "Jesus, man, you're burning up."

Looking on and listening, Jack frowned deeply and said to his brother, "I thought he wasn't running a fever?"

"He hasn't been. Not up to now." Boyd looked clearly distressed. "I thought I had the bleeding stopped, too, but..."

Bigbee's eyes brightened with heightened clarity and also with a sheen of brittle anguish. "Oh God, boys, the poison's got me, don't it? I could feel the bullet track burnin' hotter and hotter. I could stand that. But then, now. There's like little teeth gnawin' into my guts. It's the poison spreadin', ain't it, Boyd? Oh Jesus, I'm a goner."

"Somebody give him a slug of whiskey," Jack said.

Bigbee shook his head weakly. "No. Just water. Some cool water somebody. Please."

Crawford, who'd ridden up close but remained in his saddle along with the Halsey boy, unslung his canteen and held it out. "Here. This is as cool as any we got."

Boyd took the canteen. First he poured some of its contents directly over Bigbee's face, then he held the spout to the man's lips. After he had slurped thirstily, Bigbee rolled his face away and managed a lopsided grin, saying, "If ever there was a sign the end is near, that's it. Me askin' for a drink of water over a stiff belt."

"Maybe you're ready for that belt now," offered Jack.

Bigbee closed his eyes and released a ragged sigh. "Nah. No sense wastin' good whiskey on a dead man."

Boyd scowled. "Come on, Harlan. There's no need to—"

Bigbee's eyes snapped back open and he cut him off, saying, "Yeah, there is! No sense pussyfootin' around it.

None of you fellas." He swept his gaze over the rest of the gang, all gathered around close. "I been doin' this a long time, boys. ridin' the owlhoot trail. Almost longer than some of you been alive. I know how the game is played. One man can't drag down everybody else."

"You can make it, Harlan. We'll all help," said Crawford.

Bigbee wagged his head. "Make it for how long? To where? Even if we did find some kind of doctor out in the middle of all this open" —he waved one hand weakly, indicating the ocean of rolling grass that surrounded them— "what good would it do now? The poison's got me. You know it, don't you, Boyd?" His murky eyes rested on the older Gemsil brother. "And you know, too, what has to be done. Same as you'd do for an ailin' horse or dog. I beg ya. Don't leave me go in slow misery."

Boyd's face twisted with its own agony. "Oh Jesus, Harlan. Don't ask me that. I can't."

Bigbee heaved another ragged sigh. The others all looked on silently.

Until, abruptly, Jack announced "I can"—then drew his Colt and planted a .44 slug a quarter inch above Bigbee's left eyebrow. A single shudder passed through the old outlaw's body before he became very still, a halo of crimson spreading out through the grass around his head.

Boyd, Crawford, and Angel all jerked involuntarily at the crash of Jack's gun. The Halsey boy's eyes bugged huge and his mouth dropped open.

Jack re-holstered his Colt and met the gazes now locked on him with a hard, defiant glare. "Don't look at me like that. I only did what had to be done," he said. "I liked that old rascal, too. Rode with him near two years. But he knew the score, you all heard him call it. Once the poison had him, he was a goner. This way, he's spared a lot of misery and he won't be bogging us down—which we can't afford."

"Poor ol' Harlan," Crawford murmured, a catch in his voice.

Boyd straightened up and stepped squarely in front of his brother. "Alright. You did what you had to do, what I didn't have the guts for. But you damned well better be figuring we can afford the time to give him a decent burial."

The muscles at the hinges of Jack's jaw bulged visibly for a moment. Then they relaxed and he said, "A-course, big brother. Ol' Harlan deserves that much. But whoever's gonna do the digging had best commence. By the look of those clouds building up to the north and west" he tilted his head to indicate what he was talking about "we got a storm moving in on us. Before it hits, we need to try and find some better shelter than out here in all this wide open."

******

Lone lay belly down on a crest of tall grass. Through a pair of field glasses carefully shaded against giving off any glint from the late afternoon sun, he watched four men gathered around a fresh grave a hundred and eighty yards away. They were putting the finishing touches on the hump of disturbed earth, covering it over with slabs of rock to discourage scavengers from getting at what was buried there.

This, then, was what was left of the Gemsil gang. Though he knew none of them by sight, Lone was nevertheless confident in this appraisal. For one thing, he'd been following their increasingly more recent sign all day. The single distant gunshot he'd heard some forty-five minutes back (which he didn't quite know the reason for) had confirmed their nearness and brought him finally to within sight of therm. But the real identity clincher was the small figure sitting on the grass a few yards away from the burial detail. It was a young boy with his ankles and wrists bound, little Ethan Halsey.

Lone's further judgment was that the occupant of the grave had been a fifth member of the gang, identity unknown. What Lone did know was that five outlaws were reported fleeing Ogallala, and that was the number of horse tracks he'd been following since he found where Deputy Halsey's two ambushers had rejoined the others. Those five mounts currently stood grazing close by. An explanation for all of this was Halsey's mention that one of the outlaws had been reported as possibly being wounded during the Ogallala shootout. Evidently the wound was serious enough to result in what Lone was now observing.

The former scout smiled a wolf's smile. One down, four to go. However it had come about, the odds were improving. Even more important was the fact that, though tied up, the boy appeared unharmed.

Also, Lone had succeeded in closing on the gang well ahead of nightfall, exactly as he'd been hoping to do. A possible added bonus was the storm clouds now moving in from the northwest. It was Lone's experience that most people caught out in the wild by an unexpected storm, even men on the run tended to hunker down and focus most on enduring the bad turn of weather, their guard lowered in the belief that any pursuit would likely be forced to do the same.

If the storm hit and indeed became the Gemsil gang's main concern, Lone meant for them to find out that this night would present more of a problem than the inconvenience of a bad turn in the weather.

CHAPTER 26

_____

A few miles beyond Harlan Bigbee's grave, the land began to change somewhat. A smattering of low, irregular-shaped buttes could be seen poking up here and there amidst the rolling dunes of grass. With evening approaching fast and the oncoming storm clouds promising to hurry even more the darkness it would bring, Three Finger Jack steered his group toward the nearest of these outcrops in hopes it would provide some sort of shelter.

His choice turned out to be a lucky one. One of the butte's high, flat walls exhibited a concave depression worn away by swirling winds. It was shallow and only about six feet high but had a wide mouth that made it plenty roomy enough for the outlaws and their saddle gear. With a couple canvas tarps wedged into high crevices and stretched across canopy-like, it was actually quite serviceable. They were even packing enough scrounged kindling and buffalo chips to cook some coffee and warm up a pan of beans.

When the rain came it was a steady, cold drizzle mixed with slushy flecks of snow, all stirred by sporadic gusts of low, moaning wind.

"I don't know if we got enough buffalo chips left in the bag to keep a warming fire burnin' all night and still make breakfast in the morning," Hash Crawford reported as the gang huddled as tight as they could get to ailing the back of the cavern, each man with a post meal cup of coffee pressed between his palms. "Which way you want to play it, Jack, try to keep a fire goin' tonight, or make sure we got one in the morning?"

"I vote for hot coffee and some bacon come morning," said Boyd. "I can stand a cold night if we got that to look forward to and we ain't got enough fuel to build a big enough fire to keep us really warm anyway."

"Yeah, I go with that, too," said Jack sullenly. Then he added, "If we hadn't poured all of our damn whiskey down that ingrate Harlan, who up and died on us anyway, we'd at least have some of that left to pass around and warm us on the inside."

Nobody thought it wise to point out that Harlan hadn't just "up and died" without a little help.

Seeking to change the subject, Angel said, "This talk of having or not having fuel makes me think of something I have been wondering ever since we been riding over this place that is all grass and no trees."

"Wondering what?" Boyd asked.

Very earnestly, Angel replied, "With all the buffalo that once were so plentiful here but now are all killed and gone so they can no longer leave their droppings. In future times, what will people who live hereabouts use to build their fires?"

The other three men just stared at him. Until Jack said, "Are you kidding me? You really spend time rolling that kind of thing around inside your head?"

Angel shrugged. "I spend time thinking of women

also. But too much time thinking about that only makes me sit uncomfortable in my saddle. So I make my mind go elsewhere."

"So you go from thinking about women to wondering about buffalo shit." Jack wagged his head in wonderment. "Somewhere along the line, my south of the border friend, I think you must have chomped too deep into one of them super hot peppers and it fried part of your brain."

Angel grinned. "As long as I do not forget to think about women altogether. Now *that* would be a serious problem, no?"

"Like we're lacking for serious problems," Jack grunted.

"Come on, this ain't so bad," pointed out Boyd, trying to be more positive. "We're dry and out of the wind, ain't we? And this is only temporary. Think of poor ol' Harlan. Yeah, he might have soaked up all the liquor but what good's it doing him? Where he is, it's dark and cold permanent-like."

Jack sneered. "You can't be serious. Where Harlan is right about now, I'm betting it's real toasty warm and being down there is permanent, too, from what I understand."

Staring into the flames of the fire, his expression stone solemn, Crawford said in a forlorn voice, "Reckon we'll all be findin' out for sure one of these days soon enough."

******

A little over a hundred feet out from the outlaw camp, squatting behind a knee-high finger of rock that reached out from one shoulder of the butte, Lone squatted motionless and quiet. The brim of his Stetson was pulled down low above his eyes and the collar of a black rain slicker was buttoned tight under his chin, the rest of the garment flowing tent-like down over his body until it reached the ground.

Lone had been watching the gang for some time. The

hiss of the rain made it impossible for him to make out anything they were saying but, at the same time, it muted any sound he might have made moving up on them. He had observed as they ate their meager meal, which included untying the boy long enough for him to partake from a plate shoved in front of him. When he was done, they'd tied his wrists again, bundled him in a blanket and then pushed him back into the deep shadows at the rear of the cavern.

It was good to see they weren't overtly mistreating the kid, feeding him and keeping him warm and dry, but burrowing him so deep in amongst them certainly increased the problem of how to snatch the captive away.

Lone had been pondering a solution to this ever since taking up his current position. In the end, the answer was simple. Not simple to try and execute, but simple because it came down to only one plan that had any chance of working.

The way Lone had it worked out in his head was that, after some more time had passed and the men were turned in for the night (assuming they saw no need for anyone to stand watch), he would work his way over and cut the gang's horses loose from where they were picketed off to one side of the cavern. This would eliminate the mounts from being available for immediate pursuit in case the rest of Lone's plan hit any unanticipated snags and he and Ethan ended up having to make a more desperate run for it than he was hoping for. Barring that, however, after releasing the horses Lone's intent, still counting on the darkness and the muting hiss of the rain, was to slip into the cavern at one end and proceed to silently slit the throats of as many of the outlaws he came to until he reached the boy. If he got that far without rousting any of the others who might still be left alive, he would grab little Ethan and they would flee out to where Ironsides was waiting to get them the rest of the way gone.

Whether he should tarry any extra to make sure *all* of the Gemsil gang was dead, Lone was undecided. That they'd proven themselves vermin deserving of being exterminated, there was no doubt. And Lone had no qualms about being the one to handle the job. His only hesitation came from the thought of Ethan being present. How smart would it be to rescue the kid and then linger for the sake of some clean-up work that might erupt into a bit of last-stand gun play that could risk the boy maybe catching a stray bullet?

He'd make the final call if and when the time came, Lone decided. There was plenty else that had to go right before things ever got that far.

Despite all of these thoughts churning inside of him, outwardly Lone appeared totally calm, at ease. As still and silent as the rocks he squatted behind. A stalker with all of his senses honed and ready, just waiting for the right moment to strike.

CHAPTER 27

Lone was on the move.

The time was right to set his plan in motion. One by one, the outlaws had laid back in their bedrolls and should be sound asleep by now. The campfire was burned down to only an occasional stubborn flame licking up out of the coals. The rain continued to fall, its monotonous hiss blurring out other incidental sounds.

Lone shifted across the front of the picketed horses at a distance and then edged forward slowly, not wanting to spook them. He already had his Bowie knife drawn, holding it out ahead of him as he ghosted through the rain. As for the rest of his weaponry, he'd left the Yellowboy in Ironsides' saddle scabbard; it would have been too cumbersome for the stealth work he was attempting. Instead, as a backup to the Bowie and the Colt holstered on his hip, he'd taken the Smith & Wesson "Baby Russian" .38 caliber revolver he carried in his saddlebags for just such occasions and now had it tucked in his belt at the small of his back. If this wasn't enough weaponry to cut and blast his way clear of any trouble that might arise, then it would mean he'd reached the end of his string.

But Lone was a long way from being ready for such an outcome. The only string he was thinking about ending at the moment were the picket ropes restraining the outlaws' horses. He'd made it to the first of the animals now, reaching out to gently pat its rain slick neck as he softly whispered "Easy, boy." A moment later his Bowie had sliced through the rope connecting the horse to the picket line. Grabbing the trailing end of the rope, Lone whirled it and waved his arms, backing the animal away and then giving it cause to wheel around and fade off into the wet darkness.

One down. Lone moved quickly to the next horse on the line and did the same with it.

But then, just as he reached the third animal, things started going wrong. In the darkness somewhere past the horse Lone was preparing to cut free, one of the other horses suddenly emitted a loud, protesting whinny and bucked backward, jerking hard on the picket line. This caused the critter whose tether Lone had hold of with his free hand—ready to slice said tether with the Bowie in his other hand—to also pull back suddenly. Lone was thrown off balance. This was partly due to the thrust of the Bowie blade meeting nothing but air and then the unexpected yank on the grip of his left hand tugging him the opposite way. Before he could dig his heels into the wet, slick grass, Lone's feet flew out from under him and he was dumped to the ground.

He rolled frantically, his immediate concern not to get trampled by the pawing front hooves of the now alarmed animal he'd been about to set free. The roll took him almost to the next horse in line who was also stamping and switching about in an agitated manner. Lone scrambled to

push himself upright again, slipping and lurching drunkenly
in the process. Another shrill whinny cut through the rain
and darkness. No sooner had Lone managed to regain a
steady stance than a sideways lunge by the third horse, now
behind him, inadvertently slammed a shoulder against his
back and knocked him off balance once more. Only this
time when he hit the ground he landed on more than just
wet, trampled grass and mud—he ended up partly on top
of another person!

"Ow! You're hurting me. Get off!"

The voice that cried out sounded too immature, too high-
pitched to be that of a grown man. Lone couldn't buy that it
belonged to one of the outlaws. This left only one startling
possibility—it must be the Halsey boy!

Struggling to pin down the bundle of flailing, kicking
arms and legs, Lone growled urgently, "Ethan! For Chris-
sakes, kid, take it easy, I'm here to help you!"

The squirming resistance quickly ceased. "Who are you?"

But there wasn't time for any attempt to explain. The
commotion from the horses and the boy crying out had
done the damage of rousting the sleeping men over in the
nearby cavern. Even through the hiss of the rain, Lone
could hear heavy bodies thrashing about and then gruff
voices start to shout.

"What's goin' on? Who hollered?"

"Hey! Where's the kid? Can anybody see the god-
damned brat?"

So there it was. The card table was kicked over, chips
were spilling to the floor, and instead of reaching to turn
over an ace in the hole it was time to reach for hardware!

"You're gonna have to trust me, Ethan. Stay down.
Hug the ground and keep quiet,maybe I can still get us
out of this!"

That was all Lone took time to say before he shoved once more to his feet and rushed into trying to make the words come true. First, slashing wildly to his left and right with the Bowie, he finished cutting tethers and the main picket line itself until the remaining three horses were unloosed and bolting off into the blackness. Then he swung his attention to the shallow cavern and hurled himself toward it.

The glowing coals of the burned-down campfire gave enough weak light—basically the dark, rainy night's only illumination—for Lone to be able to make out jerkily shifting shadows being cast out from the depths of the depression. As Lone closed to within a few yards, one of those shadows became the looming form of a man stepping out and silhouetting himself against the low glow. Barely slowing his forward movement, Lone shifted the knife to his left hand, drew his Colt with his right and unhesitatingly triggered a round into the center mass of the silhouetted form.

The impact caused the man to hop backward a half step, emitting a grunt of pain and surprise. As he started to tip away, he twisted half around and spread his arms wide in an apparent attempt to balance himself. Lone pounded another slug into him, meaning to drive him the rest of the way down. This succeeded but, on the owlhoot's way to the ground, the clawing fingers of one of his outstretched arms snagged an edge of the tarp cover that had been spread over the interior for added shelter. This was enough to tear the tarp loose from its mooring and release it to come billowing down over the man as he toppled to earth.

This meant, however, that more than just the fallen man became shrouded by the collapsing canvas. The other outlaws as well as the smoldering campfire were also caught under its dropping folds.

"Shit! Somebody just shot Angel! Who the hell's out there?"

"How do I know, I can't see a damn thing!"

"Somebody smother that fire or we're all gonna be sitting ducks!"

But it was too late. The underside of the tarp, already warmed and dried from having been suspended over the fire for hours, was tinder primed for immediate ignition. And that's exactly what it did as soon as it hit the campfire coals. Flames burst forth hungrily, licking upward and flaring outward with incredible speed.

"Sitting ducks, hell—we're gonna be *cooked* ducks if we don't get out of here!" somebody hollered.

"Is going out there and getting mowed down any better?" somebody else argued.

But Lone had the answer. Either way, he meant for this pack of murderous skunks to pay the price they were long overdue on owing. What had looked like near hopeless wreckage to his plan had suddenly turned into an opportunity he couldn't afford to let slip away.

Continuing to move quickly, he swept out at an angle until he was centered a dozen yards back from the front of the cavern mouth. While he remained cloaked in darkness and rain, the burning tarp was filling the concave depression with ever brightening illumination. As some of the flames reached out into the dampening rain, curls of smoke began spiraling up.

Sheathing the Bowie, Lone shifted the Colt to his left hand then reached to the small of his back and filled his right with the Baby Russian he pulled from there. Planting his feet wide, he braced himself and got ready with ten rounds of lead to greet what remained of the Gemsil gang when they tried to make a break for it. He fully intended to send them from the taste of Hell they were currently getting in the blazing cavern to an extended stay in a far more intense inferno awaiting them elsewhere.

The first thing to exit from the other side of the flaming tarp was a barrage of gunfire, eight or nine rapid-fire shots spraying out blindly at wild angles and at varying levels. None of them came close to Lone. What it revealed to him, however, was a notably tight grouping of three backlit bullet holes punching through from a particular spot. This was enough for Lone to take a couple blind shots of his own, one from each of the guns he held and the gamble was rewarded by a gargling scream issuing out from where his slugs slammed back in return.

But there was only a moment's satisfaction from this. That was how long it took before a second corner of the tarp, this one still fastened as originally wedged into a high crevice on the side of the cavern opposite from where the canopy's first corner got torn down, was suddenly ripped away and flung outward. This spilled a middle portion of the burning canvas out into the rain and more plums of smoke began immediately churning up into the air.

Through this screen of smoke and scattered flames two men came rushing out. One, more to the middle of the cavern, was holding a Winchester rifle at his hip, discharging rounds as fast as he could lever in fresh ones. Toward the side of the cavern's mouth, where the last of the canopy had been torn away, a second man was brandishing his own brace of pistols and triggering them with reckless abandon.

Lone had every reason to believe neither of the men could yet see him, especially since their eyes would be adjusting to the dark after emerging from within the fire-il-luminated cavern. Nevertheless, he dropped to one knee as a precaution and once set, planted a slug from the Colt squarely into the rifleman. The man was knocked backward off his feet and sent rolling through a line of flames.

The pistoleer, perhaps locking on Lone's muzzle flash, paused momentarily and sent a pair of shots alarmingly close. One of them split the fabric of Lone's rain slicker just above his left shoulder. The former scout calmly turned his torso to make a narrower target, extended the Baby Russian to arm's length and triggered three .38 rounds into the chest area of the pistoleer, slamming him down as flat and hard as a hand slapping a mosquito.

The howls of the rifleman, still with some life left in him and now with one sleeve and a pant leg on fire after his roll through the flames, drew Lone's attention back to him. The man had discarded his rifle and was continuing to flop and thrash about, though with increasing weakness, in an attempt to smother his burning clothes. Lone straightened up and then stood motionless for a long moment, watching and listening to the wails of pain. An ice cold voice down deep inside told him to leave it go, it was a deserving and fitting fate. But, in the end, Lone couldn't do it. He raised and aimed the Colt, spent the remaining two rounds left in the cylinder to put the last of the Gemsil gang out of his misery.

CHAPTER 28

The rain quit about an hour before daybreak. By the time the sun poked above the eastern horizon, the cloud cover was rapidly breaking up and widening slashes of clear blue sky were showing through.

After dispatching the outlaws at the cavern, Lone had gone back to where he'd left the Halsey boy and was relieved to find him still there. The kid was scared, wet and cold, but he had held in place as instructed. Afterwards, he would explain this was mainly due to Lone knowing his name. "To those bad men I was never anything but 'the kid' or 'the brat'," he said. "When you called me 'Ethan', I figured my pa must have sent you and so you were somebody I should trust."

But that came as part of a later discussion. In the immediate aftermath of the shooting and bloodshed, with the stink of burning flesh starting to reach them even through the rain, Lone had thought it best to get Ethan away from there as quickly as possible. He'd wasted few words other than "Come on, I've got a horse waiting" as he reached down to help the boy to his feet and then took him by the arm and led him off toward where he'd left Ironsides.

By the time they reached the big gray, Lone was sharply aware of how hard the soaked boy was shivering and that there was no sign of the rain letting up. He knew he had to address Ethan's condition but with no shelter at hand and visibility too poor to try and hunt for any, the former scout's options were limited. He sure as hell didn't want to go back to that cavern. Thinking and acting quickly, he unlashed the heavy soogan bedroll from behind Ironsides' saddle and went to work creating what would have to serve as a suitable shelter right where they were.

With the soogan dragged to the ground and partly opened up, Lone focused his attention on Ironsides and spoke to him with the words and qlucks that urged him to respond as he'd been trained—to fold his legs and lie down, then roll partly onto one side and be still. Next came getting Ethan to lie down on one of the blankets peeled out of the bedroll—quickly before it got too soaked—then snug up tight against the warmth of Ironsides' belly. A moment later, Lone was stretched out beside him and had the rest of the thick soogan pulled up over them, its waterproof outer layer repelling the rain and blocking it from penetrating through. Within minutes, the warmth inside this impromptu cocoon, as created by combined animal and human body heat along with sustained dryness (in spite of their already drenched clothing), was enough to bring Ethan's shivering under control. Eventually, this warmth and the patter of the rain on the outer skin of the soogan seemed to take on a lulling quality.

"Try to get some sleep, son," Lone had said in the darkness. "It'll be morning before you know it and this lousy rain can't last forever."

And now, a few hours later, the prophecy of those words

had come to pass and the new day was opening up before them. When Ethan stuck his head out of the folds of the soogan, he found both Lone and Ironsides had quietly slipped away sometime prior. Ironsides was grazing in a patch of grass a few yards away, Lone was squatted beside a small fire, cooking breakfast. Luckily, he'd had a bag of dry kindling and buffalo chips in his gear to provide a limited amount of fuel.

Without looking around, the former scout said over his shoulder, "'Bout time you woke up, sleepyhead. In the blankets beside you, you'll find a shirt and a fleece-lined jacket. You'll need to roll the sleeves up and they'll still be way too big, but it's the best I can do. Gonna have to stick with your damp pants and boots, I got nothing to help you there but take off your wet shirt and put on those other items. Then come on over and we'll have a bite to eat before hittin' the trail."

When he heard the rustling sounds of the boy changing clothes as instructed, Lone asked, "You drink coffee?"

"Sometimes. If I can have some sugar in it," ca the answer.

Using a fork to turn over the strips of bacon he frying in a pan he held over the fire, Lone respond got some of that. I like to doctor my coffee with sugar sometimes, too."

When the boy came over to the fire, all but s by the coat, Lone had two plates and two steami coffee ready. Lone handed him one of the pl "Here. Still plenty brisk this morning but so a cup of hot mud will help warm you until t high enough to cut the chill."

"Thank you," Ethan said politely, tak didn't waste any time picking up one o

and biting into it.

"I was watching through field glasses last night, before the trouble broke out," Lone told him, "and I saw that those varmints appeared to at least take the trouble to feed you some."

"Beans. All they ever ate was beans. I think that's all they had."

"Well, beans can be a belly filler," Lone allowed, "and sometimes a body can find himself glad to settle for no more than that. The bacon and hardtack there on your plate ain't exactly no high tone meal. Especially not the hardtack." A corner of his mouth lifted in a faint smile. "But if you don't bust off all your teeth trying to bite into it, which is why I tried to soften it some in the bacon grease, it'll carry you down the trail quite a ways."

"Oh, I didn't mean to sound like I was complaining, certainly not about this breakfast you made," Ethan was quick to say.

"No, I know you didn't. But after what you've been put through, I reckon you'd have the right to do some squawkin' if you was of a mind to. Only you ain't, you're holdin' up mighty strong. When we get you back to your folks, they ought to be as proud as they are relieved and happy."

"You know my folks?"

"Know your pa some. Never had call to meet your ma."

Ethan's brows pulled together. "So my pa is okay then? When you showed up instead of him and I ain't saying I in't obliged you did, I was afraid something might have ppened to him. Two of those outlaws doubled back to e if a posse was following and when they returned they s bragging how they ambushed what they called a law . I was afraid they might've. That maybe…"

Your pa's okay," Lone cut him off. "Matter of fact,

it *was* him they ambushed. He got hurt some but not by a bullet, only from the fall he took when they shot his horse out from under him. But he's gonna be fine. You'll see for yourself just as soon as we get you back home."

Ethan's face brightened. "Boy, am I glad to hear that! How soon, do you think, before we get back?"

"Can't say for certain." Lone drank some of his coffee. "Those owlhoots hauled you quite a ways, to the north and some west. Place I reckon to be closest for us to get back to and where we'll be heading, is a town called Julesburg, across the Colorado line west of Ogallala. That's where I told your pa to expect us to show up. Either him or somebody representin' him will be waitin' there. If he can't make it, it'll be on account of his injury. In that case, whoever *is* there will take you by train on back to Ogallala."

"I'm betting Pa will be there," Ethan said firmly. "Him and Ma, too."

Lone admired the boy's faith and obvious affection when it came to his folks. He said, "As to the question of how long to reach where we're headed, I doubt we'll make it yet today. Probably be spendin' another night on the trail and then get in sometime tomorrow morning."

"As long as we're away from them." His tone turning grim as he said these words, Ethan's gaze shifted to look in the direction of the cavern where he'd been held captive. Lone's gaze followed his. The spot wasn't that far away. The upper portion of the butte, with only a handful of rolling hills in between, was plainly visible; the cavern at its base thankfully was not. Nevertheless, a charcoal haze of smoke rising out of it continued to stain the still morning air.

Softly, Ethan asked, "Did you kill all those men?"

"Yeah, I did," Lone answered without hesitation. "They didn't give me much choice."

"Good. They deserved it," Ethan said, his tone turning even harsher.

Lone gave him a sidelong glance and didn't say anything right away. Then: "Reckon the final decision on who deserves what gets made in some higher place. All I know for sure is that I didn't figure I deserved fallin' to the likes of them and so I did everything I could not to."

"I'm sure glad for that."

Lone took another drink of coffee. Then, turning his head and regarding the boy more directly, he arched a brow and said, "Long as we're talkin' about that little fracas, it occurs to me I got a question about how I got flung into the middle of it in a way I wasn't quite ready for. To make it plainer, what the heck were you doin' out there on that picket line in the rain and dark so's we ended up gettin' tangled together and alertin' those curly wolves by spooking the horses?"

Ethan blinked innocently. "I was trying to escape."

"How were you figurin' to do that? How did you even get loose?"

Balancing his plate in one hand, Ethan dug in his pants pocket with the other and produced a small nickel-plated jackknife that he held up for Lone to see. "I used this to cut the ropes they had me tied with," he explained. "They never searched me after they grabbed me off the street in Ogallala, so I had this with me the whole time. But always before they had somebody watching me or a guard posted, leaving me no chance to use it. Finally last night, though, in the storm and all, they didn't post a guard. After they were all sleeping and snoring, I cut myself loose and slipped away without waking any of them."

"What were you gonna do from there?"

"I was going to steal one of the horses and free the others so nobody could chase after me." Ethan paused and his face bunched into a scowl. "I think I coulda made it, too, if that stupid horse I tried slipping a bridle on hadn't balked and started making such a fuss. When he jerked away and pulled me off balance, I slipped and fell. The next thing I knew you were landing on top of me."

Lone grunted. "Yeah. I reckon both of our plans went off course in a hurry once we started slippin' and slidin' and trippin' over each other out there in the rainy dark."

"What were you doing in amongst those horses?" Ethan asked.

"I had sorta the same notion as you. I was gonna run 'em off so the owlhoots couldn't give chase, then I was aiming to snatch you out of that cavern and bring you here to Ironsides so we could both ride clear."

"I guess I almost messed everything up, didn't I?"

"Hey now. None of that," Lone said sharply. "You had no way of knowin' anybody, me or whoever, was close enough to try doing you any good. What you went ahead and did for yourself was dam—er, I mean darn—gutsy. And if I hadn't been there fallin' on top of you, you might still have pulled it off."

"I don't know about that." Ethan's expression relaxed some. "All I know is. well, it's kinda like you said. I guess I figured I didn't deserve to be another victim of those stinky old outlaws and if I didn't want to be, then I'd have to find a way to do something about it."

Lone smiled. "Sounds to me like pretty good thinkin', kid." He tipped up his coffee cup, drained it, then said, "So the thing now is for both of us to hope we deserve makin' it to Julesburg without any more trouble. Only we ain't gonna find out if we don't get packed up and set on our way."

"I'm all for that. But before we do, can I ask you one more question?"

Lone shrugged. "Don't see why not. Let 'er rip."

Ethan regarded him earnestly. "What is your name?"

CHAPTER 29

Riding double on Ironsides, they made it to Julesburg a couple hours before noon the following morning. The journey had been without incident and the second night camp they shared, in a stand of spindly, isolated cottonwood trees, was far more comfortable than that cocoon in the rain; leaving them considerably fresher and better rested on this new day.

Lone steered Ironsides directly to the marshal's office that was housed, along with the jail, in a wood and adobe box in the heart of town. Before either of the big gray's riders had any chance to dismount, the front door of the building swung open and the marshal stepped out to greet them.

Tobe Crenshaw was a heavyset man pushing forty, with a droopy gray mustache, seen-it-all-before eyes, and a perpetually guarded attitude. He came out from under the narrow porch overhang that ran across the front of his building and squinted up at Lone. "McGantry. Up until a couple days ago, I wouldn't have expected you to be showing up around these parts again so soon."

Lone lifted his eyebrows. "Mean you ain't glad to see

me, Marshal?"

Crenshaw's shoulders rose and fell a meager amount. "I got no particular cause to feel one way or t'other where you're concerned. Not until or unless you give me reason—like you did last time."

The previous time Lone had passed through Julesburg, back in the fall, he'd been on the trail of a young woman who, among her other troubles, had fallen into the hands of some flesh merchants who were operating a sleazy joint on the town's infamous Saloon Row. For the most part, Crenshaw kept things on the up and up for decent folks in the rest of Julesburg and left those who patronized Saloon Row, which included mainly soldiers from the nearby shithole outpost of Fort Sedgewick, to their own fate. On the occasion of Lone's last visit, however, the lawman had made an exception and got involved aiding Lone when violence became necessary as the only way to extract the girl from those holding her against her will.

"On the other hand, hard as it is to understand," the marshal continued now, "there happens to be certain folks not far from here who I have reason to believe *will* be glad to see you. What's more, if this young fella is who I reckon he must be" here he beamed a brief smile at Ethan "then there are others who will be even *gladder* to see him."

Ethan's face brightened. "You mean my ma and pa are here?"

"You bet they are, sonny. They, along with McGantry's friends, are all waiting down at the hotel." Crenshaw stepped out into the street. "Come on, I'll take you there. As anxious as they've all grown since gathering there, I'd advise you two getting ready to be swarmed like a couple of honey pots being pushed in front of a bunch of bees."

A handful of minutes later, the marshal's words proved

all too accurate. As they moved up the street, Lone and Ethan still astride Ironsides and Crenshaw walking alongside, word clearly spread ahead of therm. Barely had they come in sight of a large wood frame building with a sign reading LANGLEY HOTEL erected across the front than a group of people poured suddenly, excitedly out the front door, across the veranda, and came rushing into the street to meet them. Other people, shoppers and clerks from surrounding stores and businesses who'd also heard the news, also converged from all sides.

What ensued was a near melee of cheers, hugs, repeatedly stated congratulations, a few tears (of joy), and even a few kisses showered on Ethan. It was the kind of crowded jumble that made Lone, as befitting his name, feel very uncomfortable. The only thing that made it bearable was seeing the shining, smiling face of Tru and feeling her arms wrap around him in a tight embrace. "I told you I would see you here in Julesburg!" she gushed happily.

Ira was there, too, pumping Lone's hand in a hearty grip that was strong and sure and minus even the slightest hint of a tremor. Sprinkled among the equally congratulatory throng of citizens the former scout had never seen before (and figured never to again) were a few other faces that were familiar. Ethan's dad was there, of course, standing beside a handsome thirtyish woman whom Lone judged to be his wife and Ethan's mother, seeing how the boy alternately clung to each of them. Somewhat surprisingly, Virgil Sweeney, the veteran Box 50 wrangler Lone had first seen in the company of Cully and Buck back in Marshal Dalrymple's office, was also present. Standing close to Sweeney and Cliff Halsey with an air of familiarity was another man; tall and husky in build, fifty give or take, with a face that, though certainly more weathered and rugged, still bore features similar enough to Cliff's that Lone was instantly convinced he was looking at the older Halsey brother, Granger.

Exactly what he might add to the proceedings, Lone had little or no time to wonder before Tobe Crenshaw's voice raised to a volume sufficient to quell most all the others and call all attention to himself. "Everybody listen up. Quiet down! I understand this is a very exciting, very welcome moment. For the Halsey family especially, and for all you good folks who've been hoping and praying right along with them for the safe return of their son." He paused to let an excited murmur ripple through the crowd. Then, gesturing to Ethan, he added, "Well, as you can see, here he is, safe and sound!"

This brought forth cheers and whistles, even a smattering of applause.

Crenshaw let this go on a bit before he quieted it again with some chopping hand gestures before saying, "What you also must know, though some of you may not recognize the name, is that little Ethan's return was achieved thanks to the brave actions of this man, Lone McGantry."

Another hand gesture this time indicated Lone and resulted in more cheering and applause. After he got things quieted once more, the marshal went on. "Now I know everybody's excited and in the mood for a celebration and wanting to hear all the details and so forth. But surely you must understand that these folks badly want to have a little private time first, the Halseys as well as McGantry and his friends. We need to respect that and allow them to have it."

"So I want you all to break this up and go on about your own business for a while, create some breathing room. We'll arrange some kind of get-together later on where you can each extend your best wishes and maybe engage in a little chin wagging. Remember, these folks have homes to return to and destinations they'll be wanting to get on with now that this dreadful business is over."

"But can we be sure it's over?" called a voice out of the crowd. "The little boy got rescued, true enough, and that's great. But what does it leave as far as the Gemsil gang still being on the prowl somewhere out there? Now that they've moved up to these parts from Kansas, what Devil's work will they do next like that bloody business in Ogallala?"

This time it wasn't a joyful murmur that passed though the crowd, but rather an uneasy grumble.

It ended quickly, though, cut short by the boyishly pitched yet surprisingly strong voice of Ethan saying loud and clear, "There ain't no Gemsil gang to worry about no more, Lone killed 'em all!"

CHAPTER 30

Six people were gathered around a rectangular table in a low-ceilinged room just off the main lobby of the Langley hotel. Save for the Crenshaw's table and the high-backed wooden chairs hitched up to it, the room was sparsely furnished. A handful of other mismatched chairs lined the walls. The space was used for regular sessions of the city council, by planning boards for various activities that cropped up around town, and got occasionally converted into a courtroom at times when the circuit judge passed through and saw fit to hold a trial.

This gathering today was less formal than most of those others, but no less serious in nature. A little over three hours had passed since Marshal Crenshaw quelled the public hoopla over the safe return of Ethan Halsey, with the promised renewal of a celebration yet to come. This interim meeting had been called at the request of the Halsey brothers, Cliff and Granger (the rugged-faced man Lone had accurately spotted in the crowd earlier). Present, in addition to the two brothers who sat on one side of the table, were Lone, Tru, and Ira seated opposite them. Crenshaw was on his feet, pacing somewhat restlessly. Over beside the doorway, Virgil Sweeney leaned silent and motionless against the wall.

Granger Halsey was currently doing the talking. "My brother and I asked for this time and we appreciate everybody making yourselves available. Cliff and me have come to agreement on some things we feel need to be heard and made clear. We asked the marshal to be on hand as a witness."

His gaze came to rest solely on Lone as he continued. "You can probably imagine how we felt when we heard the news that you had shot and killed not only our brother but also a cousin of ours. No matter the details, the claim of self-defense and so forth, the initial response was anger and the urge for revenge. I'm not putting words in Cliff's mouth that aren't accurate, or at least were in the beginning. And although we haven't yet heard from our other brother Royce, I'm confident his reaction would be no different."

He paused, as if waiting for Lone to say something. But the former scout merely held his eyes and waited.

Granger heaved a sigh. "But now we come to this. All that's been revealed in the past few hours. The way you went after little Ethan and succeeded in bringing him back safely. Not only that, beyond the deep gratitude from our whole family for his rescue, but then for the good of the entire territory, you went ahead and also wiped out Three Finger Jack and all of his wretched gang!" He paused again and a corner of his mouth twisted ruefully. "In other words, mister, you make it mighty damned hard to continue looking like somebody deserving of revenge."

"And I think the same, as Ethan's pa, probably even more so," Cliff was quick to add. He shifted in his chair, trying to get more comfortable what with his heavily bandaged shoulder and the attached arm hanging in a sling, before adding, "And save your spiel about not expecting any kind of trade-off for going after Ethan. The way we feel as a result, is the way we feel. You got no control over it."

Lone gave it a beat and then, regarding the two brothers evenly, he spoke in response. "If you expect me to argue *against* you fellas wanting to let up on the notion of revenge, well, that ain't likely to happen. For your sake, I regret the loss of your kin. But, for my part, I stand the same as always, I did what I had to in defense of myself and Miss Chang.

"Comes to the boy, the same holds true there. I did what it felt like I had to given the circumstances. Which is to say, him not having much other chance and me being in a position to try and give him one. The way it worked out and me getting to know Ethan a little bit over our time together on the trail, I'd say it's one of the better choices I've made in my time. You got a fine son there, Deputy. He's smart and brave and tough and has all the makings of being a good man someday."

Cliff swallowed visibly. "You summed it all up right there, McGantry. I *have* got a fine son and, thanks to you, he now has the chance to grow into a good man."

Lone felt all eyes coming to rest on him, causing the heat of embarrassment to crawl up the sides of his neck.

Thankfully, Granger took the attention off him by heaving another sigh and then speaking up again. "The subject of boys turning into proper men is something else that probably needs to be touched on further as part of this conversation. I'm talking specifically about Isaac and Jerome. In the Halsey family, you see, it was pounded into our heads that blood is thicker than water and kin is kin, no matter if some of them fail to measure up the way they oughta. That came from our pa. Ma died shortly after Isaac was born and I think Pa saw early on that Isaac had some shortcomings. Jerome's ma helped raise him, Jerome being about the same age, and both boys mirrored each other's bad habits the whole time they were growing up. Lying, sneaking, stealing, bullying others, what have you. One lousy trait after another."

As Granger continued to talk, his expression grew more pained. "After Pa and Aunt Mildred passed on, it fell to me, the oldest brother, to sort of look out for Isaac and Jerome. I can make the excuse that the die was already cast, but the fact remains because they were kin, because they were blood, I kept cutting them slack for their sorry ways. Right up to hiring them on at the Box 50 and then covering for their screw-ups and laziness. All the while I feared there might be a deeper, meaner wildness in them, but I fooled myself into hoping they'd eventually grow out of it." Here his eyes came to rest on Tru. "It was you who almost paid the price for that deeper ugliness coming to the surface, Miss Chang and I'm powerful sorry for my failure to curb it sooner. Thankfully, McGantry was there to. Well, galling as it is to admit, I guess that makes another reason the thirst for revenge dries a mite easier in my throat."

Tru favored him with a forgiving look. "You cannot hold yourself responsible for the actions of others. Especially when you were many miles away at the time of the incident involving me. The breeze that cools a hot afternoon may also summon an angry evening storm. No one can control how or when it will turn."

Nobody spoke for a minute or so. Until Crenshaw cleared his throat and said, "Okay. I'd say both sides have aired things out pretty good. Sounds like nobody's looking to spill more blood or take more lives. Even though I wouldn't have necessarily had a dog in the hunt, seeing how the start and the play-out, if there'd been more to come, would've fallen outside my jurisdiction. Well, I'm glad it ain't gonna come to that."

"Not so fast, Marshal," Granger said, the pained expression remaining on his face. "I'm afraid there's more to tell."

Crenshaw scowled. "What's that supposed to mean? If there's more to tell, quit beating around the bush and get to it."

Granger and Cliff exchanged dour looks. Then Granger started explaining. "Back in North Platte, after I heard what happened in Ogallala and how it affected my brother and nephew, I took a few minutes to go pay respects to Isaac and Jerome before hopping the westbound train to get me to Ogallala so I could be part of things there. Recognizing how that trouble was bound to take priority for me and Cliff, my boss Angus Benton, owner of the Box 50, decided he would take charge of setting things in motion to address the matter of four Box 50 men getting gunned down. To do that, he started sending out telegrams to towns all across the Nebraska panhandle. Sidney. Kimball. Down into Colorado, too Sterling, likely even here to Julesburg."

"Telegrams saying what?"

"Same message in everyone. Short and to the point. Twenty-five hundred dollars to anybody who would gun down and provide proof of killing Lone McGantry."

In her chair beside Lone, Tru went rigid and issued a stifled cry.

On the other side of her, Ira wasn't so subtle. "That damn fool!"

Crenshaw barked out a coarse word. Then, after glancing apologetically at Tru, he said, "Twenty-five hundred dollars. That's enough to stir up every tin horn and two-bit gun sharp between here and Denver!"

"We know," Cliff said glumly. "The consequences could turn everything upside down in the worst way!"

"Can't you convince Benton this ain't what you want, get him to send out more wires to call off the first ones?" Crenshaw said.

Granger shook his head. "You don't know Angus Benton. He ain't much for admitting he's wrong or changing his mind. No matter what me or Cliff think or say, Benton sees it as four of his wranglers getting gunned, three dead, one badly wounded and so the man who did it needing to pay. Pay with his life. And Angus will pay with money to make it happen. Besides, even if he did try to send out new wires to call off the first ones, the damage is already done. There's bound to be a certain number of hardcases already on the trail, looking to be the first to intercept McGantry and claim the bounty."

Crenshaw swore again. Glaring at Lone, he growled, "Well, don't you have anything to say, McGantry? You're just sitting there looking like the cat who swallowed the canary."

A corner of Lone's mouth curved up. "Actually, that's sort of what I'm thinkin'. I'm tryin' to figure out a way to fake my death and claim that twenty-five hundred for myself. It's almost flatterin' I never thought anybody would reckon I was worth so much."

Cliff gawked at him. "Jesus, man. You can joke about it?"

"What am I supposed to do?" Lone countered. "Wail and moan about this bit of bad news? Be frightened by it? I've had gun toughs after me before. So I'll be cautious, alert. But I'll be damned if I show fear or alter my plans because of it. I've got commitments and obligations that have already been interrupted. For a good cause but not for this. Tomorrow my wagon rolls again for Fort Collins and the Never Summer Mountains beyond."

"But what about your traveling companions? If the gun toughs come after you," Crenshaw pointed out, "it almost certainly means danger for them, too."

"We figured we were in danger from the start," Lone told him. "But if my friends feel there's now an increased threat and want to part ways, then I'll help them as best I can to find some other means to get where…"

"I go where and when Lone McGantry goes," Tru stated loud and firm, settling the matter firmly as far as she was concerned.

It took Ira a moment longer, but then: "Reckon I feel the same. Like Lone said, our wagon rolls out tomorrow and we all go with it."

CHAPTER 31

Later that afternoon, in order to help Crenshaw save face because of his promise to the citizenry that a celebration would be held in recognition of the safe return of Ethan as well as the extermination of the Gemsil gang, Lone endured nearly an hour of standing in the hotel lobby surrounded by well-wishers and admirers. Having Tru next to him and also Ethan and his parents for part of the time, made it bearable. But, even still, he could only stand so much. Excusing himself at the first reasonable opportunity, he retreated with Tru to the privacy of the hotel room she had secured when first arriving in town.

As soon as they were by themselves, Lone flopped into a thinly cushioned chair by the room's only window and breathed deeply of the early evening air wafting in through the parted curtains. "Man oh man," he declared. "I'd rather be back up in the Sandhills fightin' Three Finger Jack all over again than stay in that lobby, standin' there grinnin' like an idiot while strangers walked up to jabber and paw at me."

Tru gave a little laugh. "You're a real live hero. People want to be near you and touch you, perhaps hoping some of your heroic qualities will rub off on them."

Lone scowled. "Maybe so. But, whether they realized it or not, a couple of them got awful heavy-handed with their pawing and what came close to rubbin' off was me popping 'em on the nose."

"In that case, your restraint was admirable," Tru said, still smiling. Then, her expression sobering, she added, "But all of that is done. What we need to think about now is getting a good night's rest in preparation of our departure tomorrow."

Lone nodded. "Couldn't agree more. Ira dodged that little shindig you and me got caught in for the sake of makin' sure our wagon is all stocked and ready. I'm gonna join him in a short while to double-check that he got everything he needed. I want to aim for rollin' out at daybreak."

"Ira insisted I take this room at the hotel while he's been sleeping with the wagon to ensure no one bothers anything it holds."

"Good man. Good thinking on his part. I'll join him there tonight."

Tru frowned. "But wouldn't it be a good idea for you to take a room also, in order to be most completely rested? You've been on the trail for days and got caught in the rain and..."

"Hey, take it easy," Lone interrupted with a gentle smile. "Thanks for worryin' about me, kid. But I'll be okay. While I enjoy a turn in a nice soft bed now and then, the truth of the matter is that in my life I've spent a whole lot more nights in a bedroll than on a mattress. That bath and shave I got at the barber earlier perked me up just fine, so the expense of a hotel room just ain't necessary."

"But it wouldn't hurt either," Tru insisted stubbornly.

"Like I said, thanks for worryin' about me. But it ain't necessary."

Tru moved over to where Lone sat. With him seated, their faces were nearly level. Tru regarded him, her expression and tone becoming very sincere. "But I do worry about you, Lone McGantry. I do so because, in case you haven't noticed, I have developed some strong feelings toward you."

Lone felt a lump rise in his throat. He gently took one of Tru's delicate hands in his. "Well, I purely appreciate that, kid. I also feel..."

"Please stop doing that."

"Doing what?"

"Calling me 'kid'. No matter what else, you surely must be aware that I am not a child."

She was wearing another of those silk-like blouses that clung so fetchingly to her sleek curves, something Lone was indeed quite aware of, an awareness that her words and current nearness were only increasing.

"No, dear Tru," he said somewhat huskily. "You're definitely not a child. You're all woman and, more than that, a very special one."

A hint of a smile returned to Tru's lips.

Lone continued. "And bein' looked on favorably by you means a great deal to me. But pursuin' such feelings, by either of us. I don't think is a good idea. Mainly, the timing is all wrong. There are too many things in the way, other matters that must be taken care of first. The time it will take to deal with them. Well, I fear would only lead to disappointment and hurt. Better to sidestep it right up front."

"But when feelings run deep, they cannot be so easily 'sidestepped'," Tru replied. "And if the feelings are genuine, then neither time nor other matters should be able to wipe them away."

Lone sighed. "I don't know how to argue that. I can't

say what you should or shouldn't feel. I can only warn you not to put too much stock in me. Again, I'm proud and honored that you look favorably on me. I just don't want you harmed because of it. I'll do everything in my power to get you safely to Fort Collins. You know that. And you also know the promise I must fulfill afterwards, to bury my friend. But what you don't know is the next promise I have to fulfill."

Tru gazed at him questioningly.

"It's something I've mentioned to no one before this. It's a promise to myself but one just as strong or stronger than any I've ever made. The promise to hunt down the horse thieving curs who killed Peg and make every mother's son of them pay."

"I, I didn't know," Tru said.

"Like I told you, I never mentioned it to anyone else before."

"I treasure that you are sharing it with me." Tru's brows knitted above her lovely almond eyes. "But so much time has passed. And, when you spoke of it in the past, you said there was never any clue who the marauders were or where they might have fled after the raid on your ranch."

"Even vermin like them had to leave some kind of sign. Just a tiny sliver, that's all I need. That'll lead to another. Then another. Gradually, a clearer trail will start to take shape, a trail I'll follow for as long as it takes. Until, one by one, I catch up with each of the bastards who made it." A strange, cold fire flared deep in Lone's eyes as he spoke. And, even deeper, was something he had been and would continue keeping suppressed ever since his final session with Peg. It was the one haunting phrase the old mountain man had uttered outside his talk of the Forever Mountain. *"Look for the man with the burned face!"*. This was the single clue Lone planned to build on when the time came, when he began his hunt for the marauders. Until then, further thought or mention of it even to Tru, would stay buried.

Lone averted his eyes for a moment. When he brought them back, his gaze had softened. "So do you see what I mean by too many things bein' in the way? It may take me months to hunt down that pack of curly wolves. And let's face it. There's no guarantee it will go my way if and when I do. Hell, that could be true even before then, if any of the bounty hunters that Box 50 boss sicced on me get lucky."

Now it was Tru's eyes that flashed. "Do not say or even think such things!"

Lone gave her hand a slight squeeze. "The point I'm tryin' to make is that you're on the brink of a fresh start, a new life. You don't deserve to get bogged down wasting your time waiting for the likes of me."

"Nor do I deserve to be told, like a child, what is right or wrong for me." Tru started to withdraw her hand from his, only then stopped and instead gave him a squeeze in return. "But I have made my feelings known. That is enough for now. In the days ahead you will have time to think about it more."

"The days ahead?" Lone's mouth twisted wryly. "For somebody who only a few minutes ago was worried about me getting a good night's rest, what you've gone and planted in my head sure ain't gonna help that any."

"You will manage," Tru replied somewhat airily, going ahead with the withdrawal of her hand. "In as much as I have packing to finish in order to be ready for our early departure tomorrow, and you need to check on Ira and the wagon. I suggest it's time for us to say goodnight."

CHAPTER 32

Lone exited out the rear of the hotel, in order to avoid running into any lingering well-wishers from the gathering in the lobby. The shadows of early evening were lengthening and deepening and the air was cooling now that the sun had been down for a while.

Lone paused on the narrow slip of a back porch and stood watching an elderly man who was lighting a pole lantern about ten yards off, half-way to the weathered, precariously tilting structure that was the public privy for the hotel. Lone recognized the man as an employee of the Langtry from having seen him earlier serving refreshments to the lobby crowd.

Once the lantern was lighted, the man turned and started back toward the hotel. He walked with a slight limp. Spotting Lone as he neared the porch, he halted and peered up at him. "Oh, Mr. McGantry," he said. "Almost didn't see you standing there in the shadows."

"Sorry. Didn't mean to startle you," Lone responded.

"Nothing on you. Guess my sight hadn't re-adjusted from staring into the flame of that lantern." The old timer emitted a sudden cackle. "Wouldn't that be something? Me making sure the way is lit for folks to do their outhouse business and me tripping and bustin' my noggin in the process. Ha!"

Another cackle was enough to bring forth a grin from Lone. "Maybe you oughta start lighting that lantern a little earlier, when you can see to navigate your way better."

"Normally I do," came the answer. "This evening, though, that shindig for you and the Halsey boy didn't break up until just a short time ago and I was busy with guests inside. But I ain't complaining none. The way you saved that boy and took out Three Finger Jack and his owlhoot gang, it was a pure pleasure to be part of you getting a small piece of recognition."

"The kid being back safe with his family, that's the main thing," Lone downplayed.

Seeing he wasn't comfortable having praise heaped on him, the old timer said, "Well, folks hereabouts will be talking about it for a long time, you can bet on that. But I don't mean to keep you, Mr. McGantry. If you're aiming to join your friend at the wagon, it's parked in an empty lot straight back behind the privy, just through that stand of tall bushes."

"Thanks. Reckon I'll find it okay," Lone told him.

The old man went on inside and Lone continued standing there on the shadowy porch for a few more minutes. It wasn't that he was putting off joining Ira at the wagon. If anything, he was anxious for that; it would mean being one step closer to getting underway again and getting on with fulfilling his promise to Peg. But so much else besides that had entered into the bigger picture. Not the least of which was this business with Tru that so unexpectedly flared up. Well, not entirely unexpected. Ma had tried to warn him, only he'd laughed it off. But what he wasn't laughing off now, the *real* unexpected part, was how he felt in response to the exotic beauty's direct overture.

The hell of it was, how he felt didn't change any of what he'd told her about all the things in the way.

Irony of ironies, Tru stirring a surge of tender feelings within him had also stirred, in sharp contrast, the harshest ones he harbored there, the ones he'd been holding so deep, forcing to lay dormant until the time was right, his smoldering determination to never rest until he'd hunted down Peg's killers and made them pay with blood.

All of which might have to take its turn, as Lone had also told Tru, if Angus Benton's bounty killers got to him first.

With a literal roll of his shoulders, Lone shrugged away this entanglement of thoughts and stepped down from the porch. He'd warned Tru against getting bogged down, neither could he afford to himself. Whatever lay in his path he would meet moving forward, just like always, not standing in one spot fretting.

Past the outhouse and through a stand of tall bushes, just as the old man had directed, he came to the edge of a grassy clearing where Ira had the wagon parked. The horses were in a livery stable down the street. Ira had explained that he could have stored the wagon there, too, but instead arranged with the hotel, since Tru was booked into a room, to park it here as a means of being able to stay with it and remain close to Tru as well.

Ira was next to the wagon now, squatting beside a small campfire that he was feeding some fresh twigs into. As he started across the clearing, Lone called ahead, "Hello the camp. Can you spare a cup of coffee to a real life, rootin'-tootin' Wild West hero?"

In the firelight, he could see Ira's mouth pull into a

crooked grin. "I dunno. This is a very humble camp with only the cheapest coffee my tightwad of a boss is willing to shell out money for. But you're welcome to share what meager fare I have, Mr. Hero, sir."

Lone had proceeded only three or four steps when, from behind him and off to the right, a crackling noise in the bushes caused him to hesitate and turn his head in that direction. An instant later, a bullet blistered the air six inches in front of his chest—exactly where he would have been if he'd taken another step. From the spot in the bushes where he'd turned to look, Lone saw the muzzle flash and heard the roar of the rifle that had hurled the slug.

"Kill the fire, Ira!" Lone shouted as he pitched to the ground, clawing for the Colt on his hip.

As he was going down, another rifle blast, this one also from behind only off to his left, barked menacingly. Another bullet sang close, a foot or so above his head.

"You got him! I think you got him, Beau!" hollered a voice from where the first shot had originated.

"Don't be so sure, keep pourin' it on!" the second shooter hollered back as he took his own advice.

Lone rolled frantically toward a patch of shadows out beyond where the campfire illumination reached. Bullets chased him, some pounding into the ground, some sizzling through the air.

At last the light from the fire sputtered and died as Ira was able to kick enough dirt to smother the flames. This was of benefit to Lone, but it quickly threatened to turn unhealthy for Ira.

The second shooter cursed angrily, saying, "Get that sonofabitch by the wagon, if he wants to be part of it, we'll gladly accommodate him!"

The first rifleman responded obediently, immediately

shifting his aim to Ira and cranking two rapid-fire shots his way. The slap of the slugs striking the side of the wagon was a relief to Lone's ears, indicating they hadn't scored on Ira. Almost as important, they also indicated something else, the flash of the rounds as they were triggered gave Lone a target to take aim at. Having cleared leather with his Colt by now and no longer caught in any illumination from the campfire, he quickly pushed to one knee, steadied himself for the briefest moment and then poured two .44 slugs at the muzzle flashes he was locked on.

A stifled whimper of pain followed by the crunching thud of something heavy collapsing within the bushes signaled that one or both of the rounds had done significant damage. But knowing that the tongues of flame from his Colt had marked his own location, even in his new cloak of shadows, Lone had no time to take satisfaction. The fight wasn't over and he didn't mean for it to end with him being home for the next bullet.

Barely had he thrown himself to one side and gone into another roll than the second rifleman sent lead punching through the spot he had just vacated. "God damn you! Did you shoot my pard? Hec! Can you hear me? Oh God, Hec, don't tell me you're a goner!"

"Hec's past telling you anything, you ambushing snake!" Lone taunted. "I did like you said, I accommodated him for wanting to be part of this!"

"Go accommodate in Hell, damn you! And while you're shoveling coal for Satan, I'll be doin' twenty-five hundred dollars' worth of celebratin' for sendin' your scurvy soul down there!" This angry outburst of words came with another burst of lead meant to make the words come true. But, as before, the shots were aimed where Lone no longer was. In so doing, this also gave Lone his first glimpse of the second shooter's position, something the former scout tried to take advantage of by immediately returning fire. Trouble was, his target also knew the trick of shifting away from his muzzle flashes so Lone's shots did nothing but slash empty bushes.

As he went into another roll, Lone was keenly aware that he had only two rounds left in his Colt. Wearing the back-up Baby Russian tucked into his belt had hardly seemed warranted for the hotel lobby gathering. But some-thing else he was aware of was the loaded Winchester in the seat box of the wagon that was so near and yet so far. This was enough for him to call out, "What the hell are you doing over there, Ira saving bullets? Give me some damn cover!"

"Fixing to do just that!" Ira hollered back. And from the other side of the wagon came two quick blasts sending another pair of slugs chewing into the bushes where the remaining ambusher was. Not waiting to judge the success of these shots, Lone made the most of getting the cover fire he'd asked for by shoving to his feet and rushing the handful of yards it took for him to reach the hulking shape of the wagon.

He scrambled around and came skidding up next to where Ira was crouched behind one of the front wheels. As Ira triggered two more rounds, Lone's hands rapidly, nimbly began replacing spent cartridges in his Colt, saying between puffs to catch his breath, "You hitting anything?"

"Doing a real good job of pruning those bushes some, otherwise I can't tell," replied Ira. "But he ain't shooting back, so maybe…"

His words were cut short by the sound of somebody emitting a truncated curse in combination with a loud thud and then once again the crunching of a heavy object collapsing within the bushes. Lone and Ira both froze, straining to see or hear something more.

Until a vaguely familiar voice called out to them. "Hold your fire! Just take it easy, McGantry. This hombre ain't dead but, trust me, he's out of the fight. I'm gonna step out now, so don't shoot. You know me, it's Virgil Sweeney."

CHAPTER 33

"The one Sweeney bent his pistol barrel over the head of," Marshal Crenshaw was saying, "goes by the name of Beau Pulford. His partner, the one you shot dead over in that other clump of bushes, was Hector—Hec, everybody called him—Crumley."

Lone listened to this report with a dark scowl. "Too bad I wasn't able to make 'em a matched set. As soon as I got my Colt reloaded, I full intended to send ol' Beau where he was threatenin' to send me."

"Not much doubt he'll still end up there. Just gonna take a little longer, that's all," Crenshaw replied.

Lone grunted. "Like I said, too bad."

Standing nearby, Cliff Halsey said, "You know those two men, Marshal?"

"Afraid so. Couple of long in the tooth old rascals who showed up over on Saloon Row a few months back. Rumor had it they was a pair of bad hombres down Texas way in their prime." Crenshaw made a sour face. "I kinda took that with a grain of salt because I figured they were at least smart enough not to try any funny business in the decent part of town."

"Maybe they wouldn't have, if I hadn't shown up over here to tempt 'em after they got wind of that bounty Angus Benton is offering," Lone allowed.

"You're sure that's what their motive was?" Cliff asked.

It was Ira who answered, saying, "The one called Beau didn't leave much doubt about it. Said he was gonna send Lone to Hell and then do twenty-five hundred dollars' worth of celebrating over it."

"That's right. I heard him say that too," confirmed Sweeney.

This discussion was taking place amidst a new gathering of people drawn by the sound of gunfire to where it had occurred, the lot out behind the hotel. There were twenty or so in total, a handful brandishing lanterns against the deepening darkness. In addition to Crenshaw and the participants, present also were the Halsey brothers (minus, thankfully, Ethan and his mother), some hotel staff members and several just plain gawkers looking to add a little excitement to their otherwise dull evenings.

Tru was there, too, naturally drawn by the indication of trouble from where she knew the wagon to be. She stood quietly by now, watching and listening, a mixture of relief and concern showing on her lovely countenance.

"Angus and those damnable wires he sent out!" Granger Halsey lamented loudly. "If only I'd known he was hatching such a crazy notion and could have had a chance to stop him."

Crenshaw's sour expression didn't improve any. "Yeah, and if I'd realized that bounty talk was already circulating through Julesburg, I could have done things different, too. But what's done is done and there's no sense crying over spilled milk. We can just be thankful the spilling wasn't any worse."

"I'll go along with that," Lone said. "And on the subject of thanking" here he cut his gaze to Sweeney "reckon some needs to be aimed your way for showin' up and lendin' a hand like you did. Considering our history, it wouldn't have been surprising for some fellas in your position to have just turned away and let things play out between Beau and me."

"Excuse me for butting in," spoke up Granger before Sweeney could reply for himself, "but you only say that because you don't know Virgil. He's not just 'some fella'. He sees right and wrong mighty clear, no matter what else."

"Not very hard to see an ambushin' skunk as being in the wrong," Sweeney picked up from there. Meeting Lone's gaze, he continued, "And as far as our history, if you're thinkin' about the Box 50 men who've fallen to your gun, you ain't wrong to believe I don't take that lightly. Ain't been doin' much else but grindin' on it since the first. What I got it wore down to, matter of fact, is what I was on my way to come talk to you about when I walked up on the ambush takin' place. Plain to see that needed takin' care of first."

"When you say you were on your way to 'talk' to Mc-Gantry," said Crenshaw, arching a brow, "you mean with words or did you have something different in mind?"

"I ain't one to beat around the bush with my meanin', Marshal," Sweeney told him. "When I say I'm lookin' to talk to a man, that's what I'm lookin' to do."

"I can vouch for that," Granger interjected again. "Plus, I happen to know what Virgil was coming to talk to Mc-Gantry about. And it wasn't to stir up any bad blood over the trouble back in North Platte. Far from it, in fact."

"Maybe," Lone said, "everybody oughta let Sweeney say what's on his mind so me and him can get whatever it is settled between us."

"Alright, you do that," Crenshaw agreed tartly. "While you two are having your little chat, I'll clean up the mess of getting Beau put behind bars and seeing to it Hec is hauled off to the undertaker. In the meantime, McGantry, try to stay out of the gunsights of another bounty hunting team, at least until I finish tidying up after this one, okay?"

"I'll do my best. While you're doing your tidying," Lone suggested, "how about you tidy up this pack of gawkers? They all heard what happened, no need for 'em to hang around trying to soak up more. Plus, in case somebody else *does* show up looking to collect that bounty, an innocent onlooker could get caught by flying lead."

In a matter of minutes, Crenshaw had the scene cleared. He collared a couple of men to help him take Beau to the jail and sent another to fetch the undertaker. This left behind Lone, Tru and Ira to hear what Sweeney had to say and also Granger, remaining with his veteran wrangler. Cliff went ahead and returned to his wife and child.

"How about you bring that fire back to life, Ira?" Lone said. "We can talk over there."

Ira nodded. "Can do. That pot of coffee should still be pretty warm, too. Will heat the rest of the way plenty quick if anybody wants some."

After answering that he could go for a cup, Lone looked questioning at Sweeney and Granger. "You gents?"

They both responded affirmatively and so all five relocated over nearer the wagon. Ira got the fire re-started quickly and in no time Tru was pouring cups for everybody but herself.

"All this buildup," Sweeney said, abruptly looking somewhat sheepish as he held his cup before him, "may make what I got to say seem like not such a big deal."

"Only one way to find out," Lone told him. "You had

something in mind when you headed over here to begin with. Go ahead on with it."

Sweeney took a sip. Then: "Okay. For starters, I reckon you should know that I've gave my notice at the Box 50. I no longer ride for the brand."

"Not to anybody else's liking, in case you'd like to know, most of all me," said Granger.

Sweeney went on as if he hadn't heard him. "Lot of years now I've had me a hankerin' to see what's past the Rocky Mountains. Maybe all the way as far as California and the Pacific Ocean. As I got older and grew comfortable at the Box 50, I guess I came to accept it was never gonna happen. But then, events of the past week or so changed my mind. Things didn't feel so comfortable no more. And I came to realize, inside myself, that it was finally time to move on. For my own sake and maybe for some others, too."

Nobody said anything for a few beats. Until Lone asked, "These events that changed your mind. I take it that would be the shooting of the other Box 50 riders?"

"Uh-huh." Sweeney drank some more of his coffee. "But don't go thinkin' I'm workin' up to blamin' you. Yeah, a-course you played a part. Woulda been easy to stop there. But after I ground on it like I done, I saw that there was plenty of blame to go around. Those young fools who put themselves in your way and forced your hand, each shouldered their own share. But so did I. That's the thing."

"I was there right at the start when we all stopped at your cabin the first time and found Miss Chang there alone. I shoulda shut that down a whole lot quicker and firmer than I did. No physical harm came to the gal, thank God, but she still had to listen to nasty talk and threats that must have hurt plenty in their own way."

"You stood up to the others, all four of them," Tru said encouragingly, from where she sat beside Lone. "If you hadn't done that, I would not have had the chance to make it to my rifle in order to finally make everybody leave."

"But there's the word. Finally." Sweeney said it like it tasted bitter in his mouth. "Like I said at the start, I should've stopped the whole ugly business a whole lot sooner and firmer. And then, what did I do the very next day? I sent Isaac and Jerome out to round up strays. I shoulda known the hungover little shits would've headed back to that cabin. Maybe, down deep, I *did* know. Maybe I knew, but I was so sick and tired of ridin' herd on that pair of slackers that I didn't care. At least not enough. Yet that was at the very top of the things Granger and Mr. Benton left me in charge of lookin' after while they was away and it also left Miss Chang in a bad position to be bothered all over again. So what did that make me? Who was really to blame, then, for the whole chain of events that came next?"

"I've tried to convince him and so has Cliff, that there's no call to feel this way. But he's too damn proud and stubborn to change his mind." Granger's mouth pulled into a grimace. "Nobody knows better than me how hard it was to keep my boneheaded little brother and cousin in line. I should have clamped down on them myself, a lot harder and a lot sooner than I ever did. Comes to slinging blame around, you'd have to say I've got my share coming, too."

"That's your call to make," said Sweeney. "All I can say is for myself. The way I see it, when a man can no longer make his hand then it's time to ride on. So that's what I'm doing."

Once again everybody went quiet for a stretch. And once again it was Lone who broke the silence. "Reckon I know a thing or two about ridin' on. But what I don't know, what's got me puzzled, is why you gents are layin' all of this out for us. What does it have to do with what brought you here tonight, Sweeney?"

"Everything. It's the explanation behind it," the old wrangler answered. "Now that I've decided to act on my long put-off hankerin', it struck me that the first leg is makin' it as far as the Rockies, same as where you folks are headed. Now if I ain't welcome company, I understand. But I'm lookin' at it as a way for me to maybe make amends for some of what I let slide."

"Still not sure I'm followin' you," said Lone.

Sweeney held up a pair of work-thickened fingers. "Two things. This bounty business Mr. Benton has set in motion. I figure it's all a piece of those things I didn't rein in sooner. You havin' me along with you, in the face of that unfortunate decision by Mr. Benton, would amount to one more gun sidin' you in case any would-be collectors showed up. I don't claim to be no gun sharp or nothing of the kind, but I fought in the war and if need be I know how to plant a bullet where I aim. What happened here a little bit ago ain't an especially strong example, but it showed that bounty offer *is* gonna stir some interest and it showed I'm willin' to step in if called on."

When Sweeney paused, Ira reminded him, "You said two things."

Sweeney inclined his head toward Tru. "The other is Miss Chang. On two occasions she had to suffer verbal abuse and threats when, well, when I shoulda been quicker to stop or limit 'em from takin' place. I feel powerful low about that. And I'd consider it a particular honor to serve in any way I could to help make sure she gets the rest of the way safely to her destination."

Lone prided himself on not being caught by surprise

very often. And by making quick and accurate appraisals of people he met. Yet here was this weathered old wrangler setting him back on his heels in both categories. Not that he'd ever read Sweeney as a *bad* sort, really especially not in comparison to the snotty pups Cully and Buck he'd first met him in the company of. But neither had Lone sensed any particular depth to the old cowpoke, either; certainly not to the level of introspection he was showing now. And then topping that by offering to throw in against the bounty hunters hired by the boss of his former brand. It all added up to a mighty eye-opening turn.

"So what do you say, McGantry? I'll admit that I'm hoping you won't accept Virgil's offer. Maybe that'll cause him to change his mind about staying on at the Box 50." Granger sighed wistfully. "But I know that ain't likely, either way."

"What do I say?" echoed Lone. "For starters, I say that I think Mr. Sweeney is bein' too hard on himself. But that's for nobody but him to decide. Then, what I'd say next is that any man who holds himself to those kind of tough standards is somebody I'd be foolish not to want riding at my side. But I've got two other folks already with me. Reckon it's only right they also have a say."

"No objection out of me," Ira was quick to state. "He sure came in handy tonight. And times past, back in North Platte, even though Sweeney didn't put in too many appearances at the kind of dives where I hung out, when he did, he was never one who shoved me around and treated me like dirt the way a lot of others did."

When all eyes swung to Tru, neither did she hesitate to say, "I also have no objection. Though Mr. Sweeney feels remorse for what he considers his shortcomings, I remember quite differently. I remember his stern voice reprimanding the others for what they were saying, what they were wanting to do. It gave me my only hope and then gave me the chance to reach my rifle and chase those pigs away. So no, I have no reluctance to travel in the company of Mr. Sweeney."

With a mixture of sadness and gratitude filling his eyes, the old wrangler said softly, "Bless you, child, for recallin' it that way."

CHAPTER 34

____

They rolled out of town with the first curving edge of sunlight slicing up into the base of the sky at their backs and the night's chill still brisk on their faces. Ira had the reins of the pulling team, Tru sat on the wagon seat next to him. Lone and Sweeney rode their horses on either side.

The grassland west of Julesburg grew steadily, gradually flatter as they angled slightly south away from the reach of the Sandhills. It was still largely barren of trees, except for a few lining the scattered creeks and watercourses that snaked for short distances between the blunted hills.

The hours and miles fell away, leaving Lone pleased with the progress they were making. It crossed his mind more than once, though, how different these circumstances were from the many previous distances he had traveled almost always in solitude more befitting his name. Just him and Ironsides. And while the makeup of his traveling companions—an exotic Chinese beauty, a drunk struggling to reform, and an old cowboy chasing a dream—might be viewed as creating an even starker contrast, it was an assemblage that Lone actually felt quite comfortable with.

Well, there was the matter of the feelings simmering between him and Tru. It wasn't exactly comfortable thinking about having to find a way to resolve that. But, regardless of who felt how, Lone was steadfast in his determination to fulfill the other commitments he'd been up front in warning her about. Plus, like he'd also warned her, a failure to overcome the unpredictable conditions of the Never Summer Mountains or to get past the unknown number of hardcases he was going after, not to mention dodging the bounty hunters potentially coming after *him*. Add it all up, it made counting on him to be part of any long-range plans a mighty iffy roll of the dice.

Yeah, he'd warned her. And he would remind her again. But he had a pretty good hunch it wasn't going to be that easy. What was more, he recognized that some cockeyed emotion down inside him didn't want her to give up on him *too* easy.

Even with these thoughts drifting in and out of mind, Lone didn't slack off on being alert, vigilant to their surroundings. As they neared the middle of the morning, he pushed Ironsides three or four miles ahead to scout what they were approaching; then he dropped back almost as far to check their back trail. In the middle of the afternoon, he did the same thing all over again. Each time he saw nothing but a gently undulating sea of greening grass.

It went like that for two more days. The weather remained fair, warm and sunny in the daytime, clear and cool at night. They stayed above the meandering South Platte, encountering no one else. Passed through a few clumps of branded cattle, saw a ranch house or two off in the distance.

In the beginning, as the newcomer to the group, Sweeney was somewhat reserved, acting almost shy around the others in spite of his request to join them. It didn't take long, though, for Ira's talkativeness and Tru's quiet warmth to start putting him at ease. Around the mealtime campfires, he was soon opening up and participating more and more in the conversations that took place.

On the third night, they camped near the base of a gentle slope with a flat-faced ridge of rock jutting out to shield them against a chill north wind that had come prowling down with increasing force late in the afternoon. A growing number of such rock outcrops had begun dotting the land as they drew nearer to the mountains and this one presented itself at a particularly opportune juncture.

When supper was done, the four travelers were wrapping up the day with some small talk around the campfire before crawling into their bedrolls. "If this wind don't stir up a turn in the weather that affects visibility," Lone was saying, "I'm thinking that by tomorrow afternoon, Sweeney, we should be well in sight of those Rockies you've been longing to see."

The old wrangler's eyebrows lifted. "I'll be dogged. That's excitin' news to hear." He paused and grinned a little sheepishly. "That probably sounds kinda silly comin' from an old goat like me, don't it? Like a little kid lookin' forward to untyin' the ribbon on a present."

Tru said, "It doesn't sound silly to me. I'm excited about seeing them too. Although, technically I guess I should say seeing them *again*. I traveled over them once as a babe in arms, when my Uncle Pao came and got me in California, after my parents died and brought me to live with him and my aunt in Council Bluffs. But I was too tiny to have any awareness back then—so, for me, experiencing them again now will seem like something entirely new."

Ira gave an indifferent shrug. "I've seen plenty of mountains. The Rockies and some others, too. They're kind of impressive the first time or two but, after that, it always seemed to me that if you've seen one then you've seen them all. Just great big piles of rocks, some with snowy peaks, some without."

Lone grinned wryly. "Reckon there's those who feel like you. But plenty of others I've known, ones who've actually spent time in and around the mountains like my pal Peg" he jabbed a thumb, indicating the wagon and the bolted-down box that was part of its cargo "have a powerful feeling quite the opposite. It's almost like a wild, special kind of love. In fact, Peg told me once that he saw the mountains that way—like a big, bawdy, beautiful woman that you knew you can never tame but who you also can never get out of your blood."

His gaze seemed to drift through the campfire flames and focus on something far away for a moment before he added, "Come to find out, what the old rascal never mentioned until just recently, was that another reason the mountains held a piece of his heart was because of the flesh and blood beauty whose spirit has been waiting there all this time for him to return."

When he paused, Tru said softly, "That is a truly beautiful story. And, thanks to you, your friend's spirit soon *will* be rejoined with his beloved's."

"Ask me," stated Sweeney, "it sounds like we all got good reasons for wanting to see those Rockies hove into sight tomorrow. Well, except for Ira, I guess."

"Aw, come on now. Don't make me sound like some kind of sour puss," protested Ira. "It ain't like I got anything *against* making it to the mountains. I just look at 'em different, that's all. And as far as seeing anything romantic about 'em, with all due respect to ol' Peg. Hold on. Wait a minute. Maybe if I think on it real hard I can find some romantic angle. How about this? Peg called the mountains big, bawdy, beautiful and untamed; well, my rip of an ex-wife was big, bawdy, beautiful and unfaithful. And, to boot, she was as cold and hard as the highest damn peak! How's that for a romantic connection when it comes to thinking about mountains?"

Tru rolled her eyes. "It may be *a* connection, but I'd hardly call it a romantic one."

"Well, I'm afraid it's the best I can do on short notice," Ira told her. "Me and romance haven't traveled in the same circles for a while. I've been in love twice in my life, once with my rip of an ex-wife and then with whatever I could suck out of a whiskey bottle. The two combined to damn near kill me. I'm trying to go forward, not backward. So let me steer clear of romance for a while, okay?"

To which Sweeney drawled with mock remorse, "Aw shucks, Ira. Just when I thought you and me was startin' to hit it off."

It took a minute, and then everybody broke into a round of howling laughter that made a very enjoyable cap to the evening.

CHAPTER 35

As it turned out, the bitter north wind did play a part in what was revealed the following day. But hardly in the way Lone had expressed concern over. It played no role in adversely affecting visibility but, rather, by dying out in the middle of the night, the stillness it left behind made it possible for Sweeney to notice something more immediately important than any sighting of distant mountains.

"I smelled it first," the old wrangler was explaining in a low voice as he and Lone crouched atop the rock ridge above their camp. "As a young man, my first year cowboyin', I got caught in a prairie fire that most near ended not only my cowboy career but almost my life. That was down in Kansas. Ever since then, the slightest whiff of smoke anywhere out on the open prairie that I don't know the source of, my sniffer most always warns me long before I see any sign of the fire causin' it."

"Well I can't claim to smell it," Lone replied, also whispering as he peered through his field glasses at a faint glimmer of light away off to the southeast. "But that's a fire, sure enough. A campfire, not much doubt, the way it's holding to one spot."

"I make it down mighty close to the river," Sweeney judged. "If that wind hadn't died off and left everything so still like it done an hour or so back, the smoke smell would have kept gettin' carried clean away and not even my fidgety sniffer would've tripped to it. Once it did, though, I climb up here for a better look-see and was able to spot what your glasses are now showin' even clearer."

Sweeney had been manning the last watch of the night (him, Lone and Ira each taking three-hour turns) when the scent alerted him. It was an hour or so ahead of daybreak, at which time he would have started waking the others. As it was, he'd rousted only Lone and left Tru and Ira continuing to sleep, as they remained doing now.

"Whoever they are," Lone said, finally lowering the binoculars and letting them dangle around his neck on a leather strap, "they must be camped in amongst some trees or brush. I can see the flames lickin' up, but I can't make out any shapes connected to 'em."

"Whoever they are," Sweeney echoed. "Since we didn't see any cattle or wranglers or ranch buildings all day yesterday, you pretty much gotta figure it's somebody on the move. Like us. Wouldn't you say?"

"Seems like."

"And since you didn't see any sign of anybody on our back trail when you made your rear sweep yesterday afternoon, that kinda suggests to me they must have moved up pretty fast and settled in down there late, maybe even after dark. That sound about right to you?"

"What it sounds like to me," Lone said, a corner of his mouth quirking upward, "is that you think there's a good chance whoever's down there might be up to no good. I pickin' up the right idea?"

Sweeney expelled some air. "All I'm sayin' is that considerin' our circumstances, make that *your* circumstances, if you want to be exact, I think we oughta look at it as there bein' at least a chance they're showin' up with bad intentions."

"I got no argument for that," Lone said. "The trick is gonna be figurin' out a way to determine for sure what they're up to and then, in case bad intentions is the answer, be prepared to ruin any such plan."

******

Ira's forehead was laddered with deep seams of worry as his eyes darted back and forth between Lone and Sweeney. "Are you sure that's a good idea? The two of you riding over there and confronting them, I mean?"

"Whether or not it turns into a confrontation," Lone replied, "is strictly up to what the purpose of that outfit turns out to be. If they're just peaceful travelers like us, on their way to conduct some business in Fort Collins or maybe one of the other towns that have sprung up along the foothills, then all we'll do is bid 'em a good mornin' and wish 'em well on their way. But if they're a pack of bounty hunters on the prowl to collect Benton's twenty-five hundred. Well, then yeah, a confrontation will likely happen instead."

"How will you know for sure if they are bounty hunters?" asked Tru.

"They'll have a look about 'em that I'm pretty sure I can spot," Lone told her. "If that ain't enough, me and Sweeney have a plan to bait 'em, if need be, for the sake of makin' sure."

After roughing out the details of said plan between them, Lone and Sweeney had slipped down from the ridge and awakened Tru and Ira even though it wasn't yet quite daybreak. They told them about the nearby presence of others and of their suspicions that it might signal trouble. Then Lone added how he and Sweeney intended to ride over and see for sure what was afoot.

That's the part Ira was having trouble accepting. "Why put it to a test at all? Why force their hand?" he wanted to know. "You said they don't seem to be aware we're even over here, right? So why not leave it at that? We can just stay put for a few hours, maybe all morning, another half day isn't that crucial to us and give them time to move on. That way, no matter what their purpose, they will have passed by with no risk of trouble."

Sweeney eyed him under a sharply arched brow. "And you think, if they're men with enough bark on 'em to be willin' to kill for money, they'll be satisfied with that? Fooled by it? The way they came up on us so fast late yesterday shows they been ridin' hard toward something. If that something is McGantry and us with him, they got to know we're travelin' by wagon and therefore coverin' ground a lot slower than them. Meanin' if they don't catch up with us in another day or so, they're bound to figure out they overshot us and then swing around and backtrack for another try."

"Which could result in them catchin' us in the wide open, the worst position for us to find ourselves in," Lone said, aiming to add some extra impact to Sweeney's words. "If we had to fight them as a group, we'd be better off forting up and doin' it right here where we at least got the ridge at our backs."

"Maybe we should do that, then," Ira came back, his voice taking on an excited tone. "You could do something to draw their attention, make them aware we *are* over here. When they come to investigate, you can make your assessment and if it turns out they're what you suspect, then we can all confront them like you said, from a forted up position."

Lone was getting annoyed. "So put Tru and you, too, you damn fool unnecessarily in the path of flyin' lead? That's your idea of a good plan? We have no idea how many are in that bunch or how well equipped they might be to keep us pinned down for a prolonged length of time. Came to that, there'd be the factor of them havin' access to the river for water and us eventually running out if it dragged on for very long. So you see, just because making a stand here might be better than gettin' caught in the open. It sure as hell ain't something to bring on if we can help it."

"You need to get hold of yourself, Ira," Tru said sternly. "Hasn't Lone proven often enough that his judgment can be trusted?"

"I know, I know." Ira's face twisted with anguish. "But with so much riding on the line, what if his judgment is off this time? What if him and Sweeney ride over there but don't make it back? Where does that leave you and me?"

"Same as you'd've been if I hadn't made it back from going after that Halsey boy," Lone answered. "Remember? Like I told you then, in the first place I don't plan on failin' when I set out on something. But if I should, now like then, you and Tru got it in you to finish okay without me. Hell, you're in even better shape here than you were that time. You're only two, two-and-a-half days out from Fort Collins. Just drop down and follow the river the rest of the way in. Far as that bunch over there, if they're bounty hunters and they manage to cut down me and Sweeney then I don't see 'em having much interest in the pair of you. They'll be in too big a hurry to haul me somewhere to show proof of death so's they can collect their money."

Ira swallowed visibly and had trouble meeting Lone's eyes. "Jesus, Lone. If you're trying to reassure a body, you go about it by painting an awful grim picture."

"I'm just tellin' it straight, that's all." Lone's gaze bore into him all the harder. "But if you want to talk reassurance. The last time we went through this, I figured if things went bad for me, I could still count on you to do right by Peg. But the way you're acting now…"

The color drained from Ira's face. He opened his mouth as if to protest sharply, but then halted whatever it was he was going to say. The anguished expression returned to his face. Several beats passed and then, when he finally did speak, his voice was low and raspy. "You're right. I had that coming. And Tru was right, too I need to get hold of myself. I don't know what came over me. After all you two have done for me, I almost let the old despair back in. But I won't. I've shut that door again now. Permanent. And no matter what else, I want you to believe once more that you could count on me to do right by ol' Peg if for any reason you wasn't there."

An expressionless Lone held Ira's eyes for another long count. Then, with a measured nod, he said, "That's more like it."

Next he swung his attention to Sweeney. "You ready to saddle up and go say good morning to our new neighbors?"

Sweeney grunted. "Long as it ain't no formal affair, I plumb forgot to bring along my Sunday-go-to-meetin' suit."

"That's okay. I got a hunch that wearin' a six-gun with a full wheel is the smartest way to dress for this shindig," Lone told him. "Let's find out."

CHAPTER 36

With the sun just short of peeking above the rim of the eastern horizon, Lone and Sweeney approached the camp by the river. They could see three men milling about, appearing to be only a short time out of their bedrolls.

One was an elderly, gray-whiskered gent stoking up the campfire whose smoky, dwindling flames had earlier alerted Sweeney. He still had a blanket draped over his bony shoulders and the spindly arms reaching out from under it weren't much bigger around than some of the twigs he was feeding into the fire. Across from him squatted a husky younger man with bulging jowls and pinched facial features that at the moment were concentrating intently on the task of using the butt of his pistol to pound on a lumpy, filthy hanky laid out atop a flat rock in front of him, mashing the handful of coffee beans wrapped inside. A couple feet away, another pinch-faced hombre with a sagging gut was bent over a big iron skillet, lining it with strips of bacon he was slicing with a grimy-bladed Bowie knife.

Lone slowed Ironsides to a walk and called out from a few yards off. "Hello the camp!"

Without lifting his head, the old man responded in a voice made hoarse by too many years of pouring cheap rotgut whiskey down his throat. "What the hell you hollerin' for? You think me and my boys didn't see you comin' long before this? You figure you gotta bellow like some goddamn moose or something to get us to pay attention?"

"No. 'Course not," Lone said after exchanging sidelong glances with Sweeney. "Anybody can see you and your boys are a real alert bunch."

"You damn betcha we are," grunted the old man. Finally, he turned his head and scowled at the two riders through watery, bloodshot eyes. "What the hell you doin' out here in the middle of nowhere and why you comin' 'round to bother us?"

"We're just passin' through these parts," Lone answered. "Thing is, we're lookin' to, ah, catch up with an old friend. We missed him back in Julesburg but heard he was headed this way. Far as botherin' you folks, that sure wasn't our intent. We saw your fire, reckoned you were fellow travelers like us, thought it'd be neighborly to swing by and say hi."

"Neighborly, eh?" The old man reached up with one hand and lazily scratched under his chin, the scrape of dirt-caked nails on the tough gray whiskers sounding like a file on a horseshoe. "I had a neighbor once, long time back. A good ol' boy, he was. Full of fun yarns, fair about takin' his turn when it came to providin' a jug to pass around. Then I came home unexpected one day and caught the lowdown snake in bed with my woman. Kilt him on the spot. Her too. That was down in Tennessee, never mind 'zactly where. Ain't ever been back since, and ain't ever had no truck with neighbors since, neither."

"Mama was a no-good slut, wasn't she, Daddy?" blurted

the saggy-gutted bacon slicer with a malicious grin.

"Now damn it, Zeke, how many times I have to tell you about talkin' like that!" barked the old man. "Yeah, it's a pure fact your mama was a rotten slut. But that's for me to say. You, you need to show some respect. After all, she was your mother."

Looking on and listening, it seemed evident to Lone that he was witnessing signs of inbreeding, possibly madness. Clearing his throat, he said, "Okay. Seein's how me and my pard never meant to bother you folks, like I said, especially given your bad experience with neighbors and all, we'll just go ahead and be on our way. Before we do, though, wonder if I might ask you a quick question?"

"Such as?"

"This fella I mentioned, the one we're lookin' to catch up with. well, we can't help thinkin' we should have run into him by now," Lone explained. "That's begun to make us wonder is if it's possible, considerin' all this empty all around, we might have rode right on past at some point without spotting him. So what I want to ask you, since you appear to have come across some of the same ground, did you happen to see anybody else back that way in the past day or two?"

The old man didn't answer right away. His eyes turned shrewd as they drifted from Lone to Sweeney and then back again. "What's this fella's name?" he wanted to know.

Lone traded glances with Sweeney again before answering, "I could give you a name, sure. But the thing is, see, this rascal has got himself in a sort of situation where he might not be usin' the name we know him by. So the name I tell you might not fit some other one you heard and it could just confuse the matter."

The old man scowled. "Any fella who goes around

changin' his name sounds to me like a scoundrel, maybe an outlaw. Somebody on the run."

Sweeney tried an easy grin. "Aw, you know how it is, old timer. It's entirely possible for an hombre to sometimes get crossways of certain people in a certain place without really deservin' to be labeled an outlaw straight across the board."

"That don't make a whole lot of sense." The scowl only intensified. "And I might have a few years on you, stranger, but you look seasoned enough so that you oughta know better than to speak disrespectful to someone whose hospitality you're seekin'."

The two younger men immediately stopped focusing on their respective tasks and cut piggy-eyed glares in Sweeney's direction. "It ain't polite to disrespect people, mister," said Zeke, the saggy-bellied one. "Especially not our Daddy!" added the other one, a distinct edge of menace in his tone.

Lone went rigid in his saddle. "Now hold on a minute."

"Hold on indeed! Everybody!" the old man spoke sharply. "Zeke, Zack. It makes your daddy mighty proud to see his boys so quick to leap to his defense. But calm down, you hear? This situation don't call for nothing like that. So, I repeat, calm down. My choice of the word 'disrespect' might have been a bit too strong. In fact, much as I hate to admit it, I might have been the first to show a bit of disrespect and got this whole thing off on the wrong foot."

"For my part, me bein' no spring chicken myself," said Sweeney, "maybe I ain't careful enough about sayin' things like 'old timer'. Just 'cause it don't bother me, don't mean I shouldn't consider it might others."

"See there?" said the old man. "No harm was meant, so none will be taken. And as far as my long-standin' grudge against anybody tryin' to act neighborly. Well, maybe it's time to give that old dog another chance to hunt." He jabbed a bony finger toward the large coffee pot perched on the edge of the fire. "That water oughta be plenty hot enough ain't you got them beans mashed about sufficient, Zack?"

"Reckon so, Daddy."

"Then dump 'em on in the pot and let 'em set to brewin'." Turning to squint up at Lone and Sweeney once again, the old man said, "We're travelin' a mite poor so I can't offer you fellas any bacon or biscuits. We can stand you a few swallows of coffee, though. So if you can furnish a couple of cups out of your own gear and want to go ahead and light down, we'll pour all around and maybe jaw a bit about this scoundrel you're tryin' to catch up with."

Lone noted that, at all times except to poke out a scrawny arm or hand once in awhile, the old man was being careful to keep the blanket pulled close around him. This was enough to make the former scout strongly suspect the shrewd patriarch had a gun under there that he wanted very much to keep concealed from the new arrivals.

Nevertheless, Lone aimed to play this out. On the one hand, it was hard to see this family of inbred dullards as a serious threat, even if they *were* after the bounty on him. On the other hand, Lone had encountered more than a few simple-minded individuals capable of being plenty damned dangerous. So he still needed to determine for sure if Zeke and Zack and their daddy had in mind to try and collect Angus Benton's blood money. If so, then he couldn't afford to leave them behind as unfinished business.

Even though he caught a skeptical look from Sweeney out the corner of his eye, Lone announced, "Ain't hardly got it in me to turn down a cup of fresh, hot coffee on a still brisk morning." So saying, he swung down from his saddle and Sweeney somewhat reluctantly followed suit a moment later.

A handful of minutes after that, fisting tin cups pulled from their saddlebags, Lone and Sweeney were squatting beside the fire and holding out said cups for Zack to fill with steaming black brew from the big pot. They were positioned so that the old man was close on Lone's left; Zack, once he'd finished pouring, settled back directly on the other side of the fire; Sweeney was to Lone's right; and Zeke was just past him.

Having been served first, the old man loudly slurped his first taste and then declared, "Ah, yes. Strong and black and bitter, 'zactly how I like it. You done good, Zack."

"Thanks, Daddy. Just how you taught me," responded husky, jowly Zack, who appeared to be the younger of the two brothers.

Turning to Lone, the old man said, "Reckon this is the point, 'fore we go any farther, where we ought to do some more introducin'. I already pointed out my boys, Zeke and Zack. Me, I'm Darrell Crowder, from down Tennessee way, like I also already done said. Now I hope you fellas, unlike this name changin' scoundrel you're chasin', have got some kind of permanent handles we can call you by?"

Lone grinned reassuringly. "Of course we do. My name's O'Malley. My pard here is Virgil Sweeney."

"That's better," said Crowder. "Now this other fella. the one you're lookin' to catch up with. if you can't say a name we might recognize, how is it you figure we might know if we seen any sign of him?"

"Fair question," Lone allowed. "I should have added something right from the get-go. Should've mentioned he ain't travelin' alone. No matter what name he might go by, he can best be identified by the fact he's in the company of a young Chinese woman."

Crowder's eyes instantly hardened. "A celestial?"

"That's right. They're rolling along in a big ol' wagon. Way we was told in Julesburg was that a couple other men might also be ridin' with 'em. Can't say how long that will last, but the fella we're after and the Chinese gal have been together since back in North Platte, Nebraska."

"We ain't got much truck with no celestials, do we, Daddy?" remarked a dour-faced Zack.

At the same time, a puzzled-looking Zeke said, "But don't them sound like the very folks we…"

"Shut up!" his father cut him short. Then, frowning fiercely, he growled, "Heathen celestials. Like the Negroid race and the red savages who used to infest this land, are a people so foul that the color of their skin is tinted by the impurity of the blood runnin' through their veins."

Lone felt an immediate loathing toward this attitude. But he also sensed it might be a scab that could be picked at and lifted in order to release more of the pus underneath as a means to find out additional feelings and intentions of this miserable wretch.

"Tinted skin or not," Lone said with a wistful sigh, "the descriptions we heard of this gal made her sound like a real exotic beauty whose company would sure take the edge off some of the hardship of a long trek across these barren stretches."

"I won't hear such talk, especially not in front of my boys!" Crowder declared forcefully. "Consortin' with the mud races, practically a whole 'nother species, is an abomination. And to seek pleasure from such, as you are implyin', is disgustin' beyond even the grace of God!"

"Whoa now," said Sweeney. "You're gettin' awful het up over a straightforward answer to a question you asked, ain't you? And for somebody who was preachin' against disrespect just a minute ago, you're borderin' awful close to that as well."

"You're damned right I am," Crowder responded. "I have no respect for liars and deceivers, doubly lackin' for any who make light of consortin' with a mud race tramp!"

"What you're sayin' don't all the way make sense," grated Lone, "but I'm pretty sure you need to do some beggin'-your-pardon and be quick about it."

Crowder's eyes blazed with indignant fury. "Like hell I will! What is your sorry tale of tryin' to catch up with 'an old friend' but a total falsehood? Dare you deny it? Yeah, you're no doubt tryin' to catch up with him, but not out of friendship, you want to catch up with him for the sake of collectin' the bounty on his murderin' head! You think hidin' his name was gonna fool anybody? You think McGantry travelin' with a celestial gal was some kind of secret known only to you?"

"Okay, so you know his name and the rest." Lone scowled. "I take it that means you and your boys are also makin' a run at collecting the bounty for yourselves?"

Crowder just glared at him.

"Guess that means we're in a race," said Sweeney.

Crowder's glare shifted to the old wrangler. "Me and my boys don't see it as no game, no damn race. For us, it's a matter of survival. We been scratchin' in the dirt and livin' poor our whole lives. We mean to put those days behind us once and for all."

"Comes to survival," Sweeney allowed, "if and when somebody does catch up with McGantry that's gonna be the real key to collectin' the money, survivin' a showdown with him in order to claim it."

"That'll work itself out in time," Crowder insisted. "The

main thing is bein' the one who makes it to McGantry first."

"Which brings it right back to bein' a race. Like I said."

Crowder gave a slow wag of his shaggy gray head. "Not quite. It's gonna quit bein' a race for you and your lyin', connivin' friend because you ain't gonna be part of it no more. Take 'em, boys!"

CHAPTER 37

The two husky, jowly Crowder sons responded to their father's command with surprising speed and readiness. Zack immediately reached for the pistol he had laid close to one side after using it to mash coffee beans; Zeke's bacon-slicing Bowie once more flashed into sight, its greasy blade reflecting blurred firelight. And the old man himself, just as Lone had suspected, shrugged back his blanket and thrust forth the muzzle of a Henry repeating rifle.

But Lone had harbored more than just suspicions. He'd also been poised and ready ever since taking his place at the campfire. And his wilderness-honed reflexes took a back seat to very few men.

Before Crowder's command was all the way out of his mouth, Lone was dropping back onto his rump and kicking out savagely with his left leg. He drove the heel of his boot hard into the old man's shoulder, jarring him off balance. As part of the same motion, even as he was dropping back, Lone twisted at the waist and swept out with his right arm, flinging the scalding contents of the coffee cup he held in that hand straight into Zack's face.

The younger son screeched in agony as the hot liquid hit him. He didn't finish grasping the pistol but instead brought up both hands to wipe frantically at his stinging eyes and blistering cheeks.

Joining Zack's screech was the sudden roar of his daddy's rifle, the old man squeezing off a round blindly, even as he was being kicked over onto one side. Reacting to this, Lone twisted at the waist once more, now turning back to reach with his left arm. Grabbing the bottom edge of the blanket Crowder had been holding shawl-like up around his shoulders, Lone yanked it up in a high, hard sweep and jerked it down equally hard over the old bastard's head and face. This resulted in Crowder flailing so frantically in response that he caused two things to happen: First, he triggered another round from the rifle, even more blindly than before; second, he pitched himself forward in such desperation that he fell onto the edge of the fire.

More screeching ripped through the scene.

Crowder howled as flames licked up inside the blanket he was entangled within and, across the way, Zeke howled in pain and disbelief at what his father's second wild trigger pull had done. "Daddy! Daddy! You shot me. I think you hurt me bad."

Sure enough, the knife-wielding oldest son had been knocked back onto his right hip. He lay there, propping himself on one elbow with blood pouring down over his right arm and smeared across his chest from a gaping, gushing bullet hole about four inches in from his shoulder socket. The knife he'd been attempting to bring into play was gripped in his bloody right fist.

Sweeney, his sidearm drawn and aimed loosely at Zeke, rose to his feet and took a cautious step toward the fallen man. "By the look of things," he said, "you'd better lay back and let me try to put some pressure on that wound or you're gonna bleed out and it won't take long."

Zeke didn't say anything but appeared to sag back some. When Sweeney took another step closer, though, Zeke suddenly lunged up with a vicious curse. Switching the Bowie to his left hand, Zeke leaned into a blinding fast backhand slash that laid open Sweeney's left thigh. The old wrangler jumped back, staggering, so that a shot from his six-gun sizzled wide of Zeke even at such close range.

But an instant later, a second handgun, Lone's Colt Peacemaker, drawn unhesitatingly and swiftly when he saw Zeke getting ready to slash again, roared and spat a tongue of flame. The .44 slug hurled by this shot was not off its mark. Zeke's left eyeball disappeared, bullet-driven through his skull and exiting out the back of his head in a spray of gore and bone splinters. All of a sudden he no longer had to worry about bleeding out from the shoulder wound.

The sight and sound of his father and brother in so much strife was enough to make Zack shake off his own painful misfortune. Issuing a bellow of defiant rage, he dragged his right hand away from his scalded face and once more reached for the coffee-grinder pistol. But it was too little too late. Way too late. In as much as both Lone and Sweeney already had their hands filled and their own rage running hot, Zeke never stood a chance. His fingers barely started to curl around the grips of the pistol before a pair of slugs hammered simultaneously into him, lifting him up on his toes, driving him back a staggered half step and then dropping him flat.

This left only the old man who finally clawed free of his smoldering blanket and immediately froze, wild-haired and wide-eyed, to gawk in horror at the sprawled forms of his sons. The Henry rifle in one gnarled hand hung loose and seemingly forgotten. "My boys. My strong, beautiful boys," he rasped barely above a whisper. "You've kilt 'em."

"You're the one who set 'em in front of our guns, you poisonous sack of guts," Lone told him. "Your hand did them in as much as anybody's."

Crowder's chin quivered. "But what will I do now?"

"You can start by buryin' them," Lone said, reaching out and taking the rifle from a grip that offered no resistance. "Then you can go on with your life. One I hope is long on misery and short on time."

Crowder remained motionless, tears starting to run down his cheeks as he continued staring at the bodies of his two sons.

"How bad is that cut to your leg?" Lone asked Sweeney.

"Sore as hell and pure ruination to a good pair of britches," came the answer. "But it ain't too deep, I don't think—I'll be okay."

"Tru will fix it up when we return to the wagon," Lone said confidently. "For now, get the weight off it by climbing back up in your saddle. Then give me a couple minutes to gather up this bunch's weapons and horses and we'll be on our way."

Crowder looked around, alarm showing through his sadness. "Wait. You ain't gonna leave me out here on foot, are you?"

"That's the general idea," Lone replied tersely. "After you get done buryin' your boys, keep followin' the river. It'll eventually lead you somewhere. Or, if you want to do the world a favor, just fling your sorry old ass in and drown."

CHAPTER 38

The knife wound to Sweeney's leg was worse than the old wrangler initially thought, requiring some stitches to properly close it when he and Lone got back to camp. Lone did the needlework, Tru then gently applied some healing salve and bandages. Sweeney participated by throwing down a couple belts of whiskey from Lone's saddlebag flask. (Something, Lone couldn't help but notice, that drew a rather longing gaze from Ira; a sign the poor devil was still fighting his craving for alcohol, yet was so far holding his own in the battle.)

"That puny scratch don't worry me so much," Sweeney scoffed while he was being tended. "What concerns me more is the couple swallows of that vile coffee I choked down after watchin' Zack mash the beans in his grimy bandanna. If that don't bring on some kind of poisonin' to my insides, then this cut sure ain't gonna hurt me."

Lone made a distasteful face. "You actually *drank* some of that coffee?"

"Didn't you? You're the one who accepted that old rascal's invitation to squat and join him and his idjit sons when it came to havin' some."

"I accepted the invitation, but only pretended to drink the coffee," Lone explained. "Just touching that brew to my lips was enough to 'bout strangle me and I don't mean because it was too hot."

"Well, I'll be damned," Sweeney muttered. "That old man was right, you *are* a connivin' sonofagun."

Lone shrugged. "We accomplished what we set out to, didn't we? We found out they were for sure bounty hunters and then we eliminated 'em as a threat."

"I've got to say, it was nerve-wracking for me and Tru to hear all that shooting and then have no way of knowing for several minutes that you two came out of it okay," spoke up Ira.

Sweeney gave him a look. "*You* were nerve-wracked? Bein' in the midst of flyin' lead ain't exactly good for settlin' a body's nerves, neither. But by the time it came to that, I already had that coffee in me and half-figured I was a goner anyway. So the risk of a quick bullet didn't seem so bad."

"It appears to me," said Tru as she tied the last knot on the bandage she'd applied, "that you should have been worrying less about bad coffee and flying bullets and more about a sharp-edged knife."

Sweeney's eyebrows lifted. "You might be makin' more of a point than you know. Come to think of it, that knife of Zeke's didn't look a whole lot cleaner than his brother's bandanna. Jesus, can you get blood poisonin' from rancid bacon grease?"

"I don't know," Lone said. "But what I do know, not to sound cold-hearted, is that we can find out just as well on the trail as we can sitting here jawing about it. So since we went to all the trouble of clearing our path, at least for the time being, how about we commence getting underway again and trying to still gain sight of those mountains by tomorrow?"

Lone's urging nevertheless allowed time for some biscuits and a pot of *good* coffee before they started rolling once more. In recognition of Sweeney's injury, it was decided that him trying to sit a saddle all day would not only cause considerable discomfort but would likely interfere with the healing process. For these reasons, he joined Ira (who was an admittedly incompetent horseman) on the seat of the wagon while Tru assumed the role of the group's second outrider. In this manner they traveled through the balance of the day, steadily and without further incident, accomplishing satisfactory progress in spite of the ragged start.

When they stopped for night camp, an examination and re-dressing of Sweeney's wound revealed it to be doing well. No fresh bleeding, no sign of inflammation or infection.

"So far, so good," Sweeney self-appraised. "Looks like I'm gonna pull through and even get to keep both pins. The only problem that'll leave is the doggone scar."

"What is your worry about the scar?" Tru wanted to know. "It is in a place where no one will ever see."

"That's my point," Sweeney insisted. "I've got this swell yarn to spin, how me and Lone blazed it out with those polecats and I took a knife slash in the process but without shuckin' my britches, I got no way to back it up by showin' my scar."

"Well," said Lone, "you *could* go around dropping your drawers if you really want to show off the scar so bad. That will be sure to draw an audience for the yarn you've got to spin. 'Course it might also draw some unwanted attention from the local law. "

"Or," Ira added, "the next time somebody pulls a knife on you, you could try convincing them to take a swipe at your jaw. That would leave you with what you could pass off as a dueling scar. You know, the kind dashing heroes have in those romance novels that make all the ladies swoon."

"Fat lot of help you two are," Sweeney grumbled with mock severity. "You're just jealous you got no battle scars of your own to show, no matter what part of your mangy hides you bare."

******

Their steady, uninterrupted progress continued into the following day. And then, late in the afternoon, exactly as Lone had predicted, they came within sight of the mountains. At first they were merely a lumpy blue line along the western horizon. But they were discernible at last and seeing them after all the anticipation produced a sense of general excitement that warranted bringing the wagon to a halt long enough to drink deeply of the view.

"How long before we actually reach them?" Tru asked.

"Mountains in the distance are deceiving," Lone told her. "They're always farther than they seem. But if we keep at it like we have been, without interruption, we should make it by day after tomorrow. We'll reach where the Poudre River feeds into the South Platte, then we'll make a jog and follow the Poudre straight up to Fort Collins."

"You make that final jog sound awful easy," Sweeney pointed out. "What if there's a reception committee or maybe more than one, waitin' somewhere along in there? If word about Benton's bounty has spread, then you gotta reckon it must include about Fort Collins being your destination. For any lookin' to collect, there's bound to be some who'd think it a lot easier to set up and wait for you to show up there than it has been tryin' to catch you out here on the trail."

"Yeah, the same has occurred to me," Lone admitted. "But we didn't come this far not to do what we set out for. Tru's got business in the town, I got a matter to tend to farther up Poudre Canyon. Getting those things done is what this has been about from the start and finishing 'em is still what I full intend to do."

CHAPTER 39

They continued on through the afternoon until the sun sank behind what had become ever more distinguishable as jagged, snow-capped mountain peaks in the distance. When they stopped to make camp, Lone tended the horses, Tru re-dressed Sweeney's wound, and Ira prepared supper. It didn't take long after the meal was finished for the weary bunch to be ready to settle down for the night. Lone announced he would take first watch, leaving Sweeney and Ira to reach gratefully for their bedrolls.

An hour passed. The stars began to thicken in the night sky and a fat slice of crescent moon rose to join them.

Lone took up his watch position on a grassy slope overlooking the camp. A wind scour, where the grass had been worn away to leave a narrow vertical strip of bare, sunbaked sand and gravel, gave him a spot to lean comfortably back against. With the sun gone, the air began to cool rapidly.

Good conditioning for the high, cold reaches that lay ahead of him in order to get Peg to his Forever Mountain, Lone thought idly. So much else had happened since he'd heard his old friend's dying wish and so much else still remained to be done, that it was sometimes easy to forget what the core purpose of this journey really was. But no, Lone told himself; that wasn't true. He'd encountered some distractions to be sure, but he'd never for a minute lost sight of his main goal. Make that *two* goals. First, put Peg to rest alongside his beloved. Second, track down and settle the score with the thieving, murderous scum who'd cut short his life.

Even if accomplishing those things meant turning his back on the feelings simmering between him and Tru.

"Lone?"

At first he thought the voice speaking his name was his imagination, part of his brooding. But then he realized with a start that Tru was actually there, gliding silently up the slope toward him.

"Lordamighty, girl," he said in a harsh whisper. "Don't you know that sneaking up on a fella in the dark can be dangerous?"

"Nonsense. You wouldn't hurt me. Besides, I was not sneaking," Tru protested. "I merely came to where you are. Though I saw you appeared lost in thought. That was why I spoke."

Lone expelled a ragged breath. "Yeah, lost in thought is what I guess I was. Hell of a way for a fella standing watch to be caught."

"There was no harm done."

"But there could have been. That' the point. Under some circumstances," Lone told her, "not being alert on watch could get a fella shot. Either by whoever he was supposed to be on the lookout for or by the command he was supposed to be watching over."

"I don't understand."

"Never mind. What have you got there?"

Tru held out the object in her hands that Lone had inquired about. "It is a cup of coffee. I heated up what was left in the pot and then poured this for you. It is probably quite strong but I thought you would still welcome it against the chill."

"You're right, I do," Lone told her, taking the cup. Then: "But why ain't you asleep? You must be exhausted. It's been a long day and I mean to push hard again tomorrow in order to bring this trip to a close."

"I tried to sleep, but could not," Tru replied.

"Yeah, I reckon you've got plenty on your mind. All that's happened already, plus the big changes yet to come as you get settled into your new place." Lone drank some of the coffee. It had indeed grown pretty stout but was still good.

Tru said, "Yes, I have been thinking about all of that. But mostly I have been thinking about the things you and Mr. Sweeney spoke of earlier this afternoon, how there likely will be still more men waiting to try and collect the bounty on you when we get to Fort Collins."

"It only makes sense that will probably be the case." Lone made a sour face. "Was I on their end of the situation, I figure that's how I'd probably play it."

"But you never would be—*could* be—killers like them."

Lone's mouth pulled momentarily into a tight, straight line. "In case you ain't noticed, kid, I have a kinda bad habit of not being exactly shy when it comes to killin' men."

"But never just for dirty money. Blood money. And I asked you to quit calling me 'kid'!"

"Okay, strike the kid part. But there's no getting around the rest of what I said." Lone gazed earnestly into her eyes. "In fact, as we approach Fort Collins I'm gonna have my eyes peeled sharp and I'll be hair-trigger primed. Any so-

and-so who gives me the stink eye for more than half a second or otherwise looks like he might have hard feelin's toward me, I'm apt to shoot first and ask questions later. I don't care how many other coffins I have to fill in order to clear a path for me to get that one down there in the wagon to where I promised to take it. Understand?"

Tru met his gaze and for the first time since they'd left North Platte she was looking back at him with something less than full adoration.

After an uncertain pause, Tru said, "Yes, I understand. Completely. What I also understand. What I felt so urgent about coming to discuss with you. Is how arriving in Fort Collins in my company will greatly increase the chances of you being targeted."

"Not sure I follow you," responded a frowning Lone.

"It's not like the money Angus Benton has offered is accompanied by a legitimate Wanted posted, something containing an image of you," Tru explained. "All anyone has to go on is a name and a rough description. And while you are large and rugged looking, such traits are not entirely lacking in other men on the frontier. In a setting like Fort Collins, where you are not commonly known, your appearance alone will not make you stand out. Nor will your name unless you go out of your way to announce it."

"If you have a point to make, I wish you'd get to it."

"The point is *me*," Tru came back somewhat tartly. "A stranger arriving in town accompanied by a young Chinese girl that is what will make you stand out for anyone seeking to collect the bounty on you! Don't you see? The way you and Mr. Sweeney told how things erupted with those three men back at the river. It all changed after you mentioned me. The *celestial*. Isn't that how it went?"

Lone scowled. "As a matter of fact, yeah. It turned real

nasty real quick. But that evil old man had a particular hate for Chinese. That don't mean everybody we run into…"

"I'm not talking about how anyone feels toward me being Chinese," Tru cut him off. "I'm saying that word has clearly spread to those looking to collect the bounty on you that the way you can be spotted is to watch for a man traveling with a Chinese girl."

"By God," Lone growled, his scowl deepening, "I think you might be on to something."

"I'm certain I am," Tru said confidently. "That means the only thing to do is for us to separate before we arrive in Fort Collins."

Lone nodded thoughtfully. "Yeah, we could work out something like that. You, Ira, and Sweeney could go on in with the wagon, I'd hold off a while and then maybe under the cover of darkness follow along and meet up with you at your uncle's…"

Tru interrupted him again. "No, that won't work either."

"Why not?"

"I think we have to consider that anyone traveling with me might be mistaken by an over-anxious bounty hunter as being you," Tru said. "Maybe not Ira, but Mr. Sweeney comes close in appearance to a somewhat older version of you. And isn't it reasonable to think that the kind of men we're talking about might be prone to, as you said yourself a minute ago, shoot first and ask questions later?"

Lone regarded her. Despite the somberness of the subject under discussion, it was not lost on him how lovely she looked in the silver-bluish wash of illumination from the moon and stars. He wanted to take her in his arms, but instead he just said, "You've been thinking about this from all the different angles, ain't you?"

"I told you, I could not sleep. Yes, I've been thinking

about it a great deal."

"So did you come up with any better ideas than mine?"

Tru was ready with a prompt answer. "The only way I can see is for me to be the one who goes in separate."

Lone was shaking his head before she was even done speaking. "Oh no. I don't like the sound of that at all."

"Why not?" Tru challenged. "Uncle Hai has written that Fort Collins has a sizable Chinese population, so there is no reason to think I would draw any undue attention. Same for you men and the wagon, without me. Freighters of all kinds come and go regularly in any busy town."

"All that may be true," Lone allowed. "But turning you loose on your own with everything that's goin' on. You gotta understand how hard that goes against my grain. There must be some other way."

A brief smile touched Tru's lips. "I appreciate your concern. But you looking out for me, I fear, is something we both may have gotten too used to. It is only fair to remember that I have also demonstrated some competency on my own, up to and including the fact that one of the bullets that killed Isaac Halsey came from my rifle."

"That's something you must never speak of," Lone said sternly. "It's known only to you and me, and best it stays that way."

"I can accept that," Tru replied. "But what I cannot nor will not accept is being treated like a delicate flower, a child. Especially not if me showing some strength and independence can help keep you safe."

Lone heaved a sigh. "Okay. Look, you've raised some really worthwhile points. Some angles I might not have thought of otherwise. But let's not rush into a plan on how we're gonna react, okay? We've still got a day, day-and-a-half to mull on it until we can agree on a way that suits everybody. Deal?"

Tru gave a small nod. "Again, I can accept that. But remember also what I said I will not accept."

"Fair enough," Lone told her. "I hope now you can get some sleep. I guarantee as soon my watch is over, that's what I intend to do." He tipped up the coffee cup, draining it, then handed it back to her. "Thank you for this. It sure hit the spot."

Tru took the cup but did not turn away. She gazed up at him with her wondrously exotic eyes. And then, tossing the cup aside, she did what Lone had restrained himself from doing minutes earlier. Her arms glided up over his chest and around his neck and she pulled him into a warm, longing embrace. Lone responded, his arms encircling her supple form. Their lips met eagerly, hungrily. When the kiss ended, Lone exclaimed breathlessly, "Now that *really* hit the spot!"

Pressing her velvety cheek to his, Tru whispered, "I know not what the future holds for us, Lone McGantry. I can bear it if the things you must do are destined to keep us apart. But I could not stand to see you cut down by awful men out for dirty blood money."

"I ain't crazy about that notion, neither. I'll do my darnedest not to let it happen," Lone promised her.

And then they kissed some more.

CHAPTER 40

"Look at 'em. Damned woolies. Sheep near as far as the eye can see," grumbled Sweeney. "I ain't saw any beef livestock since early this mornin'."

"Yeah. It's been quite a spell since I was over this way, I'd forgotten how sheep ranching had taken hold all through this area. Looks like it's grown even bigger," said Ira. "Helping to support it, the main crop hereabouts is sugar beets. The woolies, as you call them, really thrive on beet tops as a food source along with the natural pastureland."

Sweeney made a sour face. "No wonder I never acquired a taste for beets. Some kind of natural cowpuncher instinct in me must have recognized 'em as blasted sheep food!"

It was an hour past noon. The group had stopped briefly to rest the horses and have a bite to eat. They were making good time, having turned at the Poudre River and now continuing ever closer to Fort Collins and the majestically looming mountain peaks just beyond. Lone estimated they would be in the town by about this time tomorrow. In the meantime, the landscape had grown hillier and somewhat rockier as it ascended gradually toward the foothills. Still, there was plenty of rich grassland with increasing expanses of it, as Ira and Sweeney were currently jawing about, covered by flocks of grazing sheep.

"All I know," Sweeney declared in summation, "is that if we get to town and I can't find me a restaurant that serves good beefsteak and not just mutton, I'm liable to raise seven kinds of hell!"

"There's a good chance that will fix part of your problem," Lone told him. "You raise enough hell to get tossed in the hoosegow, I hear tell Colorado jails serve real good bread and water but no mutton."

Sweeney grunted. "Anything would be better than woolie meat."

The only one not participating in this good-natured banter was Tru, who sat nearby but was even quieter than normal. Though never overly talkative, she usually had at least a few things to add to conversations during these meal breaks. And especially now, with her destination finally so close at hand—the destination that she, more than any of the others, had endured so much to reach—a brighter, more excited mood should have been on display.

Lone, of course, knew what was weighing on her. So did the others, to a degree. Over breakfast, Lone had revealed Tru's concern that her presence in their midst might trigger attention from one or more of the bounty hunters they suspected to be waiting. And while Sweeney and Ira saw the logic in that line of thought, they—like Lone—were not at all receptive to the idea of Tru separating from them and going ahead by herself. Yet, at the same time, no one had an immediate better solution. So they left the matter unresolved, for the time being, agreeing to ponder the problem individually until somebody could come up with a better idea.

In the meantime, Tru appeared to be brooding more deeply over the matter than any of the others. Only Lone had the basis to know or at least suspect that she also was brooding over something more. That being the situation between them. Her feelings toward him, the things that stood in the way of him being able to respond in kind. What happened last night had only made things worse. It gave Tru a surge of hope that Lone had to end up dashing all over again by reminding her it changed nothing; he still had to take care of those other matters before he could commit to anything else. Not even her.

And so, as a group, they pressed on.

Continuing to make good progress toward reaching their destination.

But with much else hanging fire.

CHAPTER 41

"Tru's gone."

"What do you mean gone?"

"I mean gone. Lit a shuck. She saddled up that mustang she's been riding lately and took off."

"You were on watch why didn't you stop her?" Lone demanded.

Ira averted his eyes and hung his head. "It was just a little bit ago. I got awful groggy with daybreak coming on and I must have dozed off. The sound of her mustang breaking into a gallop is what rousted me."

"Damn it all Ira!" Lone kicked off his bedroll blankets, reached for his boots, began ramming his feet into them.

A short distance away, Sweeney was also climbing out of his bedroll. "Did I hear right? Tru's gone?"

"You heard right," Lone answered. Then he muttered again, "Damn it all!"

"I double-checked, to make sure before I raised the alarm," Ira said in a forlorn tone. "The wagon's empty and the mustang and saddle are gone. But she left this inside the wagon, propped up where it was sure to be seen. It's got your name on it, Lone."

In one hand Ira was holding a lantern, in the other a folded sheet of paper which he extended out to Lone. The former scout took the paper and then, a moment later, also the lantern. The pre-dawn murkiness made it impossible to otherwise see clearly what was written. Flicking away the drop of melted candle wax that sealed the fold, Lone shook the page open and began to read:

Dearest Lone,

I am sorry, but this is the best way for me to help you be safe. From here you must take every precaution for yourself. Please do not try to contact me. Spare me the pain of seeing you again just to say goodbye. Let Ira and Mr. Sweeney bring the wagon to my uncle's shop when it is safe to do so. I wish you Godspeed. When your other obligations are finished and only then. I hope you find your way back to me.

Your heart, Tru

The message was put down in small, very neat block printing. Only the sign-off "Your heart, Tru" was in flowing cursive. Lone had known what it basically would say, of course, even before he read the words. It was clear as soon as Ira reported Tru had ridden away. Still, the impact of it the actual act, the message backing it up, hit like a gut punch.

Lone had thought they were past Tru behaving in such a reckless manner. At supper the prior evening, the night before they would be arriving in Fort Collins, they had agreed on an alternative plan to address Tru's concern about her presence in their midst being a signal to bounty hunters on the lookout for Lone. It had boiled down to Tru and Ira taking the wagon in first and then Lone and

Sweeney hanging back and not following until after sunset. Reluctantly, Tru had gone along with trying it that way. Only now it was evident that she either had never really bought in or had changed her mind in the middle of the night and reverted to her own idea.

Sweeney and Ira had stepped discreetly away while Lone read the message. Once he was finished, they turned back. "Should we saddle up and go after her?" Sweeney asked. "'Spect we could catch up before she makes it to town."

Lone set his jaw and brooded for a long beat. Then: "No. She's made up her mind to play it this way and has already set it in motion. So we'll go along. The only thing now is to decide how best for the three of us to proceed."

Sweeney eyed him. "You got something in mind?"

"I'm working on it," Lone replied. Then, after tossing a glance toward the Godspeed pale grayness starting to creep above the eastern horizon, he added, "But since any more sleep is out of the question, I reckon we can afford taking the time to iron out details over some coffee and bacon."

"I'll stoke up the fire and get some breakfast working," said Ira.

Lone aimed a scowl his way. "You do that. But be careful how you go about it."

"What do you mean?"

"I mean watch out you don't bend over anywhere near me. because I'm fighting a powerful urge to kick you right square in the ass, Ira."

******

A handful of minutes before noon, Lone rode into Fort Collins. He was astride Ironsides, leading the three horses he and Sweeney had confiscated from the Crowders. Sweeney and Ira were bringing along the wagon, about two hours behind.

In front of a large, well maintained livery barn just within the city limits, Lone reined up. The town that stretched north, off to his right, an offshoot of the now-abandoned old fort that lay farther yet to the north, appeared prosperous and busy. Brick and wood-framed stores and businesses lined a broad main street with tidy residential pockets to either side. Farther up, the buildings looked older, shabbier, more haphazardly bunched together; the rowdier part of the settlement, it was easy to assess.

Lone remained in the saddle as he took all of this in with a wide sweep of his eyes. He liked the look and feel of the place tucked into the Rocky Mountain foothills, straddling the Poudre River as it tumbled down from the towering peaks that loomed over everything and he hoped sincerely it would not be the scene of more trouble in case there were bounty hunters lurking behind the peaceful facade. For the moment it was soothing to just pause there with the warmth of the mid-day sun on his shoulders and the back of his neck, breathing in the fresh scent of pine and a crisp hint of lingering snow that carried down from the high reaches on a gentle breeze.

"Howdy, stranger. Lookin' for a place to put up your animals?"

The question pulled Lone from his reverie and drew his attention to a man emerging from the open bay doors of the barn, brushing bits of straw and grain dust from the front of his clothing as he came forward. He looked to be about forty, beanstalk build, with carrot-colored hair, pale blue eyes, and an amiable smile under a long, thin nose whose tip was tufted with flakes of peeling skin from a recent sunburn.

Responding to the liveryman's inquiry, Lone said, "I'll

be sticking with this big gray I'm riding. But these other three, I'm lookin' to sell if you or anybody you know might be interested in buying."

"I'm Rudabaugh, like the sign says" jabbing a thumb to indicate the lettering painted on the front of the barn "and I'm always in the market for good horseflesh at a fair price. Looks like those critters you're leadin' have got some miles on 'em but appear still reasonably sound. Mind if I take a closer look?"

"By all means. Help yourself," said Lone, swinging down from the saddle. "I expect you're right about these animals having some miles on 'em. But the recent ones have all been pretty easy and they've been fed and watered good along the way. Before that, the two sorrels were packin' around a couple of plenty husky fellas so, yeah, I think it's safe to say they're sound and sturdy."

Rudabaugh began examining the first of the sorrels. "Their previous owners," he asked in a casual tone, "they give up ridin', did they?"

Lone considered a moment before replying, "You might say that. The whole of it is, they gave up living. No sense beatin' around the bush about it, I had a hand in bringin' that about. Me and a couple pards of mine. The three owl-hoots who belonged to these horses went by the name of Crowder, an old man and his sons Zeke and Zack. They came lookin' for trouble, ended up findin' a bigger dose than they could handle."

Rudabaugh continued examining the horses, showing no outward sign of alarm or concern. "Crowder, you say?"

"Uh-huh. Not sure where they hailed from."

"Not around here, I don't think. Leastways it ain't a name I'm familiar with, and I've been around a while. You mentioned a couple of partners. They get lost too in your, er, run-in with these Crowders?"

"No. They'll be along," Lone answered. "We're freighting some goods in from over Nebraska way. They're following with the wagon, I came on ahead to get the lay of the town and see if I could make a deal on these horses."

"Well, if you've ever been here before you'll find the town growin' and changin'. For the better mostly, what with the sheep and beet business growing up around it and the families that has brought in, to sort of balance out the rougher minin' element. You don't mind my sayin', you're maybe in the freightin' business nowadays but you got the look of a fella who's worked cattle in his time. You ain't got no hard feelin's toward sheepers, do you?"

"You're right about me having done some beef wranglin' among other things," Lone allowed. "That don't leave me no hard feelings against sheep or those who raise 'em, though. Never been around woolies all that much, to tell the truth, but none ever did me any harm so I'm happy to call it even."

"Good to hear," said Rudabaugh with a nod. "We don't get much of that kind of trouble any more these days, not since the sheeping has taken hold so solid, but every once in a while there are still some cowboys who come through riled about what they see as the ruination of good graze land."

Lone shrugged. "That old saw ain't my fight. I'm just here to help deliver a wagonload of stuff. And, ahead of that, see if I can find a buyer for these horses."

Rudabaugh turned from the steeldust he'd worked around to examining last. "I'm interested in bein' that buyer, if we can agree on a price. To tell the truth, I was a little iffy at first about makin' a bid. But I figure your ownership claim must be on the level, elsewise you wouldn't have been so up front about shootin' their former owners. So what are you askin'?"

Lone shook his head. "I ain't done no horse tradin' in a coon's age. You kick it off. Make me an offer."

"Okay. Thirty each."

"Whoa," Lone exclaimed. "I didn't say I've *never* done any horse tradin'. When I was twelve, I woulda balked at a lowball offer like that one. Reach a little deeper into your buying pouch, friend, and try again."

Thy went back and forth for five or six minutes before arriving at a price for the saddles as well as the horses that was reasonable though still somewhat favorable to Rudabaugh. But making a big profit from the animals was never Lone's main goal. More importantly, he was looking to use some business transactions to get a feel for the mood around town. If word of Angus Benton's bounty offer had spread widely enough, then it seemed likely that the prospect of its target eventually showing up ought to create a certain amount of anxiety among the general citizenry, apart from any who had in mind to try and claim the pay-off. It had been Lone's experience that liverymen, barbers, and bartenders were often good sources for local gossip that would convey a sense of that kind of anxiety if it existed.

In this case, liveryman Rudabaugh hadn't provided much. He was friendly and talkative enough but not even a couple broad hints from Lone nudged loose anything that resembled an awareness of the bounty business. That could be taken as a good sign that there *wasn't* an army of blood-thirsty bounty hunters waiting to pounce or it could just mean that Rudabaugh either wasn't in the know or simply didn't choose to speak of it.

CHAPTER 42

Lone rode away from the livery barn still wanting to try and get a better read off the town, as well as needing to take care of some other matters. Part of his transaction with Rudabaugh had included the purchase of a mule, knowing that one would be necessary for hauling the crate containing Peg's body up the mountain. Lone hadn't explained this to the liveryman in any detail other than to pass it off merely as a "special delivery" apart from the main freight load.

The task would also require a smaller wagon or hauling cart of some sort and for that Rudabaugh directed Lone to a blacksmith down the street who'd acquired a collection of spare wagons. One of them, a single-axle cart with a brace of sturdy, steel-rimmed wheels and a mule hitch was perfectly suited. And while Rudabaugh had suggested the blacksmith might also be interested in the Crowder guns that Lone was additionally looking to sell, that turned out not to be the case. The blacksmith, in turn, directed Lone to the proprietor of a nearby hardware store who was indeed interested in acquiring the guns and made a fair enough up-front offer to negate any reason to haggle.

Both the blacksmith and the hardware proprietor were friendly, talkative sorts but, like Rudabaugh, neither made any remark that suggested to Lone they were aware of the bounty or anticipating any trouble due to it. The closest either one came was the hardware man saying, "I can always count on making gun sales, sooner or later. If nothing else, to some of the hardcases who wander down from the north end of town. As long as they go somewhere else to use 'em, I don't mind taking their money."

Though he hadn't yet checked with a barber or bartender, Lone was feeling relatively comfortable in thinking that at least Fort Collins didn't appear to be *teeming* with a horde of gunnies seeking to claim his life. That didn't mean there couldn't still be one or two lurking quietly in the shadows, but that was considerably better than what might have been. With a little luck helped along by the diversion Tru had created, it looked like Lone actually stood a good chance to slip in and out of town barely noticed.

Only the thought of Tru gave a sour twist to his outlook. No, not the thought *of* her rather, thinking about how things stood between them. Which was to say the gap holding them apart, the request by Tru that they remain apart for an indefinite length of time. *"Spare me the pain of seeing you again just to say goodbye."* Lone understood this sentiment, saw how it was probably for the better; yet it didn't come without an emptiness, an ache down deep. Never mind he was the one who'd set the boundaries, made it clear time and again how he couldn't commit in any meaningful way beyond the other obligations he felt bound to. Maintaining those boundaries still took a toll.

At one point, after finishing up in the hardware store and stepping back out onto the boardwalk, Lone stood gazing up the street for a long moment, thinking he might be able to spot the storefront of Tru's uncle's business. He entertained a thought of mounting Ironsides and taking a pass down the street, hoping to maybe catch a glimpse of Tru through a store window just to make sure she'd made it okay, he tried telling himself. But no, that would still be betraying what her note had asked him to honor. And if he did get a glimpse of her and maybe her of him in return then it would only cause a fresh stab of the pain she wanted to avoid.

Besides, checking his pocket watch, Lone saw that it was going on two-thirty. Sweeney and Ira ought to be rolling in any time now. He needed to follow through on his part of the arrangements they'd put in place for meeting back up once all were in town together.

******

The way they'd set it up was this: After Lone had finished his business dealings and made an appraisal of the town, he would pick an easy to spot cafe or restaurant on the main street. Leaving Ironsides prominently displayed at the hitch rail out front, he would go inside and sit down for a leisurely bite to eat, awaiting the arrival of Sweeney and Ira. If by that point he had determined things looked relatively calm, he would leave his Yellowboy rifle in the big gray's saddle scabbard, positioned the standard way with the trigger guard down. That would be the signal it was okay for Sweeney and Ira to come inside and join him. If he sensed there was any kind of trouble brewing, however, he would leave the Yellowboy positioned with the trigger guard facing up that would alert the pair in the wagon to roll on by and wait for him to contact them later.

The restaurant Lone chose was a modest little spot called HOMESTYLE FIXIN'S just a block down from the livery stable. In as much as he'd sensed no trouble looming, the

Yellowboy out front was positioned trigger guard down and he sat nursing a cup of coffee and a slice of cherry pie, waiting for Sweeney and Ira to show up. It being mid-afternoon, it was a lull time for the establishment's business and the only other customers in the place was an elderly couple huddled at a table across the room. Lone guessed that the plump, middle-aged woman who served him might be the owner and was probably doing double duty as both cook and waitress until things got busier toward evening.

He was nursing a third cup of coffee and considering ordering another piece of pie when the clumping of bootheels on the boardwalk out front announced some new arrivals and then a moment later Sweeney and Ira came through the door. In a matter of minutes they were seated at the table with Lone and the plump waitress was pouring them mugs of fresh coffee.

"Did that used to be a slice of cherry pie?" Sweeney asked, pointing at the crumbs and red smear on the otherwise empty plate in front of Lone.

"That's right," said the smiling waitress.

"I hope that wasn't the last of it."

"Not at all. I've got more cherry. I've also got some apple and peach."

"Seeing how good mine was," said Lone, "I doubt you could go wrong with any of 'em."

Sweeney nodded. "I'll try some peach then, for starters."

"How about you, mister?" the waitress asked Ira.

Ira looked almost startled by the question. He'd been acting a bit fidgety and looking anxiously all around ever since coming in. "Uh, no. No thanks," he said. "I'm good with just coffee."

Lone frowned. "What's the matter, Ira? You look like you're on pins and needles about something."

"He's been like that all the way in," said Sweeney. "I told him he was acting like somebody passing through Injun country, expecting a redskin to jump out from behind every bush."

"Ain't this almost the same?" Ira snapped back. "Rolling in here, thinking there might be no telling how many gunnies waiting to claim that bounty on Lone's head?"

"But it's my head on the line, Ira," Lone pointed out. "Don't that make it me who ought to be actin' so nervous?"

Ira snorted. "You? Be a cold day in Hell before you ever went around acting nervous."

"In that case, there've been plenty of times when Ol' Scratch must've got his toes frostbit some. But this ain't one of 'em," Lone stated. "Far as my sniffer can detect, things are awful calm around here. If word of Benton's bounty offer has reached this far, it sure don't seem to have stirred up much of a crowd lookin' to collect."

"Well I, for one, don't mind hearin' that at all," said Sweeney. He took a loud slurp of his coffee. "Matter of fact, with things bein' that calm, I might take time to sample all three of those pies."

As if on cue, the waitress returned and placed a generous-sized, golden-crusted wedge in front of him. Before Sweeney had a chance to lift the first forkful to his mouth, however, the front door opened and three men walked in. At the sight of them, Sweeney's hand stopped its upward motion and his eyes widened with sudden alarm.

"What is it? What's wrong?" Lone wanted to know.

Sweeney's eyes followed the trio as they shuffled to a table in the middle of the room and began pulling out chairs. In a low, hoarse whisper he said, "Those men who just came in. The one wearing the red string tie is Royce Halsey."

CHAPTER 43

"Royce. The third Halsey brother. The one everybody was having trouble getting in touch with," muttered Lone.

"He's bound to recognize me if he looks this way," said Sweeney. "That means, dependin' on whether or not he *has* been got in touch with yet, you gotta think he might figure out who you are, too."

"Comes to that, let's just hope…" Lone started to say.

But, before he got any more out, Ira shoved his chair back from the table and thrust suddenly to his feet. In his right hand he held a large bore over-under derringer that he aimed squarely at Lone as he shouted loud enough to make sure it could be heard all through the room, "It don't matter *what* you hope, Lone McGantry! Your luck has run out and if you don't keep both hands flat on the table it will be over even quicker!"

"Ira! What the hell do you think you're doin'?" demanded Sweeney.

"Same for you, Sweeney!" Ira said through clenched teeth. The fidgety, nervous mannerisms from a few minutes ago were all at once gone and in their place was a focused, wild-eyed intensity. "I got two slugs in this pea shooter and one of them will be yours if you don't keep those pie-eating paws where I can see 'em plain!"

Lone's own eyes blazed. "For the bounty, Ira? You? That what this is about?"

"Shut up! You damn right it's for the bounty," Ira snarled. Then, without ever taking his glare off Lone or Sweeney, he called over his shoulder, "You hearing this, Royce Halsey?"

"I hear you," said the man in the red tie, looking puzzled and very ill at ease. "But I don't understand…"

Ira cut him off, same as he had Lone. "The only thing you need to understand is that this is Lone McGantry, the man who killed your brother and cousin back in North Platte. Surely some of the telegrams your other brothers sent must have reached you by now and so must news of the bounty money being offered for proof of McGantry's death."

Royce frowned. "And I'm supposed to be your witness, is that it? After you gun him down, I provide the testimony to earn you the money."

"That' right. I earn the bounty, your family gets its revenge."

His glare continuing to be locked with Ira's, Lone rasped, "You ungrateful wretch. This is how you repay gettin' pulled out of the gutter and being hauled to safety from the Box 50 wranglers?"

"*I'm* being ungrateful?" sneered Ira. "Who saved you from getting caught in a crossfire between Cully and Buck? And it was Tru, not you, who insisted on bringing me along to keep me safe from the Box 50 bunch. Even at that, I never set out to serve you like this. Not in the beginning. But once I heard about Benton's bounty offer, I couldn't stop thinking about that twenty-five hundred dollars. I've been carrying this derringer around in my pocket ever since I took it off Cully when I clobbered him in that alley. That became the other thing I couldn't stop thinking about using it on you to claim the bounty money. You were right there, practically at arm's length, every day. It would have been so easy. But I knew I couldn't count on either Tru or Sweeney to back me up, to be witnesses for my proof of death. So I had to wait."

"I not only wouldn't have been a witness for your filthy deed," Sweeney told him, "but I'd've killed you for it."

"Which is why I never gave you the chance."

"And that explains the why of something else, too—you bein' so squirmy all mornin'." Sweeney's lip curled in disgust. "With Lone comin' into town on his own, ahead of us, you were afraid somebody else might beat you to him, wasn't you?"

"So what if I was? It don't matter now," Ira said smugly. "Nobody *did* beat me to him. Now I'm the one with him under my muzzle and, by holding off, I end up with the perfect witness to provide a proof of death statement that Angus Benton can't doubt for second."

"There's just one problem," Royce Halsey said with an icy calmness.

For the first time, Ira almost—*almost*, but not quite—took his eyes off Lone. "What problem? What do you mean?"

"I mean if you pull that trigger, then the only testimony I'll provide is at the trial to see you hanged for cold-blooded murder," came the answer.

"This man killed your brother! You saying that means nothing to you?" Ira wailed. His voice became shrill with outrage. "What's more, on the trail between here and North Platte, McGantry has killed seven or eight other men. Nobody's gonna hang me for cutting down a mad killer like him especially not with Angus Benton's money backing me!"

And then Ira finally did what Lone had been so desperately wanting and hoping for he momentarily averted his gaze. So distraught was he by Royce's balk that he couldn't keep his eyes from darting angrily in the man's direction.

It wasn't much, but Lone sensed it was the only chance he was likely to get. Acting on it, he shifted his hands to grip the edge of the table where he sat and then thrust his arms straight out in a hard shove, ramming the table into Ira just below waist level. At the same time, Lone launched from his chair and bulled forward, continuing to push the table ahead of him. On one side, Sweeney was knocked off balance and sent toppling out of his own chair.

Directly ahead of Lone, Ira was also off-balanced as he got driven backward by the hurtling table. He folded at the waist, flinging his arms out for balance and support. In the process of doing this, he desperately triggered one round from the derringer. But even at such close range, it was too wild. The slug sizzled past Lone's right ear, close enough for him to feel the heat but otherwise doing no harm.

Continuing to be driven back by the table, Ira's feet became tangled in the legs of the chair he'd abandoned earlier, tripping him and spilling him to the floor. With the resistance against the table he was shoving suddenly gone, Lone was thrown abruptly off balance himself. He staggered forward a ragged couple steps, grabbing at the table with his left hand to keep upright while his right hand was reaching for the Colt holstered on his hip.

At the same time, Ira was scrambling with surprising nimbleness to regain his footing. And he was still clutching the derringer. Locking his wild-eyed glare once more on

Lone, he raised the deadly little shooter and extended it at arm's length well ahead of Lone's Colt clearing leather.

A shot roared, shatteringly loud in the cramped confines of the low-ceilinged dining room. Ira was jolted by the impact of the slug. His arm dropped, he stood teetering. Then, slowly, stubbornly, he tried to raise his arm again. A second shot roared and this time the bullet it sent knocked Ira immediately flat and lifeless.

Lone looked around. Through the curls of bluish powder smoke now drifting upward in the air, he saw Royce Halsey standing beside his table, feet planted wide, with a short-barreled, nickel-plated revolver extended at waist level.

CHAPTER 44

"I was in Cheyenne when word from Granger and Cliff finally reached me about what had happened," Royce was explaining. He bore a resemblance to both of his brothers, a bit more so to Granger, though was more carefully groomed and dressed in finer threads, right down to the red silk tie. "I'd just finished a pretty good run at the tables up there," he went on, "and, coincidentally, was planning to head down this way anyhow. Me and a couple other fellas the two men you saw me with at the restaurant are looking to open up a place of our own."

He paused and held Lone's eyes for a long moment before adding, "Had you and I crossed paths at that initial point, after my receipt of those first telegrams, I'm sure you can understand me saying that my reaction to finding myself in your presence then would have been quite a bit different than it was today."

Meeting his gaze evenly, Lone replied, "That being the case, I reckon I'm glad our trip from Nebraska took as long as it did. Not to mention the gratitude I've already expressed for the way you *did* react today."

The Halsey brother shrugged indifferently. "A snake is a snake, no matter who it's threatening to bite."

This conversation was taking place in the office of Tom Nantz, the sheriff of Fort Collins. Present were the sheriff, Lone, Halsey, and Virgil Sweeney. Nantz, a beefy specimen with streaks of gray in his walrus mustache, was leaning back against the front of his desk, arms folded, facing out at the three men sitting in wooden chairs before him. A fifth man, a portly, elderly Negro who'd been introduced only as Hiram, the jailer, slouched on a three-legged stool over by the window, looking on and listening in silence.

Some hours had passed since the shooting at HOME-STYLE FIXIN'S. The sun had dropped behind the mountain peaks. A lantern on the corner of Nantz's desk filled the room with a soft glow and, outside, a man in a stovepipe hat was making his way down the shadowy street lighting sporadically spaced pole lamps.

"By the time I arrived here in Fort Collins," Royce continued, "there was a stack of new telegrams waiting for me. No doubt you can guess that their tone was quite a bit different from the original ones. Frankly, I didn't have as much trouble accepting that change as I perhaps should have. You see, I recognized a long time ago what Cliff and especially Granger refused to acknowledge that Isaac was a mouthy, petty little turd and it was just a matter of time before he would push somebody too far."

He paused, took a deep breath that he exhaled loudly through his nostrils. Then went on. "Still for the sake of the family name, revenge, whatever I was ready to do what was expected of me if I ran into you. Thankfully, that got resolved by you saving little Ethan and my brothers coming to their senses about Isaac and Jerome reaching the ends they'd been bound for too long."

"But that wasn't all the batch of telegrams contained," spoke up Sheriff Nantz. "Some of 'em were addressed to me informing me about the bounty that had been placed on your head and warning me, since your destination was also well advertised, to be on the lookout for hardcases who'd likely be gathering to try and collect."

"Too bad," Lone muttered wryly, "nobody warned either one of us to be on the lookout for the double-crossing weasel I hauled in with me."

Wagging his head at the irony, Nantz said, "Especially due to him being out on the trail with you and not getting the follow-up word that came through about Benton calling off his bounty the way it left him practically the only one remaining to worry about."

"You sound awful sure of that. I hope you're right, but what makes you think so that the hardcases who were gathering all heard about the bounty being called off?" Lone asked.

"Because me and two of my deputies made sure the word got spread by spending two nights traipsing through every saloon and dive in the area, that's how," answered Nantz. "I can't swear we reached every single gunny along the front range, but we by-God got to most of 'em. And I know for a fact that plenty of the riff-raff we had our eyes on right here in town took off for other pursuits."

This explained Lone's earlier appraisal giving him no sense of brewing trouble like he'd expected.

"What you had no way of knowin', Sheriff, was that all your effort would leave things wide open for our Ira," Sweeney said bitterly. "The little bastard sure had me fooled, I actually grew to like him. Too bad about the close call for Lone, but at least the way things went this afternoon served to get rid of the snake before his true colors came out in some other way and to the harm of somebody even less suspecting maybe Miss Tru, for instance. After me and Lone moved on, she was plannin' on lookin' after Ira in order to help him stay on the straight and narrow. No tellin' how he might have tried to take advantage of her."

Nantz frowned. "Miss Tru? Advance descriptions on McGantry all mentioned he was traveling in the company of a Chinese girl. Is that who you're speaking of?"

"It is."

"Mind if I ask what happened to her? I haven't heard mention of a girl being part of anything that happened today."

"That's because the girl neither was nor is any part of today's trouble," Lone told him. "She parted ways with us a while back and came on ahead to tend to her own affairs. She deserves to be left out of this for the sake of doing just that."

Nantz unfolded his arms and straightened up, scowling. "Now hold on a minute, mister. You or at least the threat of trouble stirring up on account of you have put my town in the grip of quite a bit of tension over the past few days. Then, when that seemed to have tamed down, you finally show up and immediately there's a shooting and a killing. In spite of that, I've been mighty reasonable with both you and Halsey here mainly because of wires I've received vouching for the two of you from a couple lawmen I trust and respect. That would be Tobe Crenshaw from Julesburg and Halsey's brother Cliff from Ogallala. But none of that stands in the way of me being the one who decides what does or doesn't get included in any questions I take a notion to ask in my own goddamn town!"

Grudgingly, Lone relented. "All right. The girl in question is named Tru Min Chang. My association with her was strictly one of convenience discovering we were headed for the same place and deciding to make the trip together. That was before the bounty got put out on me. For exactly the reasons you just said because we figured any hunters looking to collect but not knowing me by sight might have heard to be watching for somebody traveling in the company of a Chinese girl Tru broke off on her own to give me more of a chance. She's got kin here in Fort Collins and is looking to start a new life with them. All of which leads me to say again: She don't deserve to be sucked into any more bad business involving me."

The scowl on Nantz's face eased up some. "Hai Chang is a successful businessman here in town. He owns a clothing store, does tailoring and laundry. Nice fella. I know that for some time he's been expecting a brother and niece from back east. Is that the girl we're talking about?"

"The same."

"And her uncle—Hai's brother?"

"He didn't make it. Died from a rattlesnake bite outside North Platte," Lone said. "That left the girl on her own. But she was bent on not letting it stop her from coming on. She's what you might call high spirited."

"Sounds like," the sheriff allowed. He dragged one hand along his jaw. "Also sounds like she don't need no more trouble any time soon. So I'm agreeable to not bothering her about this shooting she was no part of. But where does that leave any more business between you and her?"

Lone shook his head. "Nowhere. Our traveling arrangement is completed. There's a wagonload of stuff still parked out on the street that belongs mostly to Miss Chang. Once we're free to go, I've got one item to offload and then the rest Sweeney here will see gets proper delivered."

Nantz considered for a long moment, his gaze coming to rest briefly on each of the three men before him. Then:

"Okay. I reckon I'm satisfied. I can't see no reason to keep any of you any longer. Halsey, you say you and your other friends may be starting a business here in town. I'll welcome you and wish you luck, but at the same time I'll warn you that any more use of that nickel-plated revolver of yours may not be so easily excused in the future. As for you two, McGantry and Sweeney, did I hear you say you'll both be moving on?"

"Sheriff," Sweeney drawled, "it took me a lot of years to make it here to see these mountains of yours. Way I'm figurin' now is that I'll hang around for a few days just to drink in the sight. After that, yeah, I'll be moseyin' on farther west."

"As for me," said Lone, "once I claim that item I mentioned, I'll be heading up into the mountains for a while to take care of a personal matter. Plan on leaving at first light tomorrow. When I come back down, I don't expect to be passing this way again, if ever, for quite a spell."

Nantz regarded him. "Probably unreasonable for me feel this way, McGantry, can't say a direct thing you've done to rankle me. But neither can I say I'm sorry to hear you'll be soon gone."

CHAPTER 45

Daybreak found Lone rolling out of Fort Collins, headed up into Poudre Canyon. He sat working the reins of the mule cart with its nameless jughead plodding steadily in front, Peg's crate lashed securely in the bed of the cart behind him, and Ironsides bringing up the rear on a tether. The morning air coming down off the mountains still had a bite to it, but a bright sun rising in a clear sky promised to bring offsetting warmth.

Lone felt exhilarated, finally being at this stage of the undertaking that had started so many days ago back in North Platte. There, at the start, it had been just him and Peg's remains facing the journey to grant the old mountain man's last request. Now, after everything that had happened in between, it was back to those basics only at nearly the end of the journey.

Glancing over his shoulder now and then at the town of Fort Collins sinking lower and more distant, Lone also felt a trace of sadness for the things he was leaving from that in-between time. Tru, of course, most of all. But Sweeney, too, and the genuine friendship he'd formed with the old wrangler. In a curious way, the same could almost be said for Ira up until his loathsome swerve. And then, in another curious vein, there was his relationship with the Halsey brothers—Cliff, Granger and, to a lesser extent, Royce. Good men all, who had justification for hating him yet through a twist of ironic coincidence, his rescue of little Ethan being one of Lone's proudest personal accomplishments in addition to what it meant to the boy's family, had proven big enough to re-assess and forgive.

Royce perhaps summed it up best when, upon parting ways after leaving the sheriff's office, he said, "If we had to face each other on a regular basis, McGantry, I doubt we could ever be close friends. The weight of Isaac's death and Jerome's would always be pressing down to some degree. But distance and time have a way of balancing a person's outlook for the wiser and better."

The parting with Sweeney, over a steak supper and several mugs of cold beer, had been more drawn out and more pleasant. Though still with a bittersweet edge to it.

"When I deliver that wagonload of stuff tomorrow," the old wrangler had said near the close, "are you sure there ain't some message you want me to give to Miss Tru?"

"No," Lone replied, quiet but firm. "Her and I know where each other stands. There's nothing more to say."

Sweeney considered this, then heaved a ragged sigh. "I know it won't make no difference, but I'm gonna tell you anyhow what a dern fool you are. The way that gal looks at you. There's men all over this country who'd give anything to have a woman, a good woman, look at 'em like that. And you're runnin' away from it."

"I ain't running away," Lone insisted. "I'm running toward something. Something I've got to do beyond this trip up the mountain. Tru can't be part of it, and I can't *not* be. She understands, no matter how hard it is."

Sweeney regarded him. "Hard. That's the word for you, Lone. You're a fair and decent man, but also hard and uncompromisin'. Reckon that's part of what makes your name suit you so good."

And so that's what it came down to. The former scout on his own once again. And while there was an undeniable measure of melancholy to the moment, at the same time it somehow felt right.

******

For the next two days and nights, Lone made his way up the canyon following the twists and turns of the Poudre River that cut through it. The name "Poudre" as applied to both canyon and watercourse stemmed from an incident back near the turn of the century when a party of French fur trappers, to keep from being slowed too much during their flight to beat a snowstorm down the mountain, had buried a portion of their bulky supplies including some cases of gun powder, on the banks of the river. From that, the term "hide the powder" or "cache la poudre" in French eventually boiled down to Cache la Poudre River or, more commonly these days, just Poudre River.

Lone thought of that old story as he trudged along and wondered how many other tales of trappers and Indians who'd passed this way could be told if they had ever been handed down. And while this passage of his would likely never be handed down either, he thought with a grim smile, he'd be willing to bet that the purpose behind it was as strange or stranger than any that had come before.

On the third day, as the river angled more toward the south, Lone veered away and continued to ascend due west into the northern reaches of the Never Summer Mountains.

While the banks of the Poudre had been rocky and rugged in many places, there'd also been plenty of grassy areas with the snow melted away sufficiently to provide Ironsides and the mule decent graze. The river still carried bits of ice flow from higher up and many of the sudden crooks held icy build-ups along the edge, but the flow was steady enough and had enough whitewater stretches to be mostly open. Before departing the Poudre entirely, Lone lingered long enough to catch a half dozen good-sized trout which he cleaned and pouched and took with him; they'd make a tasty supper and breakfast.

A brief snow squally hit that night but Lone found a deep notch between some fingers of high rock that did a good job of keeping him and the animals out of the stinging wind. They had to break trail through about eight inches of fresh snow the next morning, though, before reaching clearer ground above where the squall passed through.

On the fourth night, Lone camped at the mouth of Hitchins Pass. Before the light faded, he got a good look at a well broken-in trail leading up through it. This, he knew, had been made by silver miners who had worked the region up above the pass about a dozen years back. There was a spurt of activity and even a handful of settlements formed before the low quality of the ore and the difficulty in transporting it down to a smelter curbed most of the mining almost as fast as it began. There were still a few stubborn stragglers sprinkled through the area, Lone had heard, though not many. Nevertheless, he was hoping for the chance to run across one or two who might be able to provide him a bit of added guidance for completing the final leg of his journey.

******

Dutchtown was an offshoot of Lulu City, the area's initial silver mining camp. It came into being when a group of perpetually rowdy Dutchmen got fed up with Lulu's rules and regulations and left or got kicked out, depending on who was telling the story, to start their own settlement a few miles to the northwest. The remains of this settlement was where Lone found himself after coming up through Hitchins Pass. There were only four cabins still occupied and only one of them displaying any signs of welcoming a stranger. This came in the forms of Oscar Wurblatz, a stout, limping, bullet-headed old German, and his equally stout, dour-faced (in spite of her hospitality) wife Anna.

"Yah. I think I know just the spot you are seeking," declared Oscar as he and Lone sat at a sturdy table inside the Wurblatz cabin with mugs of strong coffee laced with homebrew whiskey in front of them. "I used to run a trap line up on Hawk Creek back when there were miners still around to buy the pelts for hats and fur wraps to warm them from the cold. The old cabin was badly run down already then, so it can only be in worse shape now."

"I'm not interested in the cabin," Lone told him. "I just want to reach the general spot."

He paused, taking a deep pull from his mug, and then decided there was no way to fabricate any logical explanation for needing to get to the place in question, so he simply went ahead and told the truth. The Wurblatzes listened without interruption, Oscar showing no change in his expression, Anna a gradual softening in hers to the point of a moist, dreamy gaze forming her eyes.

When he was done, Oscar said, "I have heard talk of an old one-legged mountain man and his Indian wife. That was before any mining came to the area. Those who spoke of it believed they had either died in a harsh winter or simply went away."

"That's partly true," Lone allowed. "One of them died, the other went away but now he wants to come home."

"That is a tender, touching tale," Anna said. "Some would call it crazy. And you even crazier for following through on it. But you are not. You are a good, kind man to honor the request of your friend. And my husband will help guide you all that he can."

Oscar scowled. "Any other time I would lead you right on up to where you want to go. But a couple weeks ago my ax blade slipped off some frozen wood I was splitting and whacked me a lick across my shin bone." He slapped the thigh of his right leg, the one he'd been limping on, to emphasize this. "I nearly became a one-legged man myself. It is healing, thanks to my Anna, but I'm in no shape to make a hike up Hawk Creek."

"Maybe next year," Anna scolded, "you'll split sufficient wood in the fall so you don't have to try and chop through wood *and* ice later on."

"If you didn't keep it so hot in here to nearly blister the walls, we wouldn't go through so much wood," Oscar countered.

Lone smiled secretly to himself as he listened to this exchange, recognizing it as containing absolutely no rancor but rather the comfortable banter of a couple truly quite fond of one another. He wondered if he would ever experience or *give himself the chance* to experience any such relationship.

The Wurblatzes insisted Lone spend the night at their cabin. While Anna began preparing supper, Oscar produced a sheet of coarse paper which he spread out on the kitchen table and, with a stub of pencil, sketched out a map to guide Lone the rest of the way to Peg's old cabin and the nearby burial platform where Silver Dove lay waiting.

When he was finished, the old German tapped a finger on the crooked line he had drawn representing Hawk Creek. "There are several places where it's mighty tight going along the water's edge. Your cart will never make it. Best go on from here with your mule and a travois. There are some young trees out back of the cabin we can cut poles from, and I've got some good tough bear hides we can lace between them to make a hauling bed that will hold the crate containing your friend."

Lone nodded. "Sounds like a good idea. But I'll go ahead and use my horse rather than the mule. Me and that big gray have traveled many a tough trail together, I trust him to get me through."

******

After a warm, comfortable night's sleep on a floor pallet next to the fireplace and a delicious breakfast of fried mush and venison sausage, Lone got an early start up Hawk Creek. He sat astride Ironsides with the drag litter containing Peg's temporary coffin scraping along behind.

The creek was narrow but very ancient and cut very deep in the mountain granite. And as Oscar had warned there were several places where the space between a high, sheer rock wall and an equally sheer drop-off into the churning water was mighty slim. For the worst of these, Lone dismounted and walked ahead, leading Ironsides by his reins. The big gray never balked and never demonstrated anything less than sure-footedness, solidifying Lone's faith and trust in him all the more.

With the late afternoon sun sinking fast, the creek made a sudden juke off to the left. This was the point, according to Oscar's map, where Lone and Ironsides turned away from the water and instead proceeded up through a shallow, natural gorge. By the time they emerged at the top, the sun was gone and the pale pinkish light of dusk was rapidly fading.

But with the high rocks abruptly dropping away on either side, there was enough light to see a broad, flat meadow stretching out ahead, rimmed by a line of fir and birch trees on the far side. His heart quickening, Lone knew that in amongst those trees he would find the remains of Peg's and Silver Dove's cabin and, close by, Silver Dove's burial platform. And, just beyond, looming over the whole scene, was what Silver Dove had dubbed *Weeping Hawk Peak* the signature marker for their Forever Mountain.

What some people's imagination sees in a natural feature or shape is often lost to the view of another. But, in this case, Lone saw it immediately and distinctly. The way the peak rose up, sloping to the north, and then ending in a blunted, broken-off tip with one side as seen from the vantage of this edge of the meadow forming the ragged, sharp-beaked profile of a bird, a hawk. And streaming down from approximately where the raptor's eye might be, reached a fluted pattern of bluish lichen, distinct against the otherwise dark granite. The tear track of a weeping hawk.

Lone got slowly down out of his saddle. He walked back to where Peg's crate rested on the travois hides. He placed both hands on the crate and patted it gently as he hung his head close. "Well, we made it, you old scalawag," he said in a quiet voice. "Your Weeping Hawk Peak, your Forever Mountain. I'm too tired to trudge across that meadow yet this evening, and by the time we got to the other side it would be too dark to see to do anything anyway. So I'm going to camp here tonight. Sorry, but you'll have to wait just a little longer to rejoin your beloved Silver Dove. But you soon will. Just like you asked, just like I promised."

EPILOGUE

In the light of a new day, Lone crossed the meadow and easily found the overgrown old cabin and then the burial platform. It took a while to clear debris and reinforce the latter. When he had it sufficiently strengthened, he climbed up and very gently and respectfully, so as to not disturb her remaining earthly spirit, he wrapped Silver Dove's remains in a thick, heavy bearskin that Oscar had provided. Her previous wraps were badly weathered and decayed.

Next, with the aid of a rope draped over a sturdy branch extending out from a nearby tree, Lone pulled Peg's embalmed, shroud-wrapped body up onto the platform. After first dressing it in the fringed, bleached doeskin jacket Lone had recovered from Peg's hidden war bag back at the Busted Spur soddy, the jacket a gift from Silver Moon many years earlier, chewed to a pliable softness by her own teeth, sewn and bead-decorated by her own hands. Lone then wrapped it in another heavy bearskin. Finally, he spread the durable, protective hides from the travois over both forms, corners weighted down with heavy stones to keep it from easily blowing away.

Climbing down, Lone built a small ceremonial fire close beside the platform. When it was burning and crackling good, he seated himself cross-legged before it. Lifting his face to gaze up and out at Weeping Hawk Peak and the higher snow-capped mounds and blue sky beyond, he spoke these words:

"Oh Father Mountain
A devoted son has returned home
Please welcome him
Hold him and his beloved Silver Moon
together in your embrace.
Forever"

When he was done, Lone remained sitting silently until the fire burned down to a trail of smoke bending off in the meager breeze. Rising, he walked over to Ironsides and swung up into the saddle. Without the burden of the travois and armed with the familiarity of having already traveled the route, he figured he could make it back to Dutchtown by nightfall. There, he expected the Wurblatzes would insist on putting him up for another night.

In the morning, he would offer them payment for their hospitality and assistance which he had little doubt they would refuse. But Lone had a hunch that Oscar *would* accept being gifted with the cart and mule. The former scout no longer needed or wanted them. From here on out he planned on traveling fast and light.

Once out of the mountains, Lone's intent was to turn north away from Fort Collins for his own reasons and also in keeping with what he'd told Sheriff Nantz. He would go as far as Cheyenne where he meant to rest and indulge himself for a couple of days. Then he would re-outfit and start back to Nebraska, back to the Busted Spur soddy that would again be the starting point for what came next.

He'd fulfilled his promise to Peg.

Now remained the promise he'd made to himself.

"Look for the man with the burned face!"

A Look At: The Coldest Trail: A Lone McGantry Western

A GRITTY, ACTION-PACKED WESTERN ADVEN-
TURE

Months have passed since five ruthless men killed Lone
McGantry's partner and stole the horses from their ranch.
Now, finally free of obligations that have kept him from
taking up pursuit sooner, Lone has set out on a cold trail
to track down the killers and make them pay. He'd prefer
revenge, he'll settle for justice …

But the trail is not only cold, it is twisty and marked
by dangers at every turn, even apart from the quarry he is
after. Lone will have to fight and shoot his way through
these menacing obstacles and threats to his own life before
the real prey is finally in his gunsights.

"You will find yourself riding along with Lone McGantry, and crew when they strive to bring justice to those who
cannot protect themselves!"

AVAILABLE NOW

About the Author

Wayne D. Dundee is an American author of popular genre fiction. His writing has primarily been detective mysteries (the Joe Hannibal PI series) and Western adventures. To date, he has written four dozen novels and forty-plus short stories, also ranging into horror, fantasy, erotica, and several "house name" books under bylines other than his own.

Dundee was born March 24, 1948, in Freeport, Illinois. He graduated from high school in Clinton, Wisconsin, 1966. Later that same year he married Pamela Daum and they had one daughter, Michelle. For the first fifty years of his life, Dundee lived and worked in the state line area of northern Illinois and southern Wisconsin. During most of that time he was employed by Arnold Engineering/Group Arnold out of Marengo, Illinois, where he worked his way up from factory laborer through several managerial positions. In his spare time, starting in high school, he was always writing. He sold his first short story in 1982.

In 1998, Dundee relocated to Ogallala, Nebraska, where he assumed the general manager position for a small Arnold facility there. The setting and rich history of the area inspired him to turn his efforts more toward the Western genre. In 2009, following the passing of his wife a year earlier, Dundee retired from Arnold and began to concentrate full time on his writing.

Dundee was the founder and original editor of Hardboiled Magazine.

His work in the mystery field has been nominated for an Edgar, an Anthony, and six Shamus Awards from the Private Eye Writers of America.